Dagmara Dominczyk is an actress who has appeared in films, Broadway and TV productions. She majored in Drama at Carnegie Mellon University and graduated in 1998. She is married to the actor Patrick Wilson and they live with their children in New Jersey, USA.

The Lullaby of Polish Girls

DAGMARA DOMINCZYK

Quercus

First published in the USA in 2013 by Spiegel & Grau.
This edition first published in Great Britain in 2013 by

Quercus
55 Baker Street
7th Floor, South Block
London W1U 8EW

A CIP catalogue record for this book is available
from the British Library

PB ISBN 978 1 78087 821 8
Ebook ISBN 978 1 78087 822 5

10 9 8 7 6 5 4 3 2 1

Typesetting by Ellipsis Digital Limited, Glasgow
Printed and bound in Great Britain by Clays Ltd, St Ives plc

For Patrick,
'*. . . and the reason is you . . .*'

A NOTE FROM THE AUTHOR

On Pronunciation

Polish is a very difficult language to speak; the strings of consonants and letter combinations are daunting even to some native speakers. Below are listed some of the most basic sound and letter changes.

Consonants

C—*ts* as in *danCe*
CI—*chee* as in *CHEEse*
CZ—*ch* as in *CHalk*
DZI—*j* as in *Joke*
G—*g* as in *Goat*
J—*y* as in *Yolk*
Ł—*w* as in *Watch*
RZ—*zhe* as in French *JE t'aime*
Ś—*shee* as in *SHEEp*
SI—*shee* as in *SHEEp*
SZ—*sh* as in *Show*
W—*v* as in *Valise*

Vowels

A—*ah*
E—*eh*
I—*ee* as in *Eek*
O—*au* as in *Off*
Ó—*oo* as in *bOOt*
U—*oo* as in *bOOt*
Y—*ih* as in *In*

On Names

Polish names are tricky, as each one has many deviations. To use a person's birth name is formal, and almost every name has an intimate diminutive form. There are also *ksywy*—nicknames based on somcone's personality or a physical trait—and most young Polish people have *ksywy*. And all names in turn are conjugated to suit proper grammar. So, for a character whose name is *Jan* (John), there can be the following variations: *Jasiek, Jas, Jasiu, Janek*. It seems confusing, and sometimes it is. I have followed this convention because it is an integral part of Polish culture.

CHAPTER ONE

2002

ANNA
GREENPOINT, BROOKLYN

Looking back, Anna Baran could pinpoint the exact moment she'd fallen in love with Ben Taft. They were lying on his mattress, covers thrown off and sharing a cigarette, when Anna closed her eyes and asked him the question she'd been wanting to ask for weeks.

'Did you ever imagine you'd end up with a Polish girl?'

Ben looked at her and arched one eyebrow. 'In bed? Or in life?' Anna blushed, but thankfully Ben continued. 'Never. I didn't even know where Poland was on the map.'

'And now?' Anna whispered, placing her hands between his warm thighs.

'Now? Now I know there's a lot more to your country than meets the *kiełbasa*.'

Anna rolled her eyes but silently urged him on, hoping he would get it right.

'I know Warsaw isn't the only city there. I know not every last name ends in *-ski*. The language is tough as hell but I could listen to it all day. It's the land of amber, crystal, salt mines, and revolutionaries. And I know that the oldest oak tree in Poland is located near your hometown and that they named it Bart. There. How's that?'

'*Dąb* Bartek,' Anna whispered, feeling tingly, as if he had been talking dirty. Ben went on about Solidarity and Swedish

3

deluges, about pierogi and the Pope, about Communism and cleaning ladies. Anna interrupted him at a certain point with a kiss. '*Kocham cię*, Ben,' she said, and he didn't have to speak the language to know what she meant. But that night was years ago, and it felt as far off as the goddamn stars in the sky.

At 3:57 A.M., Anna wakes up from a bad dream. Something about the Gestapo and a defunct Captain Video – the place she used to rent VHS tapes as a girl. She stumbles out of bed and walks into the living room, shuffling blindly toward the ashtray. The familiar stench of yesterday's chain-smoking leads her to the corner of the couch, where an ashtray sits on top of Ben's old throw pillow. Her eyeglasses are nowhere to be found, but how can she look for them when she can't see a damn thing, when her own hand in front of her eyes is nothing but a blur? Anna wonders briefly if she might actually be legally blind and if there is a way she can get tested without having to leave the apartment. With fumbling fingers, she extracts one third of what used to be a handsome Marlboro Light from the ashtray, retrieves a Bic from under the couch, lights the stale tip, and walks over to open a window. The November wind slaps at her face, but it feels good, a shock to the system, and her eyes water from the cold.

Lorimer Street must be empty; she can tell from the dead silence, her ears doing the work her eyes can't. While most New Yorkers dream of white winters in theory, Anna pines for snow and means it. It smells like winter out there, crisp and clean, though there's no sign of snow yet.

'We're a dying breed.' That was Ben's opening line, on the first night they met, when Anna had walked up to him and asked him for a light. He extended his Zippo toward her and she arched her eyebrows and smiled, smitten right away. Two drinks later, they were making out by the coat check, waiting impatiently for their scarves and hats.

'So you're a New Yorker, huh?' Ben asked, when they stepped into his apartment a half hour later. Signs of three young men living on their own were everywhere, but Ben didn't seem embarrassed by the mess and his roommates were nowhere in sight. Ben and Anna sat on the dirty floor and made small talk.

'By way of Kielce, Poland, my friend – the birthplace of Polish rap,' Anna said. 'We're known in Polska as the *scyzoryki* – the switchblades. And you don't wanna fuck with us.' Ben laughed as he drummed the side of his beer can.

'Well, I'm always up for a challenge.'

Those words echo in her head like a scratch on a beat-up record. Three years ago tonight, Anna and two friends had wandered into the Turkey's Nest because their fingers were numb from the cold, and there was Ben, in that blue sweater, with an eager smile. But that Ben is gone now. He's in Omaha with Nancy and Pappy and his innumerable cousins. Ben is only gone for another day, and yet, somehow, it feels like he is gone for good.

Standing by the window, Anna can see her breath. Her flimsy T-shirt, the one she's had on for days now – Ben's old Lynyrd Skynyrd one, with the neck cut out – fails miserably to keep her warm. Manhattan glimmers past McCarren Park, its peaks and pinnacles shining like man-made constellations, like something from the future. It's beautiful, but under a blanket of snow, New York would become even more so, turning twinkly and old-timey. This concrete mess with towers sprouting like beanstalks, with subways zigzagging and crowded streets teeming with grime – all of it would be obliterated.

Anna steps back from the window, but leaves it open; she can't smoke in an enclosed space. *Hipokryta,* her father would have said. She *is* a hypocrite, dissecting everything, especially the things that bring her pleasure. Her father, on the other hand, would lie in bed, chewing saltwater taffy, reading his Polish newspaper till three A.M., and chain-smoking More Reds, as her mother silently suffered beside him. Her father, who, every so often, threatened to hang himself.

'You're a refugee? You sure don't look like a refugee,' Ben had said, eyeing her naked body supine next to his.

'*Daughter* of a refugee, if you wanna get technical. The Commies ousted my dad years ago. I was seven.'

'The Commies. Sounds so . . .'

'Dated?' Anna reached her hand toward his pretty American face.

'Sexy.'

Anna places the ashtray on her lap, hugging it gently between her thighs. Cardboard boxes stare at her from every corner, massacred by cheap utility tape. Months have passed since she and Ben moved into their new apartment, but the boxes remain untouched. She remembers that the super is stopping by today to fix the refrigerator door.

Anna's head hurts. Her nose is stuffy. The corner of her bottom lip is hot and itchy, a sure sign of a cold sore brewing. There is a weird throbbing pain near her right shoulder blade, which has come and gone intermittently during the last few weeks, and which Anna suspects might be lung cancer. Ben calls her a 'raging hypochondriac,' and he's right.

When Ben left for the airport five days ago, he begged Anna to join him. It was their tradition: Thanksgiving in Omaha.

'Come with me. Don't you miss my mom's stuffing? She misses you, Annie.'

'I can't fly, Ben. You know that.'

'Then let's rent a car and make a road trip out of it.'

'I can't, Ben,' she said and turned away from him.

Ben's mother, Nancy, always sported Birkenstocks and smelled like patchouli. She had long gray hair and all-knowing eyes that – Anna was sure – could see right through you. Nancy loved Anna from the beginning, and was always begging her and Ben to 'have a kid already, wedlock, schmedlock!' So, what would Nancy do if Anna showed up in her current state – slightly overweight and depressed? What would Anna say to her? *Missed you, Nan, but I've been real busy, what with the auditions and abortions.* It was too soon to face Nancy; the shame Anna felt was too much.

Ben had called from the airport. Even though things were strained between them, Anna had still wanted him to call her just before takeoff, in case anything happened. Since 9/11, she'd only flown twice – once to LA for a last-minute audition, and once to St. Thomas with Ben. Both times, her heart was in her throat. Anna shuffled down the aisle with her collection of crucifixes in her palm, relics from Catholic schoolgirl days, and her dad's old chain with the Polish Black Madonna medallion around her neck. She scanned her fellow passengers for dark bearded faces (it was fucked up but true), and didn't say amen till the wheels touched the tarmac again.

Ben is flying back home today. Back to what, Anna doesn't know. What can she offer him anymore? In the beginning she offered him exotic tales of growing up in the Flatbush projects, tales of a homely little Polish immigrant. She offered him daily blow jobs and Thai take-out every night. She offered him her world, a world of small but incomparable measure, a world where tanks rolled in the streets, where armed *milicja* jailed idealistic young men who fought for their freedom as their fathers and grandfathers had before them. She offered romance; it was all so incredibly romantic – the turmoil of a foreign country recounted by a Slavic-looking Marilyn Monroe.

In turn, Ben offered her a version of the New World, the uncomplicated pleasure of a boy who came from the average middle class. 'I've got four brothers,' he told her that first night, as the sun was coming up. 'Jonah, Jefferson, Simon, and Samuel.' Anna swooned over the Midwestern musicality of their names. She repeated the names in her melodious voice, tinged with the slightest trace of an Eastern European accent, as if reciting a stanza of an Emerson poem.

'Anna Baran ain't bad either.'

'Well, it could have been Żdzisława.' Anna laughed when Ben tried to repeat the word, his tongue twisting in on itself, his jaw clenched.

Last Monday, Anna had locked the door behind Ben and prepared for total isolation till his return. There would be no Thanksgiving in New York, but then again, there never had been. Her parents didn't partake in the turkey. Her father was firm in that regard. 'I steal land from the Indian, I rob his everything and put him on casino war camps and now I eat like pig to celebrate? No fuck way!' So there was no one to bother her and she was free to smoke 147 cigarettes, take one shower, and come to the realization that Ben's absence has not brought fondness or longing, just dread.

At four-twenty A.M., the phone rings. The ashtray balancing on Anna's lap flies in the air and spills all over the couch. She scrambles to the table on the other side of the room. A phone call at four in the morning can mean only a few things. *Dad,* Anna thinks, *it's* Tato.

'Hello?'

'*Ania!* Oh, Ania . . . !' Her mother, Paulina, is wailing on the other end, and Anna's heart explodes upon direct contact with the sound, a sound that pierces the silence of the room and has no business infiltrating the hush of night in such a sudden, ear-splitting manner.

'What is it? Oh God, *Mamo,* what is it?'

'He's dead! *O mój Boże,* Anna, he's dead.' This is the phone call that Anna's been waiting for since she was thirteen, waiting for on subways, in school halls, while playing Chinese jump rope, or taking a bath, or biting her nails like a zombie in front of the TV while her mother paced the dining room waiting for her father, Radosław, to turn up.

'How did he do it?' she hears herself asking before it all has sunk in.

'He didn't do it. Filip did it!' Anna's breath slows down and the walls stop closing in.

'Who's Filip?' Her mother is still crying, loudly, incessantly – and right now, in the midst of obvious confusion, it's infuriating Anna.

'Filip, Elwira's boyfriend! Anna, who do you think I'm talking about?' Anna doesn't answer but her mother thankfully plows on. 'Justyna's husband is dead, he was murdered last night, in his own house. By his sister-in-law's boyfriend. Can you believe it?'

'*Poczekaj!* Wait. Just wait a fucking second, Mother! Just hold on, okay?' Anna breathes slowly, rearranging her thoughts, smoothing down the tabletop with her hand as she does. 'Justyna? From Kielce?'

'Yes! Jesus, how many Justynas do you know? Her husband was stabbed in the middle of the night. Justyna's a widow. A twenty-six-year-old widow . . .' And now her mother is whimpering, mewling like an injured cat.

'Wow.'

'Wow?!! *Wow!!??*'

'What, *Mamo*? What do you want me to say? It's four in the morning. You caught me off guard—'

'Well, I'm sorry if this isn't a convenient time to tell you that your best friend's husband was just murdered—'

'She *was* my best friend. She *was*.'

'Oh, *Jezus,* Anka, really?'

'It's horrible. It's horrible, but I thought you were . . .'

'Were what?'

'Nothing. How did you find out?'

'Her grandmother called me from Poland. I have to go now. Their poor mother is turning over in her grave. Please call Justyna. When you stop crying, *call her.*' There are tears running down Anna's face, her neck. *How can that be?* she asks herself again, and then the dial tone signals her to hang up the phone and ask stupid questions later.

KAMILA
WYANDOTTE, MICHIGAN

They call it Downriver, these clustered neighborhoods of southern Detroit. It is below zero right now, frozen over, iced down. The snow is no longer fluffy or crunchy; it is rock solid, piled high along the road like glaciers. It's only a few days after Thanksgiving, and already merry fools are dragging Christmas trees along the curb. Kamila can't help but think that they look like corpses. America is a strange place.

'*Śniadanie!*' her mother barks from downstairs, but Kamila can't eat breakfast so she ignores her mother. Kamila has other things on her mind today, things that can no longer be put off. She's been here for weeks, and now she's ready.

The house is quiet. The modest little yellow house that her parents scrounged for is a two-story, gated little piece of the American dream, just off Spruce Street. Kamila's parents have lived here since 1997, and five years after they left Poland for good, Kamila, their only daughter, has finally come for a visit.

When Lech Wałęsa won and the world changed, Kamila's parents, Włodek and Zofia Marchewski, took full advantage of their nation's newfound freedom. They flew from Poland to Ankara for Easter, spent Christmas in Crete, and then, one summer, Włodek visited his second cousin who lived in a sleepy, leafy suburb of Detroit. And Włodek kept visiting, each time for longer periods, until finally his wife, Zofia, allowed him the courtesy and joined him, first for two weeks, then for good. Why exactly he fell in love with Michigan as opposed to Rome or London, nobody knew, least of all Kamila. But fall in love he did, and that love eclipsed all fear of laws and impunities, and so her parents became, like countless other Poles in the States, illegal aliens.

Despite her father's tales of dollar stores, central air, and the beautiful Our Lady of Mount Carmel Church (*Built in the 1800s by our people, Kamilka!*) Kamila decided to stay behind and finish college in Kielce. 'Just send me some postcards now and again, Włodziu,' she told him, half-joking. Włodek did send his only daughter postcards, one every week for the last five years, post-cards boasting sepia-toned vignettes of the quaint, historic downtown of his adopted city. Every month he sent her ten twenty-dollar bills neatly folded in half and held in place by a single rubber band. And life was good that way, it was fine and dandy, until the day Kamila needed to escape, far away, and somehow nowhere seemed farther from Kielce, Poland, than Wyandotte, Michigan.

Kamila Marchewska-Ludek has done everything in her power to recoup this past month. *You need to de-stress the situation, you need to cleanse your palate. Fuck him!* her best friend, Natalia, wrote in an email a few weeks ago. 'Fuck him.' Was Natalia being funny, or did the irony go sailing past her? Kamila had done nothing but try to fuck him for the entire length of their nine-year relationship, but Emil had always denied her. *Let's wait. Let's be old-fashioned.* And she believed his excuses, mastur-bating once a week to visions of his alabaster body pressed on hers. Later on, he proposed and they married, but nothing changed.

Kamila has escaped, as much as one can escape in a cyber

world, where everything is connected, but feels disjointed none-theless. Though her appointment at the Polish embassy was pre-planned, the actual departure was hasty – a last-minute call to the travel agency, a haphazardly packed suitcase – and now, four weeks later, she's still not sure how she made it out.

Her father met her at the Detroit airport, bouncing on his heels.

'Kamilka! Oh, Kamilka! What did you do to your hair?'

Kamila stepped back from her father, who had aged consider-ably in five years, whose frame was now as thin as ever, but en-hanced by a surprisingly corpulent gut. She touched her black bangs self-consciously.

'I dyed it. You didn't notice in the pictures?'

'Oh, but it's not what I expected in real life, *córeczko*. And your nose . . . it looks nice, Kamilka. But I expected my little girl, with that great big orange mop and those white strappy sandals on your feet.'

'I was ten when you bought me those shoes, *Tato*. I wasn't ten when you left. Now, quit crying, please, and take me home.' Włodek obliged, glancing sideways at his prodigal daughter every few seconds. Back in his fold for less than ten minutes, and Kamila was already growing irritated.

Somehow, she settled in quickly. Her parents had cleaned out the sewing room and bought a blow-up mattress for their daugh-ter to sleep on. 'For weeks or forever, Kamilka, it's up to you,' her father said, his gray eyes glistening. She had a desk, a closet, and a phone, and that's all she needed. They hadn't asked yet why her husband, who looked so dapper in the wedding album the newlyweds had mailed them five years ago, had not come with her.

The Polish enclave of Wyandotte was seven square miles small and made Kielce seem like a metropolis, but its size didn't matter to Kamila. She hadn't come to America to sightsee. Her plan was to distance herself from recent events and to make money so that she could go back to Poland clad in Ann Taylor and Banana Republic from head to toe, showing off the fabulous look that American women have perfected – chic nonchalance. To earn money she took on babysitting and a cashier shift at a local *masarnia* – a deli that paid under the table. The dollars accumulated quickly, fistfuls of crumpled Andrew Jacksons that she stuffed in her dresser, but, despite the money, Kamila was wilting.

Today was a snow day and the streets were full of suburban teens. The most formidable nation in the world closed up shop when it snowed. Solemn news reporters urged residents to stock up on canned soup and bottled water. It was so pathetic. And on the streets, hooligans flew past, outfitted in ridiculous coats that brought to mind blowfish, throwing snowballs and shouting mindless obscenities.

Now, Kamila sits upstairs at her desk, hands folded, staring down at her old typewriter, the one she lugged through three airports because she'd been afraid to check it in Warsaw. The one her grandmother bought her when Kamila was thirteen and confessed her dream of becoming a famous writer. Kamila could leave her job at the pharmacy, she could leave her husband, but there was no way in hell she was leaving her typewriter.

She hasn't written a letter in a long time, not like this, not one that wasn't sent via email. But her parents, for all their new-fangled American ways, have opted out of getting a computer. 'There's no art to it, Kamilka,' her father explained. 'I'd rather read letters from home and watch the nightly news, in the good old-fashioned way.' So Kamila walks into town and sits for hours at an Internet café on Biddle Avenue anytime she wants to check her inbox and scan silly sites about American celebrities until her brain goes numb. The Internet café, however, isn't an option for the deed at hand. No way was Kamila going to write what she had to write in a public place; there were roaming eyes everywhere, especially in this community, where the Poles rubbed their noses in everyone's business as if gossip were a vocation.

Emil Ludek is far away. He is seven hours and seven thousand three hundred and twenty-two kilometers out of her reach, and she thanks God for it. It is two in the afternoon in Kielce, and he is probably still lounging in their bed – probably with his lover. She can picture the two men, one of them her husband, snuggling under her lavender duvet. In Wyandotte, Kamila's hand shakes as she finally begins tapping the keys on her Remington. *Dear Emil, Why? Why didn't you tell me you were g—* Kamila's fingers freeze. She can't do it. Just then the door to her room cracks open and her father, her mousy little father, pops his head in.

'Kamilka? I just got a call from Poland. Some bad news.'

Kamila's heart thumps loudly in her chest. 'From who?' She told Emil never to call her again.

'From *Pani* Kazia.'

'*Pani* Kazia?'

'Yes, Kamila, remember? Justyna Strawicz's grandmother. Weren't you two good friends?'

Kamila swallows audibly. Slowly, she pulls the unfinished letter from her typewriter.

'We were.'

JUSTYNA
KIELCE, POLAND

The last twenty-four hours have brought a bloodbath upon the Strawicz home. They have brought the inevitable, but Justyna can't see that now. All she can see is that overnight, she has become someone who will be whispered about. From now on, people will whisper that she's too sad, or not sad enough. They'll whisper accusations and apologies. And surely they'll whisper if she ever finds another man, but who the fuck in this town will want to date an unemployed widow with a kid, anyway?

On the way back from the police station, walking up Witosa Road, Justyna saw her neighbors staring out their windows and clustered on the sidewalk, stealing glances in her direction. She walked past, enjoying a smoke, trying to elicit eye contact so she could wave and make them fucking squirm, but no one bit. She was ambling through a nightmare, through a haze, and nothing seemed real.

The kitchen sink is full of dishes. Rambo, her mother's dog, has left two piss puddles in the hallway that no one has bothered to clean up. Her son, Damian, is getting antsy on her lap and asks if he can go outside to play. It's cold and snowing, but Justyna pushes him off her. *And don't come back,* she thinks, as he runs out of the kitchen.

From the foyer, he yells, 'Will *Tato* be back when I come home?' Justyna shrugs her shoulders.

'We'll see!' she shouts back.

She lights another cigarette. Upstairs she hears her sister, El-wira, crying again. She hasn't stopped crying and Justyna can't blame her. Last night, Elwira's boyfriend killed Paweł, killed him in the upstairs bathroom, cold-blooded, out of the blue, just like that.

Celina, Elwira's daughter, wanders into the kitchen, a naked Barbie dangling from her skinny hand. '*Ciociu,* the dog pee-peed by the stairs.' Justyna says nothing. '*Ciociu!* It stinks!' Justyna looks at her niece, at her big blue eyes, ratty hair like tangled straw, her pretty oval face.

She hands Celina a dish towel. 'If it stinks, then clean it up.'

On the table, Justyna moves her ashtray around in a circle. She can still see Paweł's body in her head, twisted and puffy, splayed on the coroner's table. Had his last word been an angry '*kurwa!*' or a cry for her, a frantic '*Justynka!*'? No one gives a shit and Justyna doesn't blame them. Her husband was just a carcass; she could see that in the way the examiners had poked at him. Paweł would never be someone who *used to be;* to them he had never existed in the first place. He was a corpse. Justyna had stared at his gashes, as if she too had no point of reference any-more, as if she was gazing at some unfortunate stranger and not at Paweł at all.

Later, at the police station, Justyna smoked one L&M Light after the next. She stared at the puke-green walls and talked, while a middle-aged cop scribbled everything down. The cop, whose nameplate read *Kurka,* rubbed his eyes every once in a while, stifling yawns.

'Elwira's boyfriend beat up on her. Not just a slap here and there, 'cause God knows, she deserved that from time to time. I'm talking a black eye, cigarette burns, that kind of thing. I never did anything to stop him. Neither did you guys. But my husband . . .' Justyna faltered. 'My husband tried to stop him. He—'

Kurka had stopped scribbling after 'she deserved' and sat there stiffly with his lips pursed.

'Mrs. Strawicz, we need information pertaining to last night. Just last night.' Justyna tapped a cigarette on the table. How could she explain to this dimwit that the last twenty-five years of her life pertained to Paweł's death? That somewhere in the far-flung past, there was a kernel of an answer to what the fuck had happened a few hours ago.

'At about midnight, Filip came home drunk, started picking on Elwira. Told her to cook him food, or something. So she goes, "Fuck off" and he—'

'Elwira Zator, your younger sister?'

Justyna nods her head. They knew exactly who Elwira Zator was; at that very moment her sister was in another room down the hall, getting interrogated by another drab officer.

'Anyway, he smacked her and her nose started bleeding. Paweł was, like, enough of this shit. So, you know, he punched him, punched Filip, just once but it was enough.' Justyna smiled recalling the force of her husband's gallantry. 'Then Filip went upstairs. Fell asleep, I guess.' Justyna was aware of her repeated use of the term *guess*. She sighed audibly; there was no point to the interrogation and she wished Officer Kurka would just let her go.

Filip had lugged himself up the stairs, blood sprayed on his face, drunk as a skunk. He was roaring obscenities and Justyna was afraid the kids would wake up, but they were used to slumbering through fights. At one point Filip lost his footing and fell backward, on his ass, grabbing the railing at the last minute to

18

keep from tumbling downstairs. Justyna wondered where they would all be now had Filip lost his grip completely, had he tumbled backward, perhaps twisted his neck.

'We all went to bed. Around one-thirty A.M. I *guess*. Ah, goddamnit, you sure you wanna hear it? I mean, nothing I got here – nothing! – is, whattaya call it, *conclusive*.'

Kurka nodded impatiently.

'Okay, then, I *guess* Filip woke up and went down to the kitchen to get a knife. Elwira was sleeping on the couch. She heard him but thought he was just parched, sobering up, and she went back to sleep. Aren't you guys getting all this from Elwira? I mean she was the one who saw – '

'Just go on, Mrs. Strawicz. We need to hear every single witness account.'

Witness implied awareness, it implied action, but Justyna felt like a passerby at best. She exhaled loudly, her head spinning.

'Elwira heard the scream. I can sleep through anything. Obviously.' Justyna sighed and smiled dryly. 'By the time I found Paweł in the bathroom, he was facedown on the floor, there was blood everywhere and, um, I dunno, sir, just a lot of fucking blood. I just stood there. Like I . . . like I couldn't fucking move.'

'Shock, Mrs. Strawicz.'

'No shit, sir.'

Kurka pursed his mouth again. She could tell her constant cursing was irritating the fuck out of him.

'Then Elwira ran up, her throat bloody, from where Filip, uh, grabbed her, I guess. She was crying and she managed to tell me that Filip had run out the back, but not before he found her on the couch and told her if she said anything she'd be fucking next. She didn't know what he was talking about, naturally. Not then, anyway.'

'Well, try to get some rest. Kielce is a relatively small city, Mrs. Strawicz, and we'll do our best.'

Two young cops drove her home. They were nice enough and the one with the mustache was kind of cute. They told a joke about a prostitute and a blind gypsy and Justyna laughed along. She asked to be dropped off a few blocks from her house. *The neighbors,* she explained, rolling her eyes. They smiled back at her kindly and for a moment, Justyna thought that all this – her husband's death, her kid, her mother's cancer, her whole fantastic fucked-up life – that all of it was a dream, and any moment she'd wake up.

CHAPTER TWO

1989

ANNA

KIELCE, POLAND

In the backseat of the Volkswagen, Anna wakes up with a start. She wipes some drool from her mouth and stares out the window. The sun is rising quickly. It is enormous but shapeless, as if God has taken a knife to it and is spreading it across the sky. The American sun blanches in comparison.

'Are we there yet?'

'Almost. Crossed the border while you were napping.'

'So we're in Poland now?'

'*Tak*. Welcome back, Ania.' *Wujek* Adam keeps his eyes on the road when he speaks to her. Her uncle is so cute, with his thick black hair and lopsided grin, like a Polish Tom Cruise.

'Excited?'

When they left Berlin at four A.M. it had still been dark. Uncle Adam said it would take about nine hours to drive to Kielce. Anna glances at her wristwatch, does the math, and squeals in the backseat, immediately regretting it. In the rearview mirror she sees Adam shake his head.

'I guess so.' He smiles and lights a cigarette.

The road is narrow and bumpy, making it difficult to navigate. The other drivers swerve their cars maniacally, passing each other whenever there is a lapse in oncoming traffic, and from time to time Uncle Adam does the same. But Anna isn't afraid of this kind of driving; whatever brings her to Kielce faster is fine by her. They are surrounded by fields full of roaming cows, actual cows! Vast patchwork hillocks just like she's seen in Irish movies pass by endlessly. Once in a while, she spies old men on rickety bikes or old women by the side of the road with handmade signs offering *jagody* or *truskawki,* fresh berries sold in glass jars. When she rolls down the window, Anna is taken aback. She didn't know she would remember the air here. It smells like burning haystacks and fresh laundry, like sunshine and sausage, piquant and fresh at the same time. There are layers of scents in this old air; it is aged to perfection.

'*Wujku,* nobody in Kielce knows, right? *Tato* didn't ruin it?'

'Nothing's ruined. I just hope your *babcia* doesn't have a heart attack.' Anna squeals again, this time unrepentant. She sticks her face out the window, like a puppy, and everything swishes past her – a ribbon of countryside zooming by.

Last time she was in Poland, Anna was a scrawny little seven-year-old. Now she's almost thirteen, tall and curvy, with plump lips, big blue eyes, and newly permed blond hair. The tank top she's wearing shows off both an impressive bust and an adolescent paunch. Will her family even recognize her? Will she look foreign to them? Will she look American?

Six and a half years ago, when the Barans landed at JFK airport, armed only with two suitcases, standing in the line at customs and immigration felt like the end of something. They had no money, no knowledge of English, and no relations or acquaintances in New York. Their sense of loss was so huge it felt like the three of them were suddenly nothing but driftwood. A Polish woman named Aleksandra from the AFL-CIO greeted them at arrivals and escorted them to a refugee hotel on the Lower East Side, where they stayed for three weeks. At first, the city was too much for Anna and her parents to bear. There was too much noise and too much movement. For the first few days, they cosseted themselves in the hotel room and just stared at the color TV. At night Anna and her mother often woke up to the sound of Radosław stomping on roaches.

After that, the AFL-CIO helped them rent public housing in downtown Brooklyn. Anna vaguely remembers how her parents struggled. Their furniture was scavenged at night, while Anna slept. Her parents combed the streets, stunned at what people in New York City deemed garbage. They couldn't help Anna with her homework, not even the first-grade stuff. Paulina started cleaning houses to earn pocket money. Anna doesn't remember what Radosław did. She doesn't remember what it felt like not to understand a language and maybe that's why Anna has only fragments: a Pac-Man machine in the lobby of the Breslin Hotel, commercials for *CATS! The Musical,* the marvel of rubbing shoulders with black people, Chinese people, and Hasidim.

Soon, Anna was giving her father English lessons, earning a dime for every word he misspelled during their nightly dictation sessions. She was the one calling the bank, and translating the notes Paulina's employers left regarding laundry. Anna excelled in her ESL classes, and her parents, having neither the time nor money for English school, relied on both Anna and the television as teacher. They never quite caught up.

The years passed, each one quicker than the last. This September Anna will attend eighth grade at a Catholic school in Brooklyn. Her girlfriends are all Italian and prefer to have get-togethers at their houses; nobody wants to come to the projects to sit in Anna's room and stare at her posters of Elvis, New Kids on the Block, and the lone map of her homeland.

Anna tries to be all that her parents demand – studious, proud, and courageous. But she has a hard time looking people in the eye. She's in constant turmoil about her overbite and the glasses she was prescribed at age eight. When Anna laughs, she cups her hand to shield her mouth, like a geisha. She has crushes on boys but doesn't do anything about them. She's in a constant state of pining, for what and for whom she doesn't know. When Radosław yells at her for not wearing a hat in the winter she doesn't protest or raise her middle finger when he turns his back. Instead, Anna runs to her room, shuts the door politely, and quietly weeps. Radosław says crying is for pussies, but Anna can't help it.

Her father is still not allowed back into Poland; the threat of political imprisonment continues, as long as the country remains under Communist law. Radosław often recounted what the government official told him when the Barans were inquiring about asylum: 'You deserted in 1975 and in your statement wrote that there was no such thing as a "Polish" army. You were right. There is no Polska, *kolego*. There is only the Polish People's Republic. And if you ever come back here, you are fucked, comrade.' Sometimes, when Radosław gets into one of his moods, he cries about the Commie pricks who killed his father, the Commie pricks who 'castrated' him. 'Commie pricks, Commie fucks, *skurwysyny*,' he whispers as he pounds his skull with his fists. His moods scare Anna more than his belt smacking the side of the bed, and more than the times he calls her a *debil*. Her father's sadness frightens Anna the most, because she doesn't know how to make it better, and no one can tell her.

Radosław is free to travel anywhere west of the Berlin Wall. Now, he does his freedom fighting from cramped, smoky offices in London, Paris, and Amsterdam. He goes on overseas trips that last for months at a time, bringing Anna back useless gifts like yellow wooden clogs. His work, which probably includes smuggling, is shrouded in secrecy. All Anna knows is that he has a collection of passports, driver's licenses, and business cards that mysteriously read *Import/Export*. This summer, he decides to take Anna to Europe with him. Their last stop was West Berlin, where Uncle Adam lives.

Adam was going to Poland as a favor to her dad, who couldn't cross the border. The trip had something to do with a printing press that Radosław's friends in Kielce were counting on. It was only a three-day trip and, as soon as they mentioned it, Anna begged to go with her uncle. She delivered a beseeching monologue about how Radosław 'didn't raise a coward, did he?'; about how she yearned to see her homeland. When Radosław heard the word *ojczyzna*, coming from someone he clearly found lacking in guts, something must have clicked and he agreed to let her go. Anna threw her arms around her father's neck and inhaled the ever-constant mix of tobacco and sausage. 'Go,' he murmured into her hair. 'And come back.' It was an order, disguised as permission. He swatted the top of her head, pulled on her bangs, and clutched the side of her face; a series of gestures executed quickly, like a secret handshake. Then, from around his neck, he took off his chain, the one with the Black Madonna medallion on it, the one he'd gotten from a priest while in prison. He put it on Anna, tucked it underneath her blouse. '*Wracaj*,' Radosław grunted, and then he walked off without another word.

Anna idolizes her father. He is a true *bohater*, a hero of *Solidarność*. But when he yells the whole house shakes and Anna is terrified of him, terrified of his anger, which is always on the verge of bursting. The last month, traversing Europe together, has been like a tense, drawn-out blind date. Conversation does not flow. Radosław refuses to spend money on hotels, and instead they sleep in the rental car or on colleagues' couches. Anna has not been in a good mood since the plane ride, when midway over the Atlantic she got her first period. After they landed in Paris, Radosław made her buy her own maxi pads. Anna approached the nice French cashier, silently pointed to the big blue pouch of pads behind the counter, and felt like dying. When she finally managed to secure the giant foamy diaper to her underwear, she sat in the bathroom stall of a café and cried.

In the rearview mirror, Anna sees Uncle Adam wink and motion in front of him as they finally pass a green 'KIELCE' marker. She stares out the window in awe as they roll into the city and, when Adam makes a right on Warszawska Street, her heart starts walloping in her chest. Minutes later, they park in front of her *babcia*'s prewar limestone building. When Anna opens the car door and steps out onto the cobblestone sidewalk, she opens her mouth to tell Adam that she wants to go up alone, but no words come out. When she turns around Anna sees the old rug beater she used to dangle from like a *kiełbasa,* and wants to shout for joy, but again, she can't muster a syllable.

By the thicket of rowanberry trees, which are full of the bright red *jarzębiny* that she suddenly remembers picking as a little girl, Anna stares at the rug beater. The *trzepak* is made up of three iron poles that fit together like a frame, planted into the ground, with a fourth pole slicing the middle. Vacuum cleaners are still a Western luxury, and in the fifties local Communist housing administrations erected *trzepaki* in every neighborhood. When she was little, Anna remembers people dragging their rugs and carpets outside, hanging them over the poles, and thumping them with what looked like tennis rackets. Anna closes her eyes and can hear the *thwap thwap* sound that used to echo like a chorus and often woke her up in the mornings. The sudden memory is so vivid that she remains frozen until Adam speaks.

'I'll wait down here for a few, all right? So you can have your big moment. Whistle if we need to call an ambulance.' Adam leans against the car and lights a cigarette, laughing.

The stairwell in the apartment building smells the same. Anna takes her time winding up the three flights, her clammy hand gripping the bright blue balustrade, inhaling the blend of cigarettes, rain, fried pierogi, and metal. If her whole visit consisted of standing in the stairwell and breathing, it would be enough. On the third floor there are three doors. She knocks on the last one, and it opens, and there, just like that, stands *Ciocia* Ula. They stand and stare at one another. Anna is struck by her aunt's hair – a poufed bob the exact color of pumpkin. And when Ula finally asks, 'Who're you looking for?' Anna sees that Ula, despite being only in her mid-thirties, has absolutely no teeth.

'O Matko Boska!'

Faces appear behind Ula, the cries of 'heavenly mother' grow louder. Suddenly there is a mad rush, a cacophony of yelps, and Anna is pulled into the apartment by dozens of limbs; or at least that's what it feels like. Faces press into hers; people are shouting and jumping up and down and then, just as suddenly, there is an eerie stillness, as Anna's face is drawn into a warm, heaving bosom. Her grandmother's embrace is so strong that it hurts. Finally, *Babcia* Helenka breaks the clinch and takes Anna's petrified face into her hands, which happen to be the softest hands in the world.

'Aniusia. You've come back.' *Aniusia.* Nobody calls her that back in the States. But the Poles have codes and deeply rooted traditions when it comes to names. What someone calls you is

what they think of you. Diminutive, demonstrative, cautious, guarded, formal, intimate; the form of your name is a symbol of your status. So, Anna is Ania, Anka, and sometimes, once in a while, she is Aniusia: darling, sweet, little Aniusia.

Later, after they stop literally pinching themselves and her, *Babcia* tries to coax her toward speech.

'But your Polish is beautiful. Don't be embarrassed. We always talk on the phone when your mama calls, and now we can talk in person. In person, Aniu!' *Babcia* Helenka entreats as she kneels by Anna, tenderly stroking her hair. But Anna smiles through her tears and says nothing.

After the shrieking dies down, Adam comes up and fills them in on the hows and whys and then he leaves. 'I'll be back for you Sunday, ten A.M.' Anna sits on the divan with an empty plate on her lap that mere minutes ago was filled with homemade meat *pieroẓki* and sweet carrot soufflé. Her relatives, who had all come over to *Babcia*'s for *obiad* that day, hover around, offering jokes, smiles, biscuits, and tea. *Ciocia* Bronka and *Ciocia* Ula, her mother's older sisters, are there with their children Hubert and Renata. *Wujek* Leszek, Bronka's husband, stands by the balcony, smoking and asking about her dad. Anna's cousin Hubert sports a curly pompadour and acid-wash jeans, belted high above his waist. Cousin Renata is taller than Hubert and with her wide nose and small, pretty mouth she looks just like Aunt Bronka.

Hubert cuts in among the chattering women. 'People, leave her alone. *Jezus Maria,* she's exhausted. Anka, just ignore the barbarians. What do you wanna do? Wanna take a walk or something? Renata and I can take you to the *zalew.* Remember the bay? We used to go there every summer. The water's shitty now, but the Café Relaks is still open. Remember it? And that Czech circus has pitched its tent right on the—'

'Oh my God, Hubert, talk about leaving her alone!' Renata laughs and rolls her eyes in Hubert's direction. Renata took Anna to her first movie. Anna was five, and she remembers hurrying there in the rain, the almost religious hush in the theater, and images of the film, *W Pustyni I W Puszczy*. She spent weeks dreaming of the movie and the young Polish lead, her first crush. Anna remembers all of this now, in a momentary flash.

Wujek Leszek growls, 'Hubert, you *pudel,* you leave her the hell alone.'

Anna smiles. Hubert's hair does resemble a poodle's, tight black curls that extend past his head like a coiled tower. *Ciocia* Bronka starts laughing and chokes on the tea biscuit she's devouring and *Babcia* runs for a dish towel, because 'the crumbs, the crumbs, Bronka!' Anna's smile widens; she loves them so much! Her heart aches with love, but how was it that just yesterday she didn't even remember their faces? She never thought about them at all, aside from the calls to *Babcia* and the Christmas cards she signed her name on every year that were mailed along with care packages from her mom. She never really missed them, or Poland, as a matter of fact. And all of a sudden, she wants to live here, with all her relatives, in this very room, and never, ever leave.

'Actually, I *would* like to go outside.'

These are the first words she utters and Hubert and Renata jump to their feet.

'*Sama.* If that's okay.'

Babcia Helenka tells her not to wander off too far, to please stay in front of the building. Leszek says he'll be spying out the kitchen window and if she talks to any boys he'll report her to the authorities. It's just a joke, but Anna instantly recalls her father's warnings about the police. Truthfully, she just wants to go and hang off the rug beater to see if she can still pull off some somersaults.

When she opens the apartment building's stairwell door, she sees that a dozen or more kids have gathered around. Most are hanging off the rug beater, some of them are squatting in front of it; they are an army of small warriors, holding down the fort in the face of an intruder. They must have seen the German car pull up; maybe someone caught a glimpse of a tall girl in Levi's and spread the word. Anna walks tentatively toward them.

The boys, assorted ages but not sizes (with legs so skinny that it makes her sad, those giant knees), pretend to be idle with other things such as gum chewing. The girls stare at her unabashedly. They are all – boys and girls alike – clad in polyester short shorts and open-toed sandals. Suddenly, one kid, whose shorts are so small they look like underwear, squints up at her and asks, '*Mówisz po Polsku?*' Anna nods and the boy continues, 'That's a Volkswagen, right? So, are you from Germany?'

Jestem Polka, Anna wants to say, 'I'm Polish,' but it's too early to feel defensive, so she merely shakes her head no.

Then, a pretty girl, who looks to be around Anna's age and has brown hair that is cropped like a boy's, asks, 'Then, where *are* you from? Because obviously you're not from here.' The girl stands with her arms folded sternly across her chest, waiting for Anna to answer. Some of the other girls chuckle and Anna flushes pink. The folded-arms girl wears orange cotton shorts with flowers on them, an outfit that would be ridiculed in the States.

'Actually, I *am* from here. I was born here. But I live in New York City.'

A slight hush befalls the group.

'You mean, like, America?' asks another boy, whose unfortunate bangs cut right across the middle of his forehead in a perfectly straight line. Anna nods again.

'I'll be fucked!' exclaims a kid who can't be more than six. And then everybody cracks up, including Anna.

The next day, Anna runs outside as soon as she wakes up. She exchanges addresses with her new friends. The pretty brunette is Justyna Zator, whose mother was best friends with Anna's mother, Paulina. Justyna tells Anna that their moms got pregnant the same year and both of them had to quit school and that their mothers still keep in touch. 'I know everything about you, girl. I know you live in Brooklyn and that your dad drives an Audi.' Justyna pronounces it *Brroookleeen*, and Anna smiles.

That day, Sebastian Tefilski comes back from summer camp and immediately sets his sights on the *Amerykanka*. Sebastian is cute (by Polish standards at least. He wears terry-cloth socks and tucks his shirts in) and Anna is smitten. Justyna tells her that he's a total show-off and when they were dating last summer he kissed like a dog, slobbering so much that her chin broke out in a rash. Anna listens intently but doesn't care about chin rashes, she just cares that the cool boy likes her. In fact, *everybody* likes her. The feeling is overwhelming and addictive all at once.

On the third day, the day of her departure, tears are shed. Anna weeps, her cousins weep, her aunts weep while chain-smoking on the *balkon,* and *Babcia* weeps in the kitchen, kneading her rosary. Anna tries to cheer them up, and vows to return in ten months. She'll work after school and buy her own airplane ticket if she has to. An hour before Uncle Adam comes to pick her up, Anna says goodbye to the apartment. She stands in every corner, touching each wall with her palms, touching as many things as possible. 'I'll come back,' she whispers to the pink bathtub in the tiny bathroom, *'Wrócę.'*

Outside, the rug beater is occupied again, this time by an army of allies. They stare at her with sad, longing faces. Anna was never, ever this popular in New York. If her parents don't let her come back next year, she will probably kill herself.

Sebastian Tefilski arrives to the goodbye ceremony last minute, as Uncle Adam is about to load the car. He makes a gallant show of taking Anna's duffel bag from Uncle Adam and then hugs Anna, hugs her tight, even though the adults start cracking wise. Sebastian whispers in her ear, 'I can't wait for next summer. You'll be my girlfriend.' Anna gasps quietly into his neck. She will not forget his words: *Będziesz moją dziewczyną.*

As the car zooms past St. Józef's church, her childhood neighborhood of Szydłówek disappears just like that. In the backseat, Anna feels her heart breaking. Just a few kilometers away but she already feels *tęsknota* – a Polish word that describes a kind of yearning for which there is no American equivalent.

'Don't cry, *mała,*' Uncle Adam urges quietly as he steers back toward Warszawska Street, but Anna can't stop.

Kamila slams the front door, a slam so full of cuff it resounds through the whole apartment.

'*Mamo!* Did you or did you not go to school with a woman named Paulina Baran?'

Kamila bursts into the kitchen, and comes to a halt in front of her mother, who is sitting on a stool, a pail between her hefty thighs, peeling potatoes.

'What did I say about slamming doors?'

'Did you or did you not?'

Zofia stops peeling and points the tip of her knife in her daughter's direction, her face just venomous enough to shut up Kamila instantly.

'How dare you run into this house like a banshee, conducting an interrogation? I'm not your buddy, Kamila. You have more than enough *koleżanki* out there. And I hope for your sake none of them lent you that lipstick. Is that lipstick?'

Kamila taps her foot on the linoleum floor and tries to stare her mother down, failing miserably after ten seconds. She huffs into the bathroom, grabs a piece of gray toilet paper, and wipes her mouth. Lidka Frenczyk let everyone sample her Pink Seduction *szminka,* and in the uproar surrounding the Anna Baran news, Kamila simply forgot to wipe it off before running home. Zofia not only doesn't wear make-up, she doesn't *believe* in make-up. She doesn't shave her legs. She doesn't dab her wrists with perfume. She has a large mole on her left earlobe that is brown and disgusting and that everyone stares at because how could they not?

'Better.' Zofia glances up when Kamila walks back into the room, seemingly contrite. 'She wasn't Paulina Baran back then. She was Paulina Chmielinska.'

'So, you knew her? Were you friends with her? Did you know she has a daughter exactly my age?'

'We were acquaintances.'

'And!?'

'And what?'

'The daughter! What about the daughter!?'

'Cut the ruffian act, Kamila! I'm pushing your curfew up one hour.'

Kamila fights with all she's got to keep her foot from stomping the floor. It's bad enough that her curfew is already the same time as the ten-year-old Kosiak twins. Instead of wringing her mother's neck, she nods, slowly and deliberately, silently vowing to run away as soon as she has enough *złoty* saved up.

'Hand me a clean bowl. The one in the sink.' Zofia watches Kamila obey, the fighting spirit in her temporarily trounced.

'Little Ania Baran was born exactly six weeks after you were. I think you were baptized on the same day, but I can't remember. I do remember during the whole ceremony, you were bawling your head off.' Zofia allows a complacent smile. 'That was the year that Teresa Anielska, Paulina, and I all got pregnant. Of course, I was married to your father and you were completely planned, but the school kicked me out as well.'

They were baptized on the same exact day? Kamila wants to

shriek in triumph. Hah! She wants to take this information, run back to the benches, and rub it in Justyna's face.

'Guess what? Little Ania Baran isn't so little anymore.'

'Well, I would assume so. But, hopefully she's not as "not little" as you. I've warned you plenty, Kamila; girls like you cannot afford to get fat. Life's not kind to *ofermy* like you so you better break the habit now. Have you used my hairspray today?'

Girls like you. Kamila's face burns. Girls like us, her mother means: unlovable, ungainly. Girls who asked for second help-ings and snuck in thirds. Girls who didn't care for diets or re-straint in any capacity. Girls with bad hair, bad skin, and bad thoughts.

Kamila can't remember about the hairspray, she can't remem-ber anything that preceded the news that Anna Baran had come to town.

'*Mamo,* she was here. Anna was here! In Kielce! This week-end!'

'Really? The Barans were here?'

'No! Just her. It was like a super-secret trip or something. Her uncle smuggled her in from West Germany.'

'I see.'

'Point is, Mother, that I was at our stupid *działka* this week-end with Dad, picking strawberries and twiddling my thumbs when I could have been forging a lifelong friendship! Why did you make me go?'

'Because you go every weekend, and you and your father have a great time in the country. Now, stop with the theatrics and put these in a pot.'

Kamila takes the bowl of newly skinned potatoes over to the stove. God, she loves potatoes so much. She hopes her mother is making *zalewajka.* A bowl of the sour soup with juicy *kiełbasa* and a hard-boiled egg would do wonders for her mood right now.

'Anyway, Mother, now Justyna Zator is all bragging about how Anna and her totally bonded and they're best friends *and* they exchanged addresses so they can write to each other, but Justyna won't show me Anna's address! And I wanted to write her a letter saying how sorry I was that I missed her and that if she comes back next summer I want to be her friend too. And now it's all ruined because you made me go to the stupid *działka* and because Justyna is a selfish pig!'

Kamila collapses into a chair by the window and weeps. She can't help it. The single most important event of the entire summer, and she missed it because she was too busy picking berries and weaving dumb garlands with her father. Once again, the brutality of the world takes Kamila's breath away. She can't go on if things like this continue.

Zofia stands and walks over to her daughter. 'Why are you getting so excited, Kamila? It's very unattractive.' Kamila looks away and doesn't say anything.

After Jakub died, instead of clinging to the one child she had left, Zofia let Włodek do all the primary parenting. He read Kamila fairy tales at bedtime, and kissed her scrapes, and showed her how to make animal figurines from blocks of shapeless clay. Zofia wanted none of it and accepted the role of bad cop with open arms. The result was twofold: she had succeeded in keeping a safe distance should any tragedy befall Kamila and in return Kamila had grown to resent her.

'Guess what, Modrzejewska? If you want to write Ania a letter, you're more than welcome. I still get a Christmas card from the Barans every year. Why don't you finish peeling these and I'll go look for one in the credenza?'

Kamila lifts her face off the table. *Modrzejewska*. The most famous Polish actress that ever lived. If only! If only Kamila had one ounce of the beauty and grace that Modrzejewska possessed. Before her mother has time to react, Kamila throws her chubby arms around Zofia's waist and pulls her close, stuffing her face into the folds of Zofia's apron. It would be nice if Zofia would put her hand on top of her daughter's head, or stroke her hair, but Zofia doesn't.

Later that night, Kamila calls her father into her bedroom. She hands him the pages silently and he begins reading.

Droga *Aniu,*

I'm very sorry that I have to introduce myself in a letter. I wish I could have done it in person, but you see, my father and I were on our działka the weekend you visited and so I missed you. Don't think I haven't been kicking myself ever since! Everyone said that you were really nice and friendly and also, very pretty! If you are wondering how I got your address, don't worry, it wasn't from Justyna. She wouldn't share it with me and I think you should know this because real friends share everything! This letter will be short because maybe you won't want to write to me. You might be too busy with life in America or you may have too many pen pals already. But I thought I would give it a shot because I am very friendly too! I really can't get over the fact that I didn't meet you. Did you know that our moms went to school together and that we were born just six weeks apart? I thought that was really neat. I'm older!

Oh, I almost forgot, my name is Kamila Marchewska. I live in klatka 63, just a few doors up from your *babcia*'s. Just like you, I am an only child (well, I did have a brother who drowned when he was three but I was five and don't really remember him). My mom's name is Zofia. That's how I got your address, from my mom, because your mom still sends us holiday cards. And we were baptized on the same day, at St. Józef's! So, you see, we're already connected!

I am in the eighth grade coming this fall. I can't believe the summer is almost over. It makes me want to shout with despair. No more gorgeous sunsets or bonfires, and the Tęcza Pool will be closing. My grandmother died in January and I've finally gotten over it, because everything is better in the summer. But that too is over now, and I am dreading the school year. Anyway, if the rumors are true and you really are coming next year for the whole vacation, then that is so wonderful and I will wait for you and cross off the days in my calendar till your arrival! I think we are going to be better friends than you and Justyna because she can be really mean and she's also a liar. But you don't have to tell her I said that. *Proszę cię* write back!

Kamila Mariana Marchewska

Włodek folds the letter in half and delicately sets it back on his daughter's nightstand. Kamila lies on the fold-out sofa in her pink nightgown with embroidered purple roses, and a collar that's buttoned all the way up. She looks like she is eight years old again, her face shining with anticipation.

'Well? Come on, *Tatusiu,* tell me what you think! And be honest.'

'*Tatusiu?* You haven't called me that in ages, *córeczko.*' Włodek smiles and Kamila rolls her eyes.

'It's a very good letter, Kamilka. But don't you think you come off a tad too eager?'

Kamila shoots up to a sitting position. 'But I *am* eager! I can't wait to meet her!'

'Well, you sound like you somehow *did* meet her. You reveal things that normally one wouldn't say to a stranger.'

'Like what? That I told her how rotten Justyna can be? Well, I'm only being honest. Believe me, *Tato,* it will save Ania a lot of heartache once she knows that Justyna is two-faced. Anyway, you always said that in the face of adversity, honesty is the best policy.'

'*Tak,* Kamila, I did say that.' Włodek stands up now and slowly walks over to his daughter's bookcase. His eyes peruse the shelves as he continues. 'But the thing about your brother? Maybe we could, well, not include it, just yet. Some things are better left for when one has developed a strong, trustworthy friendship. Do you understand what I mean?'

'Everyone knows what happened to Jakub! Only you and Mama think it's like a big secret or something. Anyway, who cares? It happened so many years ago!'

'My daughter, when someone you love is taken from you — because Jakub didn't just die, like *Babcia* did — it doesn't matter how many years pass; your heart will always be broken.'

'Isn't it enough that we visit his grave like a gajillion times a year? It's so pointless. Sorry, *Tato,* but it's true. Anyway, I'm gonna send the letter just like I wrote it. I think it's perfect.'

Włodek turns his back to Kamila and squeezes his eyes shut. Her father's carried the guilt for her brother's death for years now. It was dumb for Włodek to take a catnap while three-year-old Jakub waded in the lake, but it happened, and it happened a long time ago. Kamila sighs in frustration as her father slumps his shoulders.

'Fine, Kamila. Just don't show it to your mother.'

'Uh, don't worry, I wasn't planning on it. I'm not retarded!'

Her father nods his head and Kamila instantly feels sorry for him. He's so schlumpy, always so keen on doing whatever is asked of him, and Zofia has no trouble asking. She suspects he hates Zofia too.

Kamila races out of bed and reaches Włodek just as he's about to leave the room. She gives him a hug, and he gratefully returns it.

'Cheer up, *Tatusiu.*' Kamila grins. 'We're still going fishing on Thursday, right?'

Włodek nods his head and combs back Kamila's hair with his hands.

'Leave it, *Tato.* Just leave it alone.'

Before she turns out the lights, Kamila spends a half hour plaiting her hair into two dozen cornrows; when she's done her head looks reticular, unbecoming, but it's the only way to tame the godawful kink in her hair. She climbs under the covers and wonders how many days it takes for a letter to sail across the Atlantic.

On the other side of the *wersalka,* Justyna feels her sister's body shift again.

'Stop that right now.'

'What? I can't sleep!' Elwira whispers in the dark.

'Then try not rubbing yourself with the pillow.' Elwira freezes and then twists her torso ever so slightly, adjusting things. 'Shut up, Justyna! I'm tossing around because I can't sleep. I'm still thinking about Ania Baran and I'm—'

'And you're rubbing yourself while you think about her? What, are you a *lezbijka,* you little perv?' Justyna's laugh is hoarse and mean.

'You're a *lezbijka*! You're the one with the webbed toes!'

'Fuck off!!' Justyna hisses into the dark. The slight deformity on her right foot is an Achilles' heel of sorts, the one obvious smudge on an otherwise flawless canvas. Her short, chestnut brown hair frames her face perfectly, and her nose is petite, which, in a Slavic country, is mighty currency. Her eyes flash like sapphires, her body is slim but ample in all the right places, and she has a beauty mark above her lip that she blackens with an eyeliner, because that's what movie stars do.

'One more word, and I'm telling Mama that you diddle yourself every night.' Elwira shuts her mouth immediately.

'Anyway, who cares about Anka Baran? She's back in America and we'll probably never see her again.' Justyna crawls out of the bed. Her hands slide under the mattress and she pulls out a soft pack of unfiltered Zefiry. She tiptoes over to the window and lights up.

'Mama and *Tato* will smell that, you know. Talk about disgusting. They know you do it.'

'And obviously they don't give a shit 'cause I haven't heard a peep from either of them on the subject. Besides, they'd be hypocrites if they did say something and I'd fucking call them on it too. Anyway, I'm out. You won't have to suffer any longer.' Elwira bolts up in bed. For a nine-year-old, she's tiny, stunted even, but Justyna knows that people consider her the prettier sister. It doesn't bother Justyna because she thinks that Elwira's pixie-like features and her short stature won't look so cute when she's sixteen.

'Where are you going?' Elwira demands.

'*Dzieciaku,* what do you care? You can go back to your pillow and dream a little dream. I got better things to do.'

And with that Justyna reaches for her miniskirt, grabs her sandals, cracks their bedroom door open, and vanishes.

In the living room, Justyna's mother, Teresa, and her father, Bogdan, are lying on the orange pullout *wersalka,* watching TV. She sees her mother's legs entwined with her father's. They're always touching each other, always smooching, pulling each other in for a quick embrace. Justyna thinks it's mildly gross, but doesn't really care. When she clicks the bedroom door shut behind her, her mother glances up and, for a minute, they lock eyes. Teresa obviously knows what Justyna is up to, but she won't come storming into the hallway now. Later there will be a fuck-filled tirade about curfews, but Justyna's mother never follows up on her threats.

The July night is unusually crisp. She should have grabbed a sweater but the walk to the Relaks is a short one. It's only nine-thirty and, already, most of Szydłówek is dark. The streetlights are shutting off, one after another, like dominoes.

Across Klonowa Street, the benches lining the walkway to the Relaks are occupied by older men from the neighborhood. The Relaks Café has become a clandestine meeting place for local drunks and for young men who aspire to be the next generation of local drunks. But they don't get their liquor from the overpriced establishment; they merely use the area as a gathering ground, bringing their own bottles of bathtub-brewed moonshine and sour, cheap wines.

Back in the sixties and seventies, the bar was busy all summer long. Families and tourists flooded the place on weekends, lounging on blankets, renting kayaks, and taking strolls uphill to the Relaks for cold beer and French fries that were served in cone-shaped napkins with tiny plastic forks. But that was back when the reservoir water was clean and you could actually swim in it. Now, people claim that the *zalew* is full of sewage and corpses from a cemetery on the other side of the bay that flooded a few years ago.

As she makes her way closer to the bar, she can see Norbert 'Lolek' Siwa and Mariusz Kowalski sitting on some benches, their cigarette tips glowing like fireflies. As she walks by them, Lolek calls out to her, 'Hey, Zator, I didn't know this was slut turf!' Justyna casually gives him the finger. 'It's not, Lolek. I heard it's pig country, so I thought I'd venture and see for myself. Guess it's true, *chrum chrum*.'

Kowalski cracks up and Justyna is pleased. Lolek is a neighborhood wiseass, who has a violent temper if you cross him on a bad night. He's a recent high-school dropout but he looks way older than seventeen. Lolek walks like a rooster, his fiery red hair is always slicked back into an outdated bouffant, and he never shaves his sparse orangey mustache. He is always borrowing money for beer and porno magazines, but he never pays it back. Last summer he brought a Russian prostitute to Kowalski's eighteenth birthday party and had her wank off the entire group, at a discount price. Lolek is a legend. And Kowalski, his sidekick, is the object of many girls' affections, even though he is as short as he is good-looking. In the land of guys in their twenties who are already losing their teeth, Kowalski, with his wide smile and pressed jeans, is a catch.

Justyna strides right up to them and grabs a wine bottle from under their bench. Without missing a beat, she takes an impressive swig, hands the bottle to Kowalski, and says, 'Cheap shit,' before sauntering past them. She can still hear them howling as she rounds the corner.

Sebastian Tefilski is waiting for her, just where he said he'd be. He is sitting on top of the hill that leads down to the water, listening to headphones. She sits down beside him and leans in.

'Depeche Mode? Is this the tape you gave me last year?' Justyna asks. Sebastian takes off his headphones and continues staring out in front of him.

'So?'

'So there's new stuff out now. It's called keeping up with the times, Tefilski. You should try it.' Justyna smiles lazily but Sebastian is impatient, thrusting his hand out.

'*Jezus Maria*, what's your problem? You should be glad I'm here. I could be at home sleeping right now, you know. Instead I'm playing postman.'

'Just give it to me.'

Justyna huffs and digs into her skirt pocket. She produces a piece of white paper, folded into a small, neat square. Sebastian grabs it, the excited smile on his face almost embarrassing. Did she ever make him that happy, Justyna wonders. But just like that Sebastian's smile fades. He stands up slowly and starts tearing the note into fragments, which drop to the ground like confetti. Justyna stands up next to him.

'Not good?'

Sebastian's silence fills the air, and for a moment Justyna actually feels bad. But, no – Anna had it coming, they both did. When Justyna told Anna about her and Tefilski, to both brag and warn, it was as if Anna didn't hear the subtext, as if Justyna's leftovers were fine by her. The *Amerykanka* just did not give a shit about other people's history, that much was clear. She was pathetically transparent, almost inhaling Sebastian when the two of them hugged goodbye. Justyna caught their whispered somethings, the looks they shared. Justyna wasn't dumb.

Sebastian Tefilski and Justyna Zator went back, way back to First Holy Communion. They were eight and assigned to walk down the church aisle side by side, one of thirteen pairs. They made their way down toward the altar just like in practice, doing a slow, methodical two-step, trying not to laugh. At one point, when she had just about had it with her itchy stockings, Justyna furtively scratched her crack and Sebastian caught her and smiled and she stuck her tongue out at him, before sticking her tongue out for the sanctified wafer. And from that day forward, Sebastian and Justyna were forever in and out of love.

Anka Baran was not just usurping an old boyfriend; she was after the first boy that ever truly loved Justyna, so what did a few forged sentences matter? Still, she wouldn't mind becoming friends with the foreigner, if only to satisfy her curiosity. So she's already planning future shopping trips with Anna to the

Puchatek mall, and sleepovers. They *will* be friends — because aside from the occasional romp with nutty Kamila Marchewska, Justyna doesn't really hang out with girls. Anna Baran would fill the gap nicely.

Sebastian recites from memory, his voice robotic, dazed. ' "Dear Sebastian, I have a boyfriend in America. It's pretty serious. I guess I felt bad for you and didn't know how to tell you but please, don't bother waiting for me. Have a good summer. Your friend, Anna Baran." '

Justyna smirks. ' "I felt bad for you"? Ewww. Who does she think she is? Right?' She tugs on his arm. 'Right?'

Sebastian looks into Justyna's face, and the shame he's feeling is too deep to hide.

'You know what, Tefilski? Fuck her. And don't even think about writing to her, unless you want to come off like a sniveling beggar.' She moves closer. 'You're better than her anyway. She wouldn't know what to do with you even if she wanted you.' Their noses are almost touching now and Sebastian doesn't say anything but he doesn't move away.

'Remember last summer when we broke up? Remember why?' Justyna's fingers find his zipper, and then quickly find their way inside his jeans. His penis feels like dough, pliant and soft. But as she starts kneading with both hands, it doesn't stay soft for long. 'We broke up because I wasn't ready, right?'

Sebastian exhales.

'Well, guess what, Tefilski? I'm ready now.'

And with that, Justyna gingerly drops to her knees.

CHAPTER THREE

2002

ANNA
GREENPOINT, BROOKLYN

In the dark, sleeping next to her, Ben looks unfamiliar, like last season's dress that no longer goes with anything. Anna stares at his receding hairline, lifts the duvet and peeks down at his belly. He's always had that little pouch, evidence of a hipster diet – low on veggies, high on hops. She used to knead it affectionately. She used to joke about it and right now she wants nothing more than to want him again; it would just be so much less complicated.

Anna reaches under her pillow and finds her glasses. She carefully places a finger on Ben's mouth and traces its contours. Yes, his mouth is very nice, with soft lips that never chap, even in the dead of winter. But Anna can't remember the last time they kissed, the last time they *really* kissed, like those high-school kids who slobbered on subways, not caring who was watching. Ben used to walk down the street shielding boners as Anna nuzzled his neck. They just couldn't stop touching each other, in private or in public. Now they kiss only when someone's watching, as if it's to prove something to their friends.

When Ben let himself in the day before, just past eleven A.M., Anna had been curled up in a little ball on the sofa with an ashtray by her feet, its rank contents spilled out on the floor. While making coffee he found her lost glasses in an empty mug in the sink. When he gently eased them onto the bridge of her nose, her eyes popped open.

'Hello there.' He leaned down to kiss her on the lips but she turned her head away from him. He didn't bother with her cheek. 'Frick came by and left a note. He seems pretty pissed you didn't answer the door. "You can fix your own damn fridge," he wrote. Nice. What, were you in a coma or something?'

Anna didn't answer, but instead started bawling. Ben put his arms around her, and when she settled down, she told him about Justyna. She wanted him to make it all better, but he just sighed and said, 'That's fucked up.' He suggested they go out to eat, said it would help Anna get her mind off things. But at dinner that night, Ben silently chewed his rice while Anna wept into her beef pad Thai.

'I can't sleep. I had a crazy dream,' Anna whispers in the dark now, tugging on Ben's earlobe to wake him up. 'I was rowing a bathtub through the streets of my *babcia*'s neighborhood and there were horses floating next to me. The whole town was flooded and I was looking for you and then I found you in some apartment, making out with Charlize Theron, but you were like, "It's okay, Anna, she's very beautiful, you understand, right?" It was horrible.' Ben's eyes open.

He turns to face her and under the covers his legs entwine hers. She hasn't shaved in over a week, and she immediately shifts away.

'Babe, you gotta do something about that tooth.'

'Oh my God! I'm telling you about my traumatic nightmare, and all you do is whine about my breath? Thanks a lot, you prick!' Anna bolts upright and swings her legs over the bed.

'Annie, come on, you want me to apologize for something I did to you in a dream? That's crazy. And don't call me a prick again unless you want me to start acting like one.'

'What is that? A threat?'

Ben tries to put his arms around her. 'It's too early for this. You're distraught. Just tell me what to do, Annie.'

'You can shut the fuck up and leave me alone.'

'Do not talk to me like that.' Ben's voice rises. 'I don't deserve it. I'm sorry for your friend, for what happened to her husband, but when was the last time you saw her? When was the last time you even spoke?'

'What's that supposed to mean?'

'It means that I think you're reaching into territory that you don't own. It means that you're displacing your grief. Besides, the last time you were in Poland, you didn't even see her, right?'

'That has nothing to do with anything. Does empathy have a fucking expiration date? I invited her to my premiere but she didn't come. I was there for only five fucking days, Ben! It was a business trip. Business!'

'I don't buy it, Annie. Poland was never business for you.'

'What the hell are you saying? I'm not allowed to be upset because we aren't pen pals anymore?'

'Stop talking to me like that! I'm not the enemy. What happened to your friend is horrible, but get a goddamn grip!'

'"What happened to my friend"? Tell me, Ben – what "happened" to her?'

'I'm going back to sleep. I have a job to go to. Remember what that's like, Annie, to actually have to rise and shine?' He's pleading now, he wants to call time-out, but Anna is persistent. She wants to hurt.

'Say it. Name the thing.' Anna's fist pounds the side of the bed.

'Her husband died.'

Anna makes the sound of a game-show buzzer. 'Wrong!

53

Sorry, Bob, the correct answer is: her husband was killed. He did not die. Big difference, right?'

Anna leans across the bed, bringing her face close to his. 'Murder and death are two very different things, my love. Or have you already forgotten?'

She pulls back swiftly, so that his fingers barely graze the surface of her cheek, and runs out of the room.

Anna's version of mourning includes slamming doors and throwing objects across the room. Her grief is the kind that makes noise. She knows that Ben used to love that about her; those mercurial moods, her passionate bellows. He used to tell their friends, in the beginning, that Anna Baran roused him like no one else had ever done. Now, Anna and Ben are just an argument waiting to happen. Two months ago, on Ben's birthday, they'd come back from a bar and had drunken sex. Ben hadn't meant to come inside her and a few weeks later, when Anna's period never turned up and, instead, two pink lines on a stick did, there was no discussion of the next step. In a moment Anna knew; not now, and not with Ben.

The afternoon Anna spent at Planned Parenthood was burned into her memory. She sat in a waiting room, in a green paper gown, with five other women. She'd felt sheepish about her engagement ring. One of the girls had a belly that was probably swollen into its fifth month and Anna fixated on it. 'What?' the girl asked and stared Anna down, before going back to her *People* magazine. Anna flushed, embarrassed by her own hypocrisy; she'd wanted to leap out of the chair and run. But Anna had stayed put until the nurse called her name and managed a small goodbye smile to the women.

Ever since that day Anna's been withering. Ben would come home from work to find her on the couch, staring at the ceiling.

'You look like your dad,' he told her one day.

'Fuck you,' she whispered, without turning her head.

When Ben leaves for work after their fight, Anna is on the couch, eating Cheetos.

'This is all getting out of hand' is the only thing he says, right before he closes the door. Anna spends the entire day in the same spot on the couch, thinking about Justyna, and about breaking free.

The next morning, Anna gets out of bed without waking Ben. In the kitchen, she boils water in a saucepan and scoops a tablespoon of Jacobs Krönung into a mug. She sips the milky instant coffee – the same kind she drank in Poland with her *babcia* – which she buys for four bucks at a deli in Greenpoint. No Starbucks in the world could ever replace it.

Anna climbs out onto the fire escape, mug in hand. It's cold but sunny. She stares across the rooftops and remembers a day, weeks after their engagement, when she had been waiting for the B43 bus after she returned from an audition in the city. It was drizzling and her hair was damp. Anna stood at the bus stop and fished out a pack of smokes from her purse, and that's when she noticed him: a young man in a leather jacket, with thick, wavy hair like Michelangelo's *David*. He looked like he was from Montenegro or Serbia, or some other war-torn Balkan state. He looked the way she sometimes imagined Sebastian Tefilski would look all grown up. He was staring at her, openly, his hands jammed in the pockets of his jeans. She looked away and smiled; it was textbook flirtation. The rain misted over her face, the bus was nowhere in sight.

'Would you accompany me for the coffee?'

Anna had been right. His accent was thick. She paused and lifted her left hand, wiggling her adorned ring finger. The man hung his head in mock despair, and placed his hands over his heart. 'Please, anyway?' She laughed as the bus rolled up.

'Sorry,' she mouthed over her shoulder, and as she boarded the B43, for a moment, she actually was.

Anna thought about that man for days. She fantasized about running off with him, and she kept her distance from Ben, confused by her feelings. The idea that Ben wasn't enough, that he would never understand, had been planted.

When she crawls back into the kitchen from the fire escape, Anna's cheeks are raw and she feels like someone realigned her vertebrae or something. The shower is running and she decides to actually make breakfast. The idea comes to her out of the blue, and, aside from piles of take-out menus in the cupboard and a few utensils, Anna is unprepared. She finally unearths a frying pan, after rummaging through a moving box marked KITCHMISC.

Minutes later, three eggs sizzle on a paper plate. It's not much, but it's something. Ben emerges from the bathroom, swathed in a towel, trailing steam. 'For me?' he asks, pointing to the table. She nods and manages a smile. The whole thing – her effort and his approval – feels lacking, as if they both know a bit of protein can't apologize for everything. Ben eats right then and there, water dripping down his arm as he digs in. Anna wishes the sight could arouse her, or at best reassure her, but she feels nothing except for a small lump of revulsion when, after the last bite, Ben burps loudly. He leans in to kiss her in thanks, and she lets him.

After Ben leaves for work, Anna goes to her desk, and pulls out an old address book. The numbers look like hieroglyphics and her fingers shake as she dials them.

'Słucham.'

Poles answer the phone in a myriad of ways: a basic *halo,* a polite *dzieńdobry,* or an impartial *słucham,* which translates literally to 'I'm listening.' When Justyna says it now, it almost sounds like a dare.

'Justyna. It's Anna Baran . . . from New York.'

'Hi, girl. How are you?'

The neutrality in her old friend's voice takes Anna by complete surprise. 'I'm so sorry. My mom told me yesterday.'

'Yeah . . .'

'I wish I could be there.'

'No, you don't.' Anna can hear the smile in Justyna's voice; she knows Justyna is trying to keep the conversation light but somehow it does the opposite.

'How's Damian? Last time I saw you, he was a baby, right? When was that? 1998?'

'Yeah.'

'And then I got that movie and I—'

'—became a star?' Justyna's voice doesn't belie any accusation, but Anna doesn't know how to respond.

'I'm sorry,' she echoes, at a loss.

'Well, you know, shit happens, right? Damian's fine. He's fine.'

'He's six?'

'Seven.'

'Is he a good – does he like school?'

'Hates it. He'd rather, you know, while away the hours whittling.'

'Whittling?' Somehow the conversation has gotten off course.

'Yeah, it was a thing he did with.' Justyna makes a sentence out of what should be a fragment. 'He's a big baby, though. Still wets the bed, but what are you gonna do? He's a handful, *wiesz?*' Anna nods her head, but, no, no, she doesn't know.

'Justyna. Really, I'm so sorry. If you and Elwira need anything, I can wire you some money and—'

'No, no,' Justyna quickly interrupts, 'we're okay. But thanks. So. How are *you*? You married?'

'Justyna, there's a Western Union near—'

'Listen, Anka, I gotta go. Tell your mom and dad *cześć*. And maybe one day you'll come to Kielce again, right? I'll tell Elwira you said hi. *Trzymaj się.*'

Trzymaj się. 'Hold on to yourself,' a casual Polish farewell, like *take care,* but it calls to mind so much more. Anna hangs up when she hears the dial tone.

The little red light on Anna's answering machine is blinking desperately. It's been blinking for weeks now. The world just won't leave her alone no matter how much she ignores it. Anna presses the play button. Message after message pours out, from Paulina, Ben, her friend Veronica. From Frick and the cable company. She listens to each one for a few seconds before erasing it. The last message is from her agent.

'Anna, it's me again, sweetie. We're worried sick over here. Been trying to reach you forever. Forever! Had to pass on a great offer you got for an indie. Other stuff too. What gives, honey? What the hell happened? Someone die or something?'

Anna takes a small breath, stares at the boxes that surround her, at the gray walls that have survived hundreds of her cigarettes, and she presses delete one last time.

The front door is unlocked and Kamila lets herself in. She tries to tiptoe upstairs unnoticed, but she hears her mother call her from the living room. Zofia has always had freakishly acute radar.

'Why are you so late? We already ate *obiad*.'

Kamila doesn't respond. She takes off her galoshes and unravels her scarf. Zofia drags her two-hundred-and-fifty-pound frame toward the entranceway. 'Your father already left for work. Want a plate?'

'No, thanks. I'm tired. Just wanna go to my room.'

'Unbelievable, that thing with Justyna. But I tell you, I'm not surprised.'

Kamila doesn't want to discuss anything with her mother, let alone the death of her old friend's husband. She starts walking up the stairs to her room.

'Were the kids good?' Zofia calls after her.

Kamila nods her head but, no, they weren't good. Jack, the four-year-old, peed on the rug again. Jack is a toddler by day and a Dalmatian by night, eating his Honey Smacks cereal out of an aluminum dog bowl in the kitchen. 'It's just a phase, Kamila, and we go with it,' Mrs. Levicky explained when Kamila started. Today, Jack's sister, Laura, asked Kamila why her nose was so big. 'Your new name is Kamila Mar*jew*ska! Get it? Get it?'

Kamila was taken aback. How was a regular ten-year-old simpleton schooled in anti-Semitic insults?

She had wagged her finger in Laura's face. 'Your dad he is the Jewish, so you not nice for him.'

'What? I can't even understand you! If you can't speakie dee Eeen-glish – go back to your own country!' Laura had sassed back. These kids were the opposite of good. They were the low point in an already shitty day.

Their mother, Mrs. Janina Levicky (*call me Jan*), was Polish, but hardly spoke the language anymore. Her dwarfish figure flaunted firm boobs and toned triceps. 'No chicken wings for me, Kamila,' she boasted, waving her arms about like a windmill. Jan was married to an American named Joey, who was of Polish-Jewish descent. Joey Levicky (born Józef Herbert Lewicki) was a partner at an advertising firm. He was rich and never around.

Jack and Laura were spoiled, their expansive rooms overflowing with things – the latest gadgets, the trendiest clothes, mounds of high-end debris. But this did not concern Kamila. What concerned Kamila was the fact that the Levicky children had no clue from whence they came. They were oblivious to war, famine, ghettos, or holocausts, and their parents believed that was a good thing; victims were powerless. Jan and Joey felt there was no need to burden their children with macabre tales of barbed-wire walls. It was a decidedly American sentiment, this onward and upward stuff.

Kamila's day had been spent cleaning up after those brats, and making sure they were at their usual station, in front of the TV. She scrutinized the neat to-do list that Mrs. Levicky had written down on the hanging chalkboard, all the while thinking about how she should call Justyna. Kamila folded the laundry, wiped down the crystal, and sorted and took out the trash. The chores had been mind-numbing and, for that, Kamila was grateful.

'Your husband called again,' Zofia rasps as Kamila makes her way up the stairs, her voice like an asthmatic's.

Again, Kamila does not respond, even though her heart starts racing. Why couldn't Emil just leave her alone?

'Did you hear me? Your husband called. Maybe it was about Justyna. You should call him back. Use a phone card.' Kamila doesn't move until she hears her mother slogging back to the kitchen. America has made her mother into an oaf; she was big before, but now there is no end to her girth. When Kamila first laid eyes on her in the States, she had to turn her head away, to blink back the tears.

Safe in her bedroom, Kamila flops on her mattress and grabs a fistful of Werther's hard candy from her nightstand. She stuffs three into her mouth. It has taken continuous effort to maintain the weight loss she first attained with pills and laxatives, but today Kamila needs the comfort that only food can bring.

The phone buzzes and she shoots up. She lets it ring five times and then, almost as if possessed, picks up, right at the same time that Zofia does on the downstairs phone.

'*Halo.*'

'Kamila? It's me.'

She glances at her wristwatch still set to Polish time. It's one A.M.; he always used to be asleep before ten. '*Kamila? To ja,*' in his plummy, sonorous voice, one of the best things about him. She's missed that voice so much that it takes all her strength not to drop the receiver, scurry under the warm blankets, and never come out.

'I know.' *Wiem.* One word. Meek and dreadful. Ignorance is bliss, that's what the Americans say, and there's no Polish aphorism that echoes that sentiment but goddamnit, there should be.

Emil clears his throat. 'Did you hear about Justyna Strawicz?'

'I did. Her grandmother called my dad yesterday.'

'Awful, right?' Emil says it quietly. Emil always liked Justyna. They went on double dates, occasionally, before Justyna's mother got sick. Kamila bites down on the candy in her mouth and says nothing.

'I got the package. *Dziękuje, kochanie.*'

Two weeks ago, without rhyme or reason, Kamila stopped into the local Gap on her way back from work. She quickly picked up two pairs of vintage wash jeans and some crew socks, boxed them up, and airmailed the package to Poland.

'They fit great. Wojtek's too.'

Something is wrong because she has imagined this conversation every day, and yet she isn't using any of the words she wants to. Words like *homosexual* and *liar*. Words like *how* and *why*.

'It's late over there.'

'Yeah, I know. But I couldn't sleep. Wojtek, on the other hand, he's—' Emil stops mid-sentence.

'He's there?'

She shouldn't be surprised. When she left for the airport, Kamila left Emil a note on the kitchen counter, along with his set of the keys, which she had taken from him the day she found out about Wojtek. *Baw się dobrze,* she'd written. 'Have fun.'

'Do you mind? His parents told him he was no longer welcome at their house.'

Kamila surprises them both by bursting into laughter. 'Would it matter if I did mind?'

'Kamilka, when you come home, we'll talk. The three of us.'

'There will never be a three of us. And anyway, I might

not come home. What's there to come home to? Wojtek in our bed?'

It's as far as she's ever gone to articulating what it is Emil has moonlighted in for all these years. When he and Wojtek, both crying, finally confessed their mutual ardor, she didn't say anything. She doesn't recall much from that afternoon, except for her silence.

Emil's voice warbles. 'I know you're angry, Kamila. And I am waiting for you to come back, to walk up to me and slap me silly, because I deserve it. But then I want us to, I don't know what I want. . . . *Kocham cię*, Kamilka. I always will.'

Kamila is afraid of what she'll say. She's afraid, and her tears are useless. She swipes at them frantically.

'*Jesteś assholem*,' Kamila says finally, conjugating in her native tongue the most befitting of English slurs, the one that's become her favorite. Her husband and their mutual lifelong friend had fallen in love. She never saw it coming even though it was there all those years, staring her in the face. Should she tell him now that when they were seventeen, Anna Baran pulled her aside and said, 'Maybe Emil's not the one for you. Don't you think he's . . . different?'

'Different how?'

'I don't know, Kamila. He's distant. And he says his *s* like *sssss*.'

'What's his lisp got to do with anything?'

'Nothing, I guess.'

You just didn't talk about the thing Anna was insinuating, not in Kielce. There were no lesbians there, only old maids. Guys acted queer but they were never *actually* queer. This was a part of Poland where most guys Kamila grew up with still exchanged nigger, retard, and fag jokes.

'Don't call me again,' Kamila instructs Emil quietly and hangs up.

The next morning, there is a lavish breakfast on the table: hazelnut coffee and toasted croissants, assorted jams, scrambled eggs with fried *kiełbasa*. Kamila gingerly walks past the cholesterol-laden table and retrieves a banana from the fruit bowl. Zofia is standing at the sink, scrubbing a frying pan.

'There's plenty.' She thrusts a wet rag toward the spread. In lieu of a response, Kamila quickly peels the soft, mottled fruit and takes a giant bite. Zofia watches her.

'Suit yourself. The more for your father.'

'He doesn't need more, *Mamo*. He needs less.' Kamila's father has given up his jogs, he's given up lettuce and his morning ritual of black coffee and calisthenics. In fact, he's abandoned all that he had in Poland, including his doctorate. Now, her father works the night shift at the Lubelski Bakery, where he manipulates dough till the sun comes up. His hands are eternally coated in a layer of flour and in another lifetime Kamila would have loved it, would have accompanied him to work every night just for the smell of warm, fresh loaves. But Włodek says he's sick of rye bread, and every night he brings home a large pepperoni pizza. Every night he and Zofia eat the entire thing at an alarming pace. Her father's American dream is nothing but menial labor and take-out.

'When you start cooking around here, then you can talk about what's good for my husband. Worry about your own.' Zofia wipes her hands on her apron and stares at Kamila.

'I'm off,' Kamila says quietly, walking around her mother.

'Look at you! Nothing gets to you, Kamila? Your friend's husband murdered, your husband . . .'

'*My* husband what?' Kamila asks lightly, but hurries quickly toward the foyer.

Zofia follows her. 'We need to talk.'

Kamila fumbles with her coat, grabbing her hat and mittens. 'I don't want to be late. What do you want to talk to me about anyway? Huh, *Mamo*? What the hell could we possibly talk about? You never liked Justyna, always called her a slut. You never liked any of my friends, so what do you care?' She wants to stop talking, fling the door open, and leave. But Zofia grabs her arm now, forcing her to turn around.

'I don't wanna talk about Justyna. I wanna talk about Emil. I wanna talk about the fact that you married a queer.'

For a moment Kamila can't move. Zofia's face is close to hers, breathing heavily. Finally, Kamila twists her arm free and yanks the front door open. She runs out into the snow.

In the rain, they huddle. No more than a dozen, all dressed in funereal best, black woolen coats that graze ankles, black felt hats, everything ironed and pleated, layers upon layers. Underneath Paweł's old leather motorcycle jacket, Justyna is wearing a long spandex dress that hugs her like a second skin. She stands off to the side, dying for a cigarette, having to remind herself every so often why the fuck she's here.

The funeral was held on short notice. Some people didn't want to come. Too soon, they said. *Too soon for what?* she wanted to ask. To acknowledge Paweł's death, or to look her in the eye? Too soon to shake hands with her sister? Too soon to have to face Damian, who no longer had a father? Maybe for them it was too soon, but for Justyna it wasn't soon enough. At least planning the funeral had kept her busy.

Kazia Anielska is wailing. Justyna cringes every time her grandmother lets loose a howl. It's outlandish, this kind of biblical grieving; people are ping-ponging looks between distraught *Babcia* Kazia and the stone-faced widow. She catches one of her uncles staring at her, and she lifts her palms toward the sky and shrugs.

'O, *mój Boże kochany! O, mój Boże kochany!*' Her grandmother is evoking God's name with such personal affront, you would think it was her own son in the coffin, or her own husband. It was no secret – to Justyna, at least – that her seventy-one-year-old grandmother harbored a peculiar crush on Paweł. She was always cozying up to him when they walked to Mass, her veiny arm linked in his, batting what was left of her eyelashes. When he told slightly off-color jokes, *Babcia* Kazia giggled and blushed like a fawning schoolgirl. It was droll at first, but it became disturbing. When Paweł didn't call *Babcia* for a few days to inquire if she needed groceries, she would pout and behave like a spurned lover the next time she saw him. The way she was always going on and on about what a wonderful catch Paweł was, how lucky Justyna was that he had proposed, when really, he could have run as soon as Justyna announced her pregnancy, was absurd.

Justyna squeezes the jacket closer to her body. She marvels at how a funeral can come together in two days, when it takes months of planning to pull off, say, a wedding. Everyone moves with lightning speed when it comes to burying the dead. *Fuck this shit,* she thinks, and wonders what people would say if the stone-faced widow took off mid-service.

She can tell the mourners think she's not acting her part. But when has she ever? When Justyna first realized she was pregnant she spent a few days punching herself in the stomach, but the pregnancy stuck. She smoked the whole nine months, in denial till the very moment a bloody skull popped out of her insides. But Paweł, Paweł was good, through and through. He wasn't a glutton for drink, he regularly woke at sunrise, didn't cheat, lie, or gamble. His shoulder-length mullet, his Hells Angels jacket, his dangly dagger earring, all hid an inherent softness. He was kind, hardworking, and he went to church most Sundays. But what turned Justyna on were the rare occasions when the savage in him surfaced, when he'd throw her on the bed and devour her.

Paweł was being buried beside his father and mother, at the cemetery off Spokojna Street. For a moment, Justyna had entertained the idea that Paweł would be laid to rest at Stary Cmentarz next to her mother, Teresa; the only two people she ever loved completely. But it didn't really matter, did it? Her husband was gone; who the fuck cared where the wooden box ended up?

'Ashes to ashes, dust to dust,' the young priest intones, glancing down at his Bible. Justyna can tell this is probably his first time at the rodeo because his face is flushed tomato red, and he trips over his tongue as he reads from the book of Psalms. Back at the church, he stuttered while reading the Old Testament passage about Cain and Abel. It was an obvious choice, but in Justyna's opinion, a tasteless one. What had God been thinking, letting that bastard simply wander the desert for a few decades when he'd committed murder? He had delivered a much more severe sentence for a simple misunderstanding over an apple.

Justyna stares at Father Bruno, wishing he'd hurry up, but he meets her eyes askance with a sympathetic smile and plods on. Perhaps his stutters have nothing to do with priestly inexperience and everything to do with Justyna's clingy dress.

'*Ciociu,* I have to go to the bathroom.' Justyna looks down and sees her niece grasping her thigh. Her scrawny legs are twisted like pretzels.

'Tell your mother.'

'I can't.' Cela points to Elwira, who is now squatting on the ground, weeping openly.

'Well, then hold it.' The coffin is being lowered now and

she knows this is her cue to walk over and drop a flower into the hole, a final farewell. But she can't bring herself to do it, and not just because she didn't buy flowers.

Cela tugs her skirt again. 'I can't!' Her whisper is frantic now.

'Be quiet, okay?' She watches as her niece's oval face crumples and contorts, and then suddenly it goes blank.

'I pee-peed,' whispers Cela, her chin trembling.

Justyna kneels down and whispers in her niece's ear, 'Don't worry, *kotku,* it's raining. We'll tell these idiots you just fell in a puddle.'

Later that night, after *Babcia* Kazia has taken the kids to spend a few nights at her apartment in Szydłówek and after every last mourner has left, an eerie silence fills the house. Elwira goes around dead-bolting all the doors, and muttering to herself like a madwoman. She tries to secure the broken balcony doors upstairs by dragging a bookshelf against them. Kielce is a small enough city, that's what the cop Kurka had told her seventy-two hours ago. There are only so many places to hide, but Filip has evaded the cops thus far. He could be on his way to Italy by now, or he could be skulking in their back garden.

Justyna finds Elwira in the living room, staring at the television.

'I wish *Tato* were here.'

'Do you?' Justyna asked, and they both knew the answer. Their father was gone, gone since the days his beloved wife lay dying in her little room on the third floor. He hadn't even been at Teresa's bedside when she took her last breath: he'd been passed out drunk at Uncle Marek's house. Right now, their father would be useless anyway. Bogdan Zator couldn't deal with death, of any kind.

Suddenly, it seems like there is nothing to do, now that the final resting place has been occupied and the bloodstains have been wiped up. For the time being, Damian has stopped asking about his father's return. He's thrilled to have a few days off from school. At the burial he asked her what was in the box, and Justyna corrected him: 'Not *what,* Damian – who,' but she did not elaborate. Of course *Babcia* Kazia insists that Justyna is damaging Damian further by not telling him outright.

Elwira breaks the silence as if they have been long in conversation. 'So, yeah, I can't believe Ania Baran called you.'

'Yeah.'

'It's been a few years, right? You missed her premiere. I forgot about that.' Two years ago, Anna Baran was in Poland to celebrate her starring role in a big Hollywood movie – something with corsets and horse-drawn carriages. A lot of their friends took the train to Warsaw for the big event and Anna had offered to pay for travel if they couldn't afford it. In Anna's interviews she told the journalists that the premiere wouldn't mean anything if her Polish friends and family wouldn't be there. But Justyna didn't go. The fact that her mother was dead and that she had a five-year-old on her hands had been reason enough to skip a reunion; but there were other reasons too, and so Justyna had steered clear of Anna Baran and her newfound celebrity.

'It's actually a good movie, Justyna. You should check it out. I totally cried at the end.'

'Yeah, that's what I fucking need now. A tearjerker.'

Elwira smiles. 'I think it's nice she called. Is she working on a new movie?'

'I don't fucking know! We didn't go over her résumé!' Justyna snaps as Elwira's face crumples. 'She offered to send us money.'

'*Na serio?*' Elwira wipes her nose on her sleeve, suddenly bright eyed.

'Yeah, she did. She's Hollywood now, right? It's the least she could have done.'

But Elwira does not catch the sarcasm in her sister's voice. 'How much is she sending?'

'Elwira? Are you fucking crazy? Like I would take one *złoty*. We're not a charity case.'

Elwira shrugs her shoulders. 'We're not?'

'Anyway, you know what surprised me? That Kamila Marchewska wasn't there. Didn't even send a *wieniec.*' It was customary to send a wreath if one couldn't attend a funeral and Justyna had quickly surveyed the ones that had been on display next to the coffin that morning, scanning the cards for *Marchewska* or *Baran.*

'She's in the States. At least that's what I heard,' Elwira answers.

'I guess it's the place to be.' Justyna sighs, wondering why she ever gave a shit.

'Justyna. I've been thinking—' Elwira interrupts Justyna's thoughts.

'And? How does it feel? Like your head hurts a little, but you can get used to it?' Justyna smiles. *Let's go back to four days ago,* she thinks. *Let's be normal again.*

'I think I should move out.'

Justyna glances up, trying to read her sister. 'Where would you go?'

'Back to Szydłówek. To *Babcia*'s.'

'You and Cela and *Babcia* Kazia, all in a one-bedroom?'

Elwira lights a cigarette and walks over to the balcony doors. 'Well, obviously I can't stay here.'

'No one's kicking you out.'

'Justyna! What if he comes back here, looking for me? He put his bloody hand around my neck and told me if I talked he'd be back. And I talked, I fucking talked! What if he does something to Cela?'

'He doesn't know where *Babcia* lives?'

'But she lives on the third floor.'

'He killed someone with a kitchen knife. I'm sure he can figure out how to climb a balcony or two.' Justyna clicks the TV off and starts for the door.

'He did. He *did,* right?'

Justyna turns back and stares at her sister.

'What you said now, Justyna. The way you said it. Kitchen knife. This is real, right? There's no going back?'

Elwira looks so small next to Justyna, like a little dove. Once again, Justyna silently curses her mother. If Teresa suddenly appeared like Lazarus in their living room, Justyna wouldn't think twice about slapping her upside the head. She was young and pretty and fun and she loved them more than anything in the world. And then she died and left them, just like that.

'I don't know what will happen if I stay here. I don't want Damian to suddenly hate me.'

'Damian lost a father. He's allowed to hate anyone he wants.'

'See, this is what I mean. We can't do this. How can we live together?'

For a second, Justyna wants to get down on her hands and

knees and beg her sister to stay. To confess that she can't face these four walls alone haunted by the past. In one room the ghost of her mother lies on the bed, where she took her last breath seven years ago, and now there's the bathroom where her husband's throat was slashed as he finished taking a piss.

'Do what you wanna do, Elwira,' Justyna says quietly. 'Just don't leave me alone tonight. Please.'

CHAPTER FOUR

1992

ANNA
KIELCE, POLAND

The lifeguards are everywhere, slithering around in skimpy orange Speedos. When wet, the cheap lycra works like a suction cup, leaving nothing to the imagination. They swagger around the pool, barrel-chested and cocksure, keeping a lazy eye on the crowd. Anna, Kamila, and Justyna are having a hard time not staring.

Around the Tęcza *Basen,* beefy grandmothers sit on blankets, in their bras and underwear, chain-smoking cigarettes while their annoying grandkids in polyester trunks run wild, breaking the no diving rule and getting fished out and carried off like flailing puppies. Kamila, Anna, and Justyna are spread out directly across from the lifeguards' station, perched on a bleacher. The Tęcza Pool's stadium seating compliments the gladiatorial pageant they are viewing. On the other side of the pool the lifeguards are surrounded by bleached-blond groupies who never dip a toe in the water. They glisten in the sun like a bikini-clad harem.

'That one, with the curly hair? He looks like Morten from A-ha, doesn't he?' Anna follows Kamila's stare, pulling back the outer corners of each eyelid; she looks like she's doing a crude Chinaman impersonation, but it's the only way she can see anything beyond a three-foot radius. Her glasses lie in her bag, where they will stay until she exits the pool.

'*Jezus!* He does, he totally looks like Morten! Take *me* on, baby.' Anna giggles.

'You're looking at their faces, *dziewczyny,* and that's not where you should be looking.' Justyna raises her brows meaningfully.

'*Fe!*'

'*Fe* what, Kamila? A face in the dark is inconsequential, even if it's ugly. It's how he makes you *feel* in the dark that counts.' Justyna pauses, and to make sure her meaning isn't lost, adds, 'It's how his *dick* makes you feel.'

'*Jezus!*' Kamila flushes bright pink.

Justyna smiles knowingly and winks, and Anna winks back, but what the hell does she know? Back in the States, all she and Miguel have done is dry hump. He sometimes managed to slide her underwear down and graze the tip of his penis against her, but she always pushed him away. Miguel wasn't the one. He had too many pimples, and he wasn't Sebastian Tefilski.

'Too many people here today,' Anna murmurs. Kielce is in the midst of an unprecedented July heat wave, and the Tęcza Pool is swarming with folks looking for relief. Everyone looks so Polish to Anna. Nobody is willowy; even the thin women give off a sense of largesse. In a sea of shiny Slavic faces, no one wears sunglasses and no one cares about the fact that their swimwear looks decades old.

'Look at that one.' Kamila points to a stocky lifeguard in imitation Ray-Bans, whose trunks bulge ominously, even from across the pool. 'It looks like there's a rodent in there.'

'*Ja pierdole!*' Justyna snickers and lies down on the bench, rubbing her concave belly with one hand. Every move she makes, every gesture, oozes sexuality. Anna finds it both mesmerizing and annoying. At the start of the summer, Justyna confessed that she'd finally done it, with a very distant older cousin who was visiting from Lublin. She told them it hurt a bit, but afterward she had felt so powerful that sex was now basically what she lived for. She'd said it so matter-of-factly, as if she were talking about the weather.

Last summer, Anna had arrived in Poland with indents at her hips, a filled-out bra, and more hair everywhere. Maybe it was her American diet – hormones in the milk or something – but she'd looked positively Amazonian next to Justyna and Kamila. At fifteen, they talked about doing stuff, but they didn't follow through with it, and that was just fine. This summer, sixteen-year-old Anna feels ready, rip-roaringly ready, to have sex. This summer, she ogles Justyna with envy. Justyna looks like a real woman, and it has nothing to do with her perky bosom. Her face looks different – all of a sudden she's got bedroom eyes and bee-stung lips. Her short hair looks defiant now, not boyish. Anna is sure it's the sex.

'I think I'm getting burned,' Kamila says, pressing on the sides of her nose. All morning she's been in a foul mood. When they first spotted the bleacher seats, miraculously unclaimed, Justyna and Anna tripped over themselves to stake them. Kamila lagged behind, griping about ultraviolet rays and insisting on a small patch of grass in the shade.

'Burned? How is that possible? You're draped in terry cloth.'

'My skin is especially sensitive, Justyna. I've always been fair. Anyway, haven't you heard of melanoma?'

Kamila is wearing a yellow tank top with matching shorts, but the ensemble is all but hidden by the strategic placement of three separate towels – one for shoulders and arms, one wound around her torso, and one hanging off her thighs. The whole getup is meant to hide the seasonal eczema from which Kamila suffers, unsightly, scaly patches behind her knees and in the crooks of her elbows that she scratches to no avail.

Kamila shifts exaggeratedly on the bench, readjusting her wrapping. 'Besides, if you must know, I'm menstruating, and I don't want anyone to see my pad.'

Justyna lets her mouth hang open in mock horror. 'You're menstruating! Heaven forbid. Where's your pad, Bloody Mary? Stuck to your bellybutton? Or do you have two, one on each arm? Jesus, I'm on the rag too. Why don't you join the twentieth century and use a tampon.'

'Yeah, right, Justyna! Some of us are virgins who intend on staying that way.'

Justyna slowly lifts her head. 'What the fuck, Kamila? You think a bit of cardboard is gonna rob you of your cherry? Anna, help me out.'

'Sorry, but I only use pads too. My mother told me it's safer.'

'Safer? Who am I dealing with here?' Justyna sits upright, no longer amused. 'Neanderthals. I'm hungry. French fries, any-one?' She extends her arms in front of her and yawns, aware that the heave and fall of her breasts is attracting peripheral glances. Anna reaches for her coin purse; she always buys. Thanks to inflation and a ridiculous exchange rate, the measly three hundred dollars she brings for her two-month vacation deems her a millionaire. Here money is of no consequence, while in the States she's the one wearing her mother's hand-me-downs and working after-school jobs.

This is Anna's third consecutive summer in Poland, not counting those first three days back in 1989, and the summers can't arrive fast enough. The rest of the year, Anna writes letters, sends care packages, and makes frequent trips to Brooklyn's Polish neighborhood, Greenpoint, just to fill up on whiffs of *kiełbasa* at butcher shops. Every day, she gets home from school and checks the mailbox. Kamila writes the most, about once a week, and reading her dispatches is like subscribing to a person-alized *Kielce Daily News*. Sometimes it still surprises Anna that life goes on after she boards the plane in late August, that sea-sons change, that school happens, and that there are holidays. She can't picture her friends in scarves and mittens, trudging through the snow. She can't picture leaves falling from the trees, or spring blossoms. To her Poland is summer and nothing else.

'Get me a Coca-Cola too,' Anna calls out to Justyna, 'and don't be so hard on Kamila. She's obviously hormonal.'

'And I'm obviously right here so don't talk about me like I'm not, *dziękuje bardzo*.'

'Oh, fuck off, Kamila!' Justyna shouts merrily and tucks An-na's cash into her bikini.

'She's unbelievable, right?' Anna mutters. It's not a judgment. It's what she loves most about Justyna. When they were thir-teen, Justyna thought Anna's buckteeth were cool. She had no qualms taking the hand-me-downs Anna shyly offered. Their mothers had been best friends and still kept in touch. Anna calls Justyna's mom *Ciocia,* even though she isn't her aunt, and some-times Justyna introduces Anna as her cousin. Justyna rarely ever writes to Anna in the States but when July rolls around and Anna returns to Kielce, the two friends simply pick up where they left off.

But this year, Justyna is no longer interested in skipping down to *Pan* Narcyz's cellar to refill seltzer bottles, or playing Chinese jump rope, or scaling the bomb shelter, or flipping somersaults on the *trzepak*. She is now interested in two things: boys and sex. It is overwhelming to Anna, and more and more she turns to Kamila for kinship. Kamila, who cuts her own bangs, draws hilarious caricatures, and devours books. With Kamila, Anna safely indulges all her childish whims; on rainy days the two girls sit on Kamila's *balkon* playing with the Barbies Kamila still collects. They talk about true love, make crank calls, and sometimes Kamila shows Anna poems she wrote. But Anna also has no problem going along with Justyna to shoplift sunflower seeds or ogle her dad's stash of nudie magazines. It is easy to switch sides because Anna Baran *has* two sides; she feels split between two languages, two places, constantly aware of the chasm in her life.

Justyna starts walking toward the snack shack, but she stops and turns around. 'I'm just trying to help, Kamila. You've been starving yourself, so why not shed that dumb getup?' Anna nods in agreement. This summer Kamila never eats actual food; instead, she carries around a giant bag of puffed corn kernels, and snacks on them all day long.

'Besides, if I were you I wouldn't worry about someone spotting your diaper. I'd worry about that booger that's been hanging out of your nose all morning.'

With that, Justyna saunters away, hips working overtime. Anna can't help but stare after her with a mixture of envy and admiration.

It's been like this all summer – Anna teetering on the brink of self-ecstasy and self-loathing. Anna waits all week for Sundays when *Babcia* Helenka goes to two P.M. Mass. As soon as *Babcia* leaves, Anna lies on the pullout, half nude, and masturbates to her heart's content. But feeling sexual and feeling sexy are two different things. Recently outfitted with a retainer (which she only wears at night), Anna's cartoonish overbite is making a slow retreat. Now, she's learning to expose enamel when she smiles. It's a small step toward sexy, but it's something. Anna remains optimistic about her hidden prowess. Just two weeks ago, she gave Heniek Żak a hand job in the stairwell. She has no idea why, only that Heniek offered to walk her home and when they got to the *klatka,* she grabbed him without a word and went to work. Heniek Żak was a nobody, a year younger than her, but he was as good as anybody to practice on.

'I won't tell anyone,' he whispered after.

'I don't care if you do,' Anna replied, and she almost meant it.

Then, at her sixteenth birthday party a week ago, when Kowalski showed up without his girlfriend, Anna did a shot in the kitchen before asking him for a slow dance. When they swayed to the melodic undertones of the Scorpions, she could feel his erection pressing on her thigh. Then, someone hit the light switch and, in the dark, she let him French-kiss her. She was so turned on it frightened her. Kowalski has potential. He's on the short list of possible candidates to lose her virginity to. But Anna's been secretly waiting for Sebastian Tefilski to finally come back to Kielce and make a woman out of her. His family moved to Germany in 1990, a week before she came back to Poland, just like she promised him. The news of his departure crushed Anna, but there wasn't anything she could do, except hope that one day he'd come back.

'Why is Justyna so spiteful?' Kamila's eyes well up as she furtively wipes her nose.

'Kamilka, she's not really. You're just extra sensitive today. When I have my period all I wanna do is eat and cry.'

'That's not it, Ania. I mean you're right, but it's more than that. Tomorrow is the anniversary of my brother's death. We have to go to his grave and then sit around the table while my parents tell stories about when he was alive. We do it every year, but I'm over it, Ania. I don't even remember him. And I don't care. Is that awful?'

'No, it's not awful. It's normal. He's dead, but you're not. Any way you cut it, it just fucking sucks.' Anna smiles and doesn't know what else to say.

Anna remembers the first letter she ever got from Kamila, remembers reading the part about her brother's death over and over again. Anna wrote Kamila back, confessing that when her hamster had suffered an untimely demise after crawling into a hot oven, she was despondent for a whole week and therefore knew firsthand what an 'accident like that' could do to a girl. If Kamila was offended at the comparison, she never let on, because the next summer the minute Anna touched pavement in Kielce, Kamila was waiting by the *trzepak*.

Kamila turns to face Anna, her face streaked with mascara.

'Will you come with me tomorrow? Please? I can't do it alone this year and you're my best friend. I don't have anyone like you in my life, Ania. You make everything better.'

Before Anna can answer Justyna returns, eating an ice cream cone, her tongue darting back and forth like a kitty cat's. The lifeguard with the rodent-filled trunks stands next to her juggling three orders of French fries and two Cokes.

'I couldn't carry all this shit. So Patryk here was gallant enough to help a lady out. Why are you crying?'

Before Kamila can fumble for an excuse, Anna chirps in with 'Cramps,' an obvious salvo.

The lifeguard smiles widely, and it's all Anna can do to keep her eyes from roaming toward his swimsuit. She can swear the contents are moving.

'I bet we have some *aspiryna* in our first aid kit. Should I get you some?' Patryk asks, unaware of the slow death Kamila's now dying. Anna forces herself to look in his face and decides, aside from his seemingly remarkable package, there's not much to look at. He's bug-eyed and his nose looks like a potato.

84

'So should I? It's no problem.' Patryk repeats his offer. Kamila shakes her head madly at the same time Justyna purrs, 'That would be so sweet of you.' Patryk gallantly places the snacks onto their bench and bows away.

'What the hell?' Kamila hisses.

'I know, I know, he's a bit of a *mól* but his friends are gorgeous, I promise you. I invited him to my birthday *balanga* next week and he's gonna bring his boys. Morten included.' And with that Justyna triumphantly digs into the soggy *frytki*. Anna is stunned and impressed.

'It was obvious she'd been crying. You think it would have been less awkward if nobody said anything about it? Take some fries or I'm gonna eat them all.'

Suddenly Kamila stands up, towels dropping like hotcakes. 'I'm going home. You two can stay and get skin cancer. It's not like you want me here anyway.'

'*Skin cancer?* You've been reading too many foreign magazines, *dziewczyno.*'

Kamila swings her mesh beach bag across her shoulder and jumps over the bench and unfortunately lands cockeyed, stumbling to the ground. Justyna does a spit take.

'Kamila! You okay?' Anna scrambles toward her friend.

'Yeah, should I call old Patryk back with a stretcher?' Justyna laughs.

'Shut the hell up!'

Justyna looks at Anna, and then lets out a low whistle. 'Shutting up. But next time you talk to me like that, you'll have my foot up your ass. And despite the rumors, you *won't* like it. Got it, *bejbe*?' Anna closes her eyes, weary all of a sudden.

Justyna stands up and wipes her greasy hands on her bottom. 'Screw this overcrowded shithole. We are gonna walk home, in the shade, so as to avoid "the cancer," take showers, refuel, re-pad, re-fucking-lax, and then have an awesome time tonight. All right, *pipki*?'

The word *pipki* does wonders, more than Justyna's backhanded apology. *Pipki*: small vaginas. It's crude and comical, and vintage Justyna. Fighting smiles, Anna and Kamila nod their heads and pack up their gear, leaving the French fries, and Patryk with his aspirin, behind.

The girls walk through the woods that surround the *zalew*, and halfway, when they pass the corrugated shed that serves as a bus stop, Anna reaches for both their hands. Neither friend fights it. They end up walking hand in hand the rest of the way.

After a cool shower, which is not really a shower but a squat in the tub and a dunk of the head under running water, and after a plate of *Babcia*'s fried *schabowy* and sweet cabbage, Anna nestles onto the sofa with some crosswords, listening to the sound of *Babcia* washing dishes and singing those Russian ballads she loves, the vibrations of the TV in the next room, the passing cars on the street below, and the slow billowy dance of the lace curtains by the open balcony. *Perfection,* Anna thinks. This is her very own personal Jesus.

Anna puts the puzzle book down onto her chest and closes her eyes. Soon, she'll meet up with Justyna and Kamila again, and they'll go meet the *chłopaki*. She'll bring her cassette deck. The boys will pass around a bottle of wine and listen to 'Words' over and over again, and Lolek will beg Anna to translate the lyrics one last time.

Babcia waddles into the living room, a muumuu-clad penguin, with a little green rag perched on her shoulder. 'Need some help, *córeczko*?'

Anna smiles and opens her eyes. She pats the lumpy fold-out *wersalka* in invitation. No one has beds here; there's simply no room for them in cramped Polish apartments, and even that thought fills her with affection. *Babcia* sits down next to her. Even though with every passing summer Anna is less inclined to hang out with family, she always makes time for *Babcia,* who calls her *little daughter.* They eat breakfast together every morning while *Babcia* recaps Anna's youth in exquisite detail, bringing up memories Anna's mother has seemingly forgotten. 'You used to steal my sewing scissors and cut up all my plants, Aniusia.' Sometimes *Babcia* gets out a shoebox full of ancient black-and-white photos, and they rifle through them gleefully. '*Babcia,* you looked just like Vivien Leigh.' Anna sighs staring at the picture of her grandmother standing on a cobblestone street, wispy and gorgeous, her dark, wavy hair falling over one eye.

Anna loves *Babcia* Helenka's soft glistening skin, pampered every morning and night with a healthy dollop of Nivea cream. She loves *Babcia*'s dainty fingers, her moon-shaped fingernails, unpolished but perfectly trimmed. She loves the way *Babcia* stands in front of the mirror, brushing her silvery hair, which she refuses to dye. She loves the array of *podomki Babcia* wears every day (braless), with the deep pockets in the front that she sews in herself. Anna adores the way she kneads dough for homemade *makaron;* the way she takes off her shoes and slips into her *trepki* the minute she walks into the apartment, one hand leaning on the foyer dresser, the other clutching a grocery bag; the fact that she always has a covered plate of *kromeczki* waiting for Anna at night: rye bread smeared with butter and thin slices of gouda cheese and smoked ham.

'Five letters, starting with *s.* "Handy holes in the kitchen"?'
'*Sitko.*'

'Oh my god, *sitko*! How did I not know that?'

'I'm the same way, *córeczko,* simple words will just fly out of my head, but I hunt them down in time. Patience is key. How do you say it in English?'

'Colander.'

'*O, Jezus!* Karender? Kawendol?'

Anna laughs and laughs.

Later, on her walk to meet Justyna, who was spending the night at her *Babcia* Kazia's in Szydłówek, Anna thinks about the camping trip they are planning. She knows that Sielpia Lake was where she was conceived; her parents went *pod namioty,* camping, for two whole weeks, by themselves, after her dad left the army. Wouldn't it be serendipitous if she made love for the first time under the same stars that shone down on her parents sixteen years ago?

The stars in Poland are bright and sharp, as if torn from a connect-the-dots coloring book. They baffle Anna and remind her of religion and faith. In New York, the neon signs and tall buildings disturb the heavens, and all Anna can make out, aside from the moon, is the lone North Star. But not here – here the grass looks and smells like grass, rampant and overgrown among the cracked stones that pave the sidewalks – it's not pretty, and it's a far cry from the well-manicured lawns in Brooklyn, but it's real. Even downtown you can sometimes inexplicably catch a whiff of cow manure and wheat. Here, nature forces its way into every corner, in its purest form, and the stars take over at night, illuminating everything the way God intended. It's all as if from a fairy tale: the blackbird's call at seven in the morning, the magpies' flight at dusk, the century-old wooden huts nestled next to the brightly painted seventies-era Communist apartment housing. Everyone smokes and laughs, but nobody smiles unless they really fucking mean it. And at the heart of every-thing is the one thing that unites everyone: *przetrwanie* – survival.

Anna knocks on Justyna's door and Justyna answers, wrapped in a towel. 'I'm not ready.' She glances at Anna. 'And you're giving me that tank top. My *babcia* made tea. Get the fuck in! The guy across the hall is a total *pedofil*.' And then she quickly undoes her towel, flashes her boobs for a second, and then sticks up her middle finger.

'You're crazy!' Anna cackles. Justyna pulls her inside and loudly shuts the door behind them.

KAMILA
KIELCE, POLAND

The bathroom sink fills up quickly. The water is so hot that Kamila can feel her pores opening up as the steam rises. She submerges her hands slowly. The water scalds, but it's the only thing that eases the itch. None of the eczema creams help one bit, not the fancy cortisone prescriptions that Doctor Poniatek scribbles, not the natural aromatherapy salves, and not the tubes of black tar that her friend Lidka Frenczyk swears by. The only thing that temporarily alleviates the pain is when Kamila dips her hands into a torrid stream and rubs her palms vigorously. Above the din of the running faucet, she can hear her parents in the kitchen, still going at it.

'There is no way, my beloved God – that – she – is – going! Running around with a bunch of boys, in the middle of the woods? Over my dead body!' screeches Zofia.

'What's another dead body in this family?' Kamila can't believe her father actually said it, but he did. Then there is a small pause before Kamila hears a loud whack and then glass shattering. Włodek lets loose a howl and then he is at the bathroom door. His knocks are gentle and few, like he simply needs to pee.

'Kamila? Can you let me in please, *córeczko*? I'm bleeding.'

When Kamila lifts her hands out of the water, they look stippled and bloated. Włodek knocks again. 'Sweetheart, she threw a glass at me. I need to get the shards out. *Proszę cię*, Kamilka.'

Kamila opens the door and regards her father with a mixture of disdain and pity. 'Why do you let her do that to you?' Her father is holding his hands to his temple, and there is a stream of blood trickling through his fingers, down his cheek.

'Can you just help me clean up, *córciu*?' Kamila shakes her head and holds up her ruined hands.

'I can't.' She walks past him and goes straight into her room. Her overnight bag is on her bed and she zips it quickly, making a mad dash for the door, her mother's strangled 'Kamilaaaa!' echoing in the stairwell after her.

The bus headed for Sielpia doesn't leave till tomorrow morning but, thank God, Emil Ludek lives only two buildings down. It's raining and she doesn't have the energy for a long walk. When she buzzes Emil's intercom, he answers immediately.

Emil makes *herbata* for her right away, sweetened with raspberry syrup, just the way she likes it. The honey-based balm he rubs on her hands feels good. She wonders briefly if her eczema is stress-related, like Doctor Poniatek suggested.

'They look terrible, Kamila. The worst yet. Are you taking your vitamins?'

'Yes, *Panie Doktorze,* I am. Nothing helps. Especially not the damn humidity. I'm ravaged by it!' Kamila pretends to faint, eyes rolling back in her head.

Emil laughs, but there is sympathy in his eyes. He's the only person she will let comfort her so openly. Long ago, it was the other way around. Kamila was the bully to all his bullies. When the other boys in third grade snickered at the tights he wore in the winter, Kamila stood up for him. When girls called him *lalus* and pulled on his golden locks and gave him Indian burns, Kamila swatted them away. But now, Emil doesn't need a bodyguard, and he has to fend off the girls for other reasons. At sixteen he is tall and very handsome, like a young Laurence Olivier. His eyes are gooseberry gray and piercing, and his blond hair is always slicked back with pomade, high off his forehead, like Rick Astley's. Kamila would do anything to be his.

'She hit him again.'

'Well, better him than you.'

'But that's the thing, Emil. I wish it were me, because I'd teach her a lesson real fast.'

Emil smiles gently. 'Your dad might seem cowardly to you, Kamila, but he's doing the right thing. It's so easy to strike back. The hard part is to turn the other cheek.'

He's almost biblical in his quiet martyrdom. Emil knows what he's talking about. He hasn't only endured beatings after school when the upper-class thugs cornered him at the bus stop. Emil's own father used to whale on him, until last year, when he fully gave over to the vodka, and became a mere shell of a man. Right now, he's probably passed out in front of some liquor store, his pants stained with day-old urine tracks.

Emil's mother moved out last year. Someone had to keep the old man from starving, and being his only child, Emil felt it was his duty. Kamila often thinks that she has it bad – drowned brother, feeble father, ravaged hands, countless unreciprocated feelings . . . but Emil takes the cake when it comes to shitty luck and somehow, he never complains.

'You sure you don't wanna come with us tomorrow?' Kamila asks, her eyes pleading.

'I'm sure, Kamila. I have work, and if I leave for more than three days, I'd come home to find Franciszek choking on his own vomit.'

Kamila nods and finishes her tea.

'Your hands will get stronger when you get stronger,

Kamilka. It's all in the mind. Trust me.' She does trust him. She more than trusts him, she adores, pines for, dreams about, and waits for him.

That night, Kamila and Emil sleep dressed in their clothes, on top of his sheets. Emil wraps his brawny arms around her torso, but his hands don't travel up or down or anywhere she longs for them to. There has been only one kiss between them, last summer, but it was sloppy and drunken and all but forgotten on Emil's part. Kamila, however, remembers every second of it.

At seven-thirty the next morning, she slips from his warm clutch and grabs her bag. In the living room, Franciszek is passed out in his clothes, his legs shuddering.

When Kamila joins the group at the bus stop she is battling many things – anxiety, guilt, and platform shoes that are one size too small. She sits quietly next to Anna, who is constantly turning around and kneeling on the seat to gossip with Justyna, who is seated behind them.

The bus is a dinosaur – a piece of shit on wheels, treading slowly and stopping and starting till it finally breaks down thirty kilometers from the campgrounds. The passengers waste four grueling hours standing around while Kamila's friends get drunk on what's supposed to be a week's supply of beer and wine. When the repaired bus finally rolls into the depot, it's dark and cold outside. As they stumble into the woods, Lolek heaves all over himself. Kamila and Anna have to hold him up the rest of the way, slowing everyone down because the girls are no match for his two-hundred-pound frame. On top of everything else, it starts to rain.

They throw their stuff down under the wooden gazebo at the site's entrance. The rain comes down with no signs of stopping, the kind of relentless downpour typical of early spring or late fall but that has no business ruining a perfectly good summer night. The boys sleep like bums on the floor, while the girls sit up on the wooden benches, taking turns keeping resentful watch over their belongings. Kamila wishes she were back in Kielce, under her afghan, reading a book.

'Why didn't we stop them from drinking all that beer when the bus broke down?' she whispers, worried about waking the other innocent campers, not her slovenly, fucked-up friends.

''Cause we're not their mommies. Relax, Marchewska. This will make a good anecdote for you someday. You'll be a hero back in Kielce, as the lone virgin amongst the savages, keeping vigil in the wild!' Justyna laughs loudly.

Kamila ignores the insult and furiously whispers, 'Be quiet! You might wake someone up and they'll—'

'They'll what? Come over and rape us all?'

It's no use with Justyna; nothing gets the girl down. Kamila activates her wristwatch's neon light. It's already past midnight. She frowns and sighs. 'Anyway, I'm not the "lone virgin" here, not by a long shot – not that it's anyone's business. I'm only saying this out loud right now because they' – she points toward the comatose boys lying on the floor – 'can't hear a word. Besides, why is everything with you about sex?'

Anna glances at Kamila and shakes her head. Anna, who always wants to be on everyone's good side. She seems to think that her greatest tragedy in life is that she's caught between two worlds. Two worlds! Can't her dear friend see what a blessing that is?

'Everything with me is about sex because everything *is* about sex. Perhaps a week stuffed into itty-bitty tents with a few happy drunks will finally make women out of you two.'

Kamila shakes her head. Her friends were not happy drunks. They were drunks that hurled empty beer cans all over the place and grabbed you by your waist too hard.

Somehow, in the morning, the tents get pitched. The guys wander off in search of a snack shack that will sell alcohol at eight A.M. It's a balmy morning. Tent mates are chosen and most of the girls change into their bathing suits and head to the water. Kamila stays behind. She sits on a blanket looking out onto the lake, the same lake that her little brother drowned in. She fumbles in her backpack for her journal, a small black notebook adorned by a collage of torn-out pages from books and quotes from her favorite poets. Kamila's going to be a junior in the fall at Kielce's fine arts high school. Her father wants her to be an artist, but even though Kamila has spent all her semesters weaving tapestries and copying paintings of fields and valleys, she has a secret dream. Kamila wants to be a writer, like Anaïs Nin, like Maria Pawlikowska-Jasnorzewska, whose poem 'The Lady Who Waits' is copied by hand a dozen times throughout her diary. *She waits, she looks at the watch of her years, she bites her handkerchief impatiently. Beyond the windows the world pales and grays . . . and maybe it's too late for the guests to arrive.* Every time Kamila reads it she feels like Pawlikowska is calling out to her.

One day, she wants her journals to be read by girls like her. She wants her words to strike a nerve, but thus far her own poetry feels mawkish and lacking. Kamila closes her eyes and waits for inspiration to strike her. When she feels droplets on her legs, she looks up and sees Anna, wet from head to toe, grinning at her as she plops down on her stomach.

'It's heaven.'

'What is?'

'The water, the trees, us in the midst of it. *Jak w raju!* All of it, it's all heaven. And I never want to come back down to earth again.'

'Why? Is Kowalski flirting with you?'

'Nah. He's all about Justyna. By the way, she's this close to taking off her top. She's trying to convince everyone to skinny-dip! In broad daylight!' Anna cracks up and flips to her back, squinting up at her friend.

'Uh-oh. You look sad. Are you upset I didn't show up yesterday? Was it that bad?'

Kamila shrugs her shoulders and closes her book. 'It's not that.'

'Oh, Kamilka, don't be sad. I bet Emil will realize what a fool he's been and come riding up here on some white horse and steal you away.'

'Don't patronize me, Anna.'

'Kamila! You've got to stop this! Stop pining and start living. Look around you. This isn't 1892, okay? It's 1992. Poland is finally free! And *we* have options too, *dziewczyno*! But you have to be in the moment.'

'I *am* in the moment. And this moment sucks.'

Anna laughs. 'The moment is ripe, my friend. I wish I never had to go back to New York.'

'Oh my God, you're crazy. New York is a gilded city. Everything is modern and ready to burst there. It's like fireworks. Here? It's like everyone is taking a perpetual nap in the name of "tradition." It's old news. It's Lolek getting wasted on some poison he brewed in his own bathtub and pissing in front of my grandmother's doorway.'

'Nah. New York is dirty.'

'Well, at least you have air-conditioning on public transportation.'

'*Dobra, dobra.* I guess the grass is always greener, but New York makes you feel alone. Besides, you wouldn't like my New York friends. I don't even know if I like them. They don't know what it's like to work for anything.'

'And Lolek does? And Kowalski? They're on the freaking dole! I wish we could trade lives, even for a few days.'

'Listen, one day I'll fly you out to New York and you can make up your own mind. For now, let's just enjoy this. We're sixteen and it's summer. The possibilities are, like, fucking endless. Now read me a poem!' Anna grabs Kamila's notebook and starts flipping through it. Anna is probably the only person in the world, aside from Emil, who is privy to Kamila's secret aspirations.

'Don't get it wet,' mumbles Kamila.

'Soon you're going to be a famous poetess and I'll make you write my Oscar speech. Pinky swear.' Anna holds out a pinky and Kamila holds out hers, and they intertwine, just like Anna taught her a long time ago.

'Peenky sweer.'

'Now let's go swimming. The water's divine,' Anna proclaims in a Joan Collins-y voice, and hops up, her long legs pumping as she runs back toward the lake. Kamila watches her get smaller and smaller until she looks like a little fish, diving in headfirst, breaking the surface. Kamila crawls inside the tent and curls up into a ball, wrapping her arms around her own torso. She pretends they belong to someone else.

JUSTYNA
KIELCE, POLAND

Justyna ignores the gooey sediment on the bottom of the lake, trying not to notice how her toes sink into what feels like piles of cow shit. The moon is full, casting a silvery shadow onto the still water. In the distance she hears Lolek singing the words to Dr. Alban's 'It's My Life.' He's wasted and the foreign words slur and slide into one another, so it sounds like complete gibberish. Justyna inches closer to Kowalski.

A small part of Justyna was surprised that her mother allowed her to go on this unsupervised trip. In June, Justyna got kicked out of school, permanently. The history teacher caught her giving Lucjan Popiel a hand job in the custodian's office. When the door creaked open and *Pani* Jesienowska walked in, Lucjan was just cumming. 'What in God's name?' she shrieked. Justyna wiped her hand off and looked up at her teacher. 'I believe God's name for it is spunk.'

A two-hour-long meeting followed between the principal of the school, Justyna's mother, and *Pani* Jesienowska. The school had a laundry list of Justyna's misdemeanors: hooky, failing grades, graffiti in the girls' bathroom, the time Justyna punched a girl who was rifling through Justyna's book bag, about to swipe a very expensive L'Oréal lipstick. 'This latest incident just proves to us, again, Mrs. Zator, that your daughter has no respect for the educators here, nor for the institution itself.

Although she's never been caught, we suspect she's cheated her way through her last two years here. Justyna's lack of interest, integrity, and effort lead us to believe that she couldn't care less about us, and so we too have stopped caring about her. Your daughter is no longer welcome here.'

Teresa just nodded and walked out; she couldn't argue with Justyna's track record. She briefly thought about filing for an appeal – Lucjan Popiel got off with a two-week suspension, which Teresa secretly thought was more than unfair. She sat on the steps outside the school, chain-smoking for twenty minutes and thinking about when she got pregnant at seventeen and the bastards at her school had kicked her out. She had bigger plans for her own children, but Teresa had made a fine life for herself despite her lack of diplomas, and Justyna could too. There was no use crying over spilled milk; she had a high-school castoff on her hands and aside from giving Justyna a good thrashing, there was nothing Teresa felt she could do. It was time for her daughter to get a job. She'd go home, smack Justyna upside the head, and place a call to her friend Janka over at the new super-market in town.

When Justyna's mother told her the outcome of the meeting, Justyna had tried to keep the relief from registering on her face. Inside, she was thrilled. The charade was over. She would no longer have to pay Tobiasz Tedoroski to write her essays for her, she would no longer have to waste time penning tiny cheat sheets. It was no accident that the subjects she was passing, geography and chemistry, were taught by the two male professors who were defenseless against her miniskirts and push-up bras. She wrote off the rest of her teachers as cunts, jealous and disgruntled, high on power trips. Education came in all forms anyway. The nerds at school, the ones who memorized and studied ad nauseam, the ones who recited facts on cue, they were the ones who stuttered and cowered through life. Once you graduated, who the fuck cared what an isosceles triangle was, or when World War I began? How was such ancient shit relevant? Justyna believed success relied heavily on simple charm, a forceful personality, and the skill of lying in the pursuit of grander dreams. So, in other words – fuck school. Both her parents had been high-school dropouts and look at them now. A year ago, the Zators bought a modern three-story house in the suburbs of Sieje, past the *zalew,* just a few kilometers from downtown Kielce, and somehow worlds away from their cramped apartment life. Come September, Justyna wouldn't be scouring flea markets for used textbooks; she'd be standing behind the till at the Super-Sam, gossiping with the other cashier girls, and that was fine by her.

At the start of the summer, Teresa made halfhearted attempts at punishment: no allowance, no partying, and an early curfew. But Justyna, being Justyna, broke all the rules, lied, whined, or just laughed at Teresa's threats. By the time the camping trip came up, Justyna didn't even have to beg. 'Just don't drown,' Teresa cautioned.

'Watch out, I hear there are snakes in this water.' Kowalski grins in the dark. 'In fact, I think there's one trapped in my underwear right now.'

'What kind of snake?' Justyna whispers as she glides closer to him.

'A python.'

Justyna dissolves into giggles, vodka swirling in her brain and swimming in her veins. 'You sure it's not a baby eel or something?' Kowalski grabs her hips under the water and roughly pulls her toward him. Their torsos smack against each other, slick and goose-bumpy. 'Well, there's only one sure way to find out,' he growls.

Justyna reaches for him. His dick feels slippery in her hands, thick and massive. He pulls her bikini bottom to the side but it takes him three tries before he's inside her. The sex is un-comfortable and quick. It hurts, like Kowalski is jamming a rubber glove inside her. Justyna feels chafed and dry. And when Kowalski finally cums, Lolek can be heard roaring the chorus to 'It's My Life' again, his bellows reverberating through the woods, 'Eetsma laaaaaaaaaaaf!!'

Kowalski leans his body against hers, his head against her shoulder, and he mumbles, 'You let me cum inside you.'

'So?'

'So you're not worried?' Justyna *is* worried, but only slightly, and only about finding a small bump on her right labia a few weeks before. It was still there yesterday, a rough, white mound, like grains of sand. It didn't look like a pimple, and if she just gave Kowalski genital warts, she feels no guilt; he probably had them already.

'There's no reason to worry.'

Kowalski lifts his head. 'What? Like, you can't get knocked up?'

'Like, I'm on my period, moron. You think I'd risk bringing your spawn into the world?' And with that, she swims toward the shore and starts heading into the forest. She glances back at Kowalski, who is sprawled out on the sand, like a beached animal.

She's cold and wet and feeling slightly remorseful, but Justyna knew she'd fuck Kowalski on this trip. She had just planned on doing it in a tent. It wasn't the first time she and Kowalski fooled around; anytime his girlfriend was out of town, Kowalski was on her, extending his cigarette for her to puff on, eyeing her silently. He was less aggressive than the others, and his finger-nails were always clean – not that Justyna cared about that shit. He also had a scar that ran from the corner of his right eye down his cheek, like the scars in the portrait of the Black Madonna. There was something mysterious about him. He almost never said a word and he laughed wholeheartedly at jokes, though he never told one himself. But Kowalski was too shy to ever make a first move, unless he was very drunk, like tonight. When he grabbed Justyna's hand and asked her to go swimming, Justyna saw Anna's crestfallen face as they ran toward the water, but she wasn't about to let anyone get in the way of her good time.

She stumbles past the dying cinders of the campfires. It's all quiet, everyone is tucked back inside his or her *namioty*.

At their campsite, there are dozens of empty beer bottles and tin cans strewn around, the cassette player quietly playing their Lato 1996 Mix, the one Anna made, and right now, as she hears the refrain to 'Jolka Jolka,' Justyna spots her tent. She doesn't want to wake Ania, and is extra quiet as she squats down to the entrance, which is unzipped halfway. She pulls back the nylon quietly.

Lolek is on top of Anna, pumping away. His hand is over her mouth, and he is whispering in between kissing her neck. 'I wanted this so fucking bad. I love you so much. I've loved you forever.' Anna is crying; she looks scared as shit. There is blood trickling down her cheek, from a scratch.

Justyna stares into the tent. They can't see her. She has to in-tervene, but she's no match for Lolek, and she doesn't want to get kicked in the face. He would pummel her. Nobody messes with Lolek when he's drunk like this: wasted, but in control of his body. At the very least Justyna should wake the others, but she knows everyone is just as drunk, if not worse. And what could Lidka Frenczyk or Kamila do? Justyna stares at Anna's contorted face. Lolek was always Anna's personal bodyguard, her biggest fan, and the one who ribbed her the most. His old man read the letters Anna sent to his son, and boasted to the neighbors that someday Anna Baran would be his daughter-in-law.

Maybe she wants it, thinks Justyna. She's been going on and on about popping her cherry, but from the look on Anna's face this is probably not how she imagined it. For reasons beyond her, Justyna quietly stands up, the world spinning for a brief moment. Somehow she finds Kamila's tent. She pushes Kamila's tent mate to the side and slips into the sleeping bag. She can still hear 'Jolka Jolka' in the distance; someone must have set the Sanyo on replay. She closes her eyes and falls asleep.

CHAPTER FIVE

2002

ANNA
GREENPOINT, BROOKLYN

Three days ago, when Ben came home from work, Anna sat him down on the couch. 'I think it's over.'

He lit a cigarette and tried to make light of the situation. 'Banana split, huh?' *Ben Anna split*. She smiled, feeling relieved, but an hour later they were both weeping. When Ben said, 'Let's just give it one more go,' she nodded her head, but she knew she was lying. And by one A.M., instead of cuddling or consoling each other, Anna was scratching off lotto tickets in her robe and Ben was on his fourth Corona, and they didn't say a word to each other.

Now, Anna is trying to hurry this awful lunch along while her agent and manager stare at her. She's supposed to meet Ben in an hour at a couples counselor's office. It was her last promise to Ben; one session before he had to move his things out of the apartment.

She takes a sip of her pinot grigio and grimaces. Dry and expensive, not what she would have chosen but the bottle was already on the table when she arrived. This was supposed to be a powwow to discuss missed opportunities, upcoming projects, and Anna's bright future. But everything – from their concerned faces to the untouched breadbasket – screams of intervention. Anna's last job was one episode of *ER,* back in August. It was supposed to be a recurring role, but the producers changed their minds. Her manager, Linda, swirls her spoon in a frothy cappuccino; Linda doesn't drink alcohol. Jeremy, her agent, clears his throat.

'So, Annie. I want to tell you a story. Years ago, I had a client –'

'Who is now starring in a very popular sitcom,' Linda interjects. Her lipstick is smudged. 'But we won't name names.'

'Right.' Jeremy smiles. Anna likes Jeremy. He's from the Midwest and even after decades in the city, his kindness is still intact.

'Come on, Jer, get to it.' Linda doesn't like to waste time. She's a shark. Her client list is small, a few soap stars, but she's tough and relentless. From the look of her, one could never tell. She shops the sales racks at Talbots and has not just one, but an entire collection of denim vests. In the beginning, Anna thought of Linda as the Jewish aunt she never had, full of quips and world-weary insight. Linda peppered her speech with Yiddish, taught Anna one of her favorite expressions: *'gehstoygen, gefloygen,'* which meant 'bullshit.' They used to meet up in Central Park before important auditions and Linda would run lines with Anna, giving her stellar pep talks.

'Anyhoo,' Jeremy continues, lighting a cigarette, 'she was such a talent, got consistently positive feedback, but she wasn't landing any gigs. Callback after callback but nothing ever happened. This went on for a year. And the reason was, and I'm not going to beat around the bush here, the reason was – her nose.'

'It was big. And not character actress big, but distracting big.' Linda wrinkles her own nose in distaste.

'So one day she came into my office and she was distraught. Like, this girl was at the end of her rope. I mean here she was, talented, terrific body, terrific face, the face of an ingénue but for this one tiny thing.'

Anna downs her wine in one gulp. 'You mean, one big thing.' She grins like an idiot and eyes the focaccia, wanting to slip it into her purse for later.

'So Jeremy, being the nice person he is, the generous person he is, he delicately let her know that he would personally, out of his own pocket, pay for a procedure. And she was so grateful. They did it quietly, she recovered quickly, and in a few weeks she was booking jobs left and right and then came an Emmy nod and, well, the rest is history.'

Linda sits back, letting her shoulders relax for the first time.

'Okay. So what's the moral of the story here, guys? You want me to get a nose job?'

Jeremy spits his wine all over the table. He frantically dabs his fancy necktie with his napkin. 'No! For god's sake, no! Your nose is perfect, so Slavic, classic nose, classic. Your face is perfect, Anna.'

It's not her face that's the problem. Anna knows what this is about. Perhaps in the real world, she could pass muster – wasn't size 10 the norm? But Hollywood sells a fantasy world where even bums have white teeth and where no one ever takes a shit, unless it's for comedic effect. Anna had never worried about her weight before. Her weight had always been fine, just this side of a size six. Now, she wants to play dumb, but it's either sink or swim, and if she's going to drown, then she wants to be the one to throw herself into the water. 'Perfectly fat, you mean.' The word hangs in the air, like it's written in a cartoon balloon above Anna's head.

'You're not fat, sweetheart,' Jeremy drawls. 'You're just—'

'*Curvy?*' Anna smiles, ruefully. 'I know I gained some weight. It's okay. Let's be grown-ups here and call a spade a spade. I've had a rough couple of weeks, you know?'

'Yes, your friend's husband.'

'That, and other things, Jeremy. So yes, I've let myself go. But what are you saying right now? Are you saying you want me to get lipo? Is my career over? I don't get it.'

Linda arches her eyebrows. 'Okay, Anna. Yes, you have gained weight. And I'm sorry for whatever it is you've been going through, but you can't afford to let yourself go like this. It just doesn't suit you. You're much too beautiful to be a character actress, especially at this point in your career. Last year was slow, after the terrorist attacks and all, so we don't blame you for that. But you starred in two studio pics the year you graduated. That's something, honey. You should be very proud of that. And things are picking up again. Things are getting green-lighted left and right. But we can't work with what you've got now and I know you're not happy about it either.'

'Duh,' Anna whispers.

'Yes, duh. So we get a trainer. If you can't afford one right now, we'll help you out, naturally. But you need to lose it, fast and furious. The point is, we support you, we believe in you. But we must do everything to get you back to *you*. Starve yourself if you have to, I don't care.'

'Now, hold on, Linda. No one is sayi—'

'*I'm* saying it. I'm saying it because pilot season will be upon us before we know it and you need to test for at least one. At least. And when we see you again on January second, I want you looking like you did in *D'Artagnan*.'

'I see.'

'We're giving tough love here, honey, because we truly, truly think you are poised to be a huge star. Really. And it would be such a shame if fifteen pounds got in the way of that.'

'Twenty.' Linda finishes her coffee in one gulp and motions for the check.

'And if I don't lose the weight?'

Jeremy fumbles with his credit card, and Linda folds her arms. 'That is simply not an option.'

When Anna graduated from drama school, she was inundated with phone calls from agents, managers, and casting directors. At her showcase performance she did a monologue from *Cat on a Hot Tin Roof,* the one about the no-necked monsters. She *was* Maggie the Cat, with her voluptuous curves and her strangled desire. In meetings her backstory read like a script itself: humble immigrant beginnings, her jailed father, her mother making ends meet by cleaning penthouses. And there was her stunning profile, her profane jokes, and her trembling confession of wanting to make it big so she could save her family.

'You're gonna be a star,' Jeremy pronounced when she had first met with him. He said it like a diagnosis, and when Anna got in the elevator afterward, she was so giddy that she couldn't stop laughing.

Her first job was a big one, the female lead in a studio feature called *D'Artagnan.* She had been lying on the sofa when Jeremy called to tell her she had landed the role. Her parents were stunned. 'What do you mean?' Paulina asked, perplexed. 'A real movie?'

'How much they gonna pay you?' her father blurted out.

Anna looked at him and answered slowly, 'Two hundred thousand dollars.'

The bigwigs at Paramount were looking to cast an unknown, and Anna fit the bill. She flew to France, first class. It was a dream, and she made sure to bring her Canon everywhere. 'They give me cash every week, *Mamo,* to spend on anything I want. It's called per diem.' Two thousand dollars a week; her parents had to work a month to make that amount.

Anna loved the set; everyone was an overworked but dutiful cog in the motion picture-making machine. It felt familiar to be a part of it. She was nervous and grateful for the opportunity, but beyond that she was at peace because she knew – she *knew* – that this was fate.

Every morning, on the steps of her trailer, before stepping into hair and makeup, Anna enjoyed a cup of coffee and a Gauloise. It was a fairy tale and she knew it would end, but Anna wisely milked it for every last drop. She called her grandmother in Poland every day.

'One day, *Babciu,* you'll fly with me to the set. They'll see how beautiful you are and put you in the movies!'

'Oh, Aniusia.' *Babcia* laughed. 'I don't want to be in movies. I just want to watch them.'

In Hollywood, a single high-profile gig causes a ripple effect, doors open like dominoes falling one after another. There is little time to think of a trajectory. In *Halloo, I Love You* – a romantic comedy based on *Twelfth Night* – Anna played Olive, a young, sensuous Manhattanite turned celibate, and her comedic, wistful performance earned her rave reviews, headlines like 'A Star Is Born (in Poland).' It was a portentous beginning.

Instead of investing her earnings and buying a home or at least a car, Anna spent it on shopping sprees: cosmetics, books, cigarettes, shoes. The rest she handed away. She signed checks recklessly, proudly, with things like 'gift for Mom' in the memos. She left her parents' apartment and rented her own gorgeous loft in Brooklyn. After she met Ben, he quickly moved in. Ben was grateful. At twenty-two, she basked in financial autonomy, the kind no one in her family had ever achieved. She let everything else fall by the wayside, including her career.

Linda had urged her to move to LA. 'The window you have is a small one, and it's closing before our eyes. Anna, I know you're in love, but sometimes that dwindles even faster than Hollywood interest, so get off your ass!' But Anna didn't listen; she had everything she wanted.

Soon Ben and Anna had to move out of their $2,000 a month rental and settle for a cramped railroad apartment in Greenpoint. It was a steep step down, and it had happened so quickly that nothing seemed certain any longer.

At the restaurant, Anna gathers her coat, hat, and shoulder bag, stands up, and tips her chin toward the drinks.

'Thanks for lunch,' she mumbles. 'I lost my footing. I just lost my footing,' and she shuffles out, tripping on the carpet and knocking into a waiter.

On the way to the subway, she wipes away angry tears. 'They chew you up, they spit you back out,' her father had said when she first told him she was going to be a star. Perhaps he'd been right. Maybe she doesn't want to do this anymore. Maybe she's done with fads and fasts, with cattle calls and climbing the ladder. Once upon a time she'd been sure that she'd stand at the Oscar podium one day. Maybe now she'll just give it all up, marry and have babies instead. She could find Sebastian Tefilski and settle down.

By the time Anna gets to her apartment on Lorimer Street, she is sweating and fuming. There is vigor in her step. She has a plan now, hatched between the Third Avenue and Bedford subway stops. She fumbles for her keys and takes the stairwell, two steps at a time.

She yanks her apartment door open. Ben is at work. As she hurries into the bedroom, she catches a glimpse of the dirty dishes in the sink, a wet towel on the bathroom floor, it's a total mess, her mess of a life. It takes her seven minutes to fill up her duffel bag, throwing in underwear, clothes, and books as if she has only a few moments to gather her belongings before a fire consumes everything. She has to run. This doesn't feel like escape, it feels like survival, and Anna is comforted by the difference. Bag by her feet, she briefly settles into a chair with her notebook in hand, and the words pour out like lava, hot, quick, and full of all the secret, ugly truths. *I'm going back. I'm going back to the beginning,* she scrawls and quickly signs her name.

KAMILA
DETROIT, MICHIGAN

In the dim light, past the white shafts of cigarette smoke, it feels as though Kamila is eyeing the man through a fog. It's like the last scene in *Casablanca,* though Kamila is no Ingrid Bergman and he's no Bogart. The bar is empty except for a few businessmen, their ties undone, and there's a bachelorette party in a girly, tiara-clad heap at the tables in the back.

From a distance, he looks a bit like Montgomery Clift, who happens to be Kamila's favorite. Oh, tortured, closeted Monty, with his angelic face torn in half and sewn back all wrong. *It's ironic,* she suddenly realizes. *I've been with a Monty my whole life.* She laughs out loud to herself. The man looks at her. He's probably in his forties and has a nice American face, even though his hairline is receding.

Kamila hasn't seen or talked to her parents since the morning, since she yanked herself free from Zofia and left her standing there. When she knocked on the Levickys' door, Jan opened it immediately. 'Kammie! Your mother's called here six times. She desperately wants you to come home. I hope everything's all right, but I'd love it if you would stay and help me decorate the tree.'

'Eet's okay, *Pani* Jan. My friend in Poland, there was an accident to her husband. But I okay.' Kamila didn't want to explain anything. She didn't want to think about Justyna or Paweł. It

115

was cruel, but that morning, hanging glass ornaments on the Levickys' fake tree, and trying not to cry, she thought only one thing: maybe it would be easier for Justyna to move on than it was for her. At least death was final.

The American man is now staring. Kamila wonders what he sees. Is it possible that in this forgiving light she looks beautiful? Her red hair is dyed black, cut into a Betty Boop bob and weighed down with Frizz-Ease. Her body is all bone and ninety-degree angles. She can count her ribs, and does often; it's like a nervous tic, like cracking knuckles. A few years ago, she got a nose job in Warsaw. Her nose was slim now, like the rest of her. She got the operation done the summer Emil had proposed, out of the blue, one day pre-op, on his knees. They got married in the fall, in a lavish, romantic ceremony. The party went on till two A.M. When they got back home, Emil said he was too ex-hausted to make love to his new bride.

The bartender pours another shot and she sips it, ladylike, very aware of this man's eyes on her. The vodka heats up her insides. Her suitor lights a cigarette, and then he's on his feet, his cashmere coat slung casually over his arm, making his way toward the empty stool beside her. She notices his stomach, drooping slightly over his belt, which seems like it's cinched a few notches too tight. He sits down next to her and takes a drag. She can smell his woodsy cologne.

'Can I buy you a drink?' His voice is not what she expected, nasal and flat. Kamila motions to the empty shot glass and nods. The bartender appears, as if by magic, and refills it without a word. 'Do you work around here? I haven't seen you before, and I'm what they call a regular.' He grins, showing off sparkling white teeth – American teeth.

'I visiting from Poland,' Kamila shares in her broken English. She is just this side of tipsy.

'Poland?' The man smiles wider. Kamila notices that even his molars in the back sparkle. 'Poland, huh? I worked with a guy from Lodz a few years ago. Tomek Cieslak. Had the worst body odor, but a good guy.' He pronounces it *Tahmik Cheese-lak*. 'Lots of Poles in these parts. We've got a few over at Schleifer now. I've always wondered why. Maybe you can tell me, Mrs. . . . ?'

'Figura. Kasia Figura.' There is no way this man can know that Kasia Figura is the Demi Moore of Poland, famous now not so much for her long, somewhat scandalous movie career as for her gravity-defying 34DDs.

'Kasha Feegoora. So tell me, Kasha, why are you here?'

It's a good question. If she were fully drunk, maybe she'd answer it honestly, admitting she was here because she couldn't face her parents, that she'd quit her job at Mrs. Levicky's that afternoon, and that she had taken the bus into downtown Detroit and had gotten off at a random stop because once again, she was on the lam. She would tell him that her husband was a homo and her mother was obese; that her father was a loser. Not to mention that her childhood friend's husband had just been murdered and that she had just made herself throw up in the ladies' room. She would tell him she was here because the Christmas lights above the entrance were so pretty.

Instead she says, 'I on my honey month,' and hopes she remembered the word correctly.

'Your honey month? You mean honeymoon?' She glances down, embarrassed. She notices the man's nails, bitten down to the quick.

'Honey month, huh? I barely lasted a week when my ex-wife and I flew down to St. Thomas. God knows what an entire month would have done! We'd have probably flown back with divorce papers ready. It would have saved us a few years.' He laughs and puffs on his cigarette. 'So where's Mr. Feegoora?'

He's back in Poland with his boyfriend. Oh, how she wishes she could channel Justyna right now. Poor Justyna, poor Kamila. The only one who made out good after all these years is Anna Baran, with her champagne life and caviar dreams.

'My husband, he no likes to go out to the bars.'

'But he has no problem letting his wife go? Tsk, tsk, tsk. I'm no fortune-teller, but that isn't a good sign.'

'I only marry him for the moneys.'

The man lets out an uproarious peal of laughter and finishes off his martini.

'Well, at least you're honest.' Neither of them says anything else for a while. They sit and stare into their empty glasses, exchanging small glances from time to time. The bridal party stumbles past the bar, singing 'A Thousand Miles' as they head out into the cold, their lacey tops and leather minis covered by overcoats and bomber jackets.

'I suppose one of us should take that girl aside and warn her, right? I'm Kevin, by the way.' He sticks out his hand and waits. Kamila tries to give him a quick handshake but he ends up holding the grip for a long time. His hand is big and warm, like a paw.

'Warn is useless. I get warn too, but it no matter. When heart says you do something, the brain is listen. This is the life, Keveen.'

He stares at her and puts his other hand over hers. 'You have a very sexy accent, Mrs. Feegoora. Has anyone told you that before?'

Kamila blushes crimson. How can she tell this man that no

one in her life has ever used the word *sexy* when referring to her? She doesn't say anything.

'They're gonna kick us outta here soon, it's a school night, you know. I've got a very hungry Dalmatian waiting for me at home. And I bet you've got a very hungry husband waiting for you.'

'No. My husband he don't eat what I offering him. He no have the appetite. But I . . . starving.' Kamila can't believe the words are out of her mouth, and in semi-coherent English at that. But Kevin smiles.

'I bet,' he says, signaling the bartender for their check.

He kisses her in the backseat of the taxicab, and she can't get enough. By the time they are in the elevator going up to the twenty-third floor, she is a puddle, melting almost. For a minute a morbid vision of her mother identifying her naked, bruised body flashes in her head. But if this is the end, she's ready to take the risk.

The sex is strange and surprising. Kevin is in turn rough and tender, biting her nipples, stroking her thighs, brushing away years of neglect. He urges her to talk dirty in Polish and she does, because at this point, why not? She arches her neck, recalling the few X-rated movies she's seen and groans, '*Więcej, dalej dalej . . .*' He pants in her ear that she is the sexiest girl he's ever fucked, that he's going to cum all over her face, which he does. It stings and she asks for a paper towel.

Later, he brings a Tupperware of cold cuts to bed and they sit up, naked, eating slices of prosciutto and salami in silence. Kamila swallows the meat with gusto, forgetting to chew. They don't talk much even though Kamila wishes she could tell him everything. Kevin's dog wanders into the bedroom, and Kamila throws him bits of ham, which he catches in his mouth every time. 'I got full custody of Pepper and my wife got the house. A fair trade, don't you think? What a bitch.' It's the last thing he says before he falls asleep. He sleeps with his mouth open, breathing heavily. Kamila stares at him for a long time, and then gets dressed. Pepper follows her to the door, and she nuzzles his neck before leaving.

It takes her a while to find a taxi, but when she does, she throws herself in the backseat, suddenly exhausted and spent. The cab makes its way through the slush, toward Wyandotte. Kamila is no longer afraid to face her mother. Just this morning Kamila had felt close to killing herself over Emil, but now it all seems petty. She must go back to Kielce. She'll give herself a week or two to sleep off the remnants of her fear, and then she'll go. It'll be easy to change her return ticket. Easy to pack up her belongings, most of which she'll leave behind anyway.

Kamila leans her head back and closes her eyes, replaying the night in her head, from the moment she first spotted Kevin ordering his martini, to the last glimpse of his glistening torso heaving softly in slumber, his penis limp, slumped on its side. Kamila wonders if the Pakistani driver can smell the sex on her. She hopes that he does.

JUSTYNA
KIELCE, POLAND

Most people get wasted for one of two reasons: to forgive or to forget. Justyna never had much reason to do either; she drank because it was fun. Other girls needed half a bottle of hard liquor to abandon their inhibition. The boys Justyna grew up with needed half a bottle to forget about their deadbeat dads and their alcoholic moms. But Justyna had always been content with her lot, simply sidestepping every pitfall that came her way. Since Paweł died, she hadn't touched a drop, but when her neighbor dropped by with a bottle of white wine to see if she was doing okay, Justyna replied, 'I'm doing fine,' and went to get two glasses.

They sat on the terrace, shivering in their winter coats, sharing a pack of smokes and talking about everything except for Paweł. By midnight the walls were spinning. Tucked in her bed, she sang her favorite Perfekt lyrics, *Nie płacz, Ewka, bo tu miejsca brak na twe babskie łzy, po ulicy miłość hula wiatr wśród rozbitych szyb,* over and over. *Don't cry, Ewka, there's no room here for your girly tears. On the streets, the wind hurls love among smashed windowpanes.* As she drifted off to sleep she imagined Paweł looking down at her, lying on their old *wersalka*.

Justyna has spent the last seven days aimless like jetsam. Thank God Damian was staying at *Babcia* Kazia's; she had no energy left for mothering. Her limbs felt like they had a life of their own now, carrying out her life. She still took a shit in the morning, still picked at food when she felt hungry, watched TV, and sometimes remembered to brush her teeth at night. She said things without even thinking (*We should get a Christmas tree soon. Can I change the channel? Have you seen my black leggings?*). She took the dog for a walk. But every day she felt a new fissure inside, as if her bones were cracking, bit by bit, and soon, soon, she would collapse into a lifeless heap.

The best part of being drunk, it turned out, was that she didn't dream. In the morning, however, she felt like an octogenarian, her joints creaking, her head throbbing. She got out of bed and prescribed herself the hair of the dog, which turned into an entire day of drinking. She could suddenly see how her dad had turned into a drunk so quickly after his wife's death.

In the afternoon, she had willed herself to go to the grocery store. The kids were coming home later, and the fridge was empty, except for some expired cheese and a two-liter of flat Coca-Cola. Justyna wandered the aisles at the supermarket, grabbing Damian's favorite junk food: Monster Munch chips and *prażynki,* chocolate Prince Polo wafers, cartons of apple mint juice and some ripe tomatoes. Damian loved it when she sliced a tomato in half, sprinkling each top with salt. He sucked on them like they were ice cream cones. At the register, she had a tough time picking out the correct change and finally just dumped the contents of her wallet onto the counter and told the disdainful clerk, 'Go for it.'

Now at her front door, Justyna finally fits the key into the lock. She kicks the door open and drops the grocery bags to the ground, realizing right away that the eggs must be goners. She pulls off her boots with effort and leaves the groceries on the floor. And that's when she notices the sound of hammering coming from upstairs. She wonders why Paweł is home from work so early, and then she remembers he can't be.

The Zator home is three stories high, each floor in a worse state of disrepair than the next. Since Teresa's death, seven years ago, Justyna can safely say the floors have been mopped twice. But the house had always been a pigsty, even when Teresa was alive. Back then, there were shoes thrown about every which way in the downstairs foyer, clothes in knotted heaps, toppling out when someone opened the closet doors. There were dishes stacked on counters, with food crusted on them. The bathrooms all smelled like public restrooms. There were mildew stains on the ceilings and coffee spills on the linoleum. Everything was sticky and filmy and in need of a scrub, but it didn't matter. There had always been laughter in the house and radios blaring. Neighborhood kids charged up and down the stairs, friends were always in the kitchen, they came over uninvited. Her mother was forever throwing parties, especially in the summers, the adults danced, grilled *kiełbasa,* clinked shot glasses, and stayed up till dawn, trying to outdo each other with dirty jokes. The younger kids would fall asleep just about anywhere and wear the same rumpled clothes the next morning, going days without brushing their teeth.

Justyna takes the stairs on her hands and knees. When she reaches the last step, the hammering stops, and she wonders for a split second if it had been in her head all along.

'What's wrong with you?'

Justyna lifts her forehead and sees her sister sitting in the middle of the floor, a long 8 × 4 piece of wood in her hand. There are nails everywhere. A few hammers and a stack of plywood sit next to Elwira. The entrance to the bathroom has been boarded up halfway. The plastic rack where she and

Paweł kept their towels, her vanity mirror, the mildewy shower curtain, and the wooden crate that served as hamper are leaning against the hallway walls. Everything that wasn't nailed down sits next to the door in plastic bags. Justyna spies Paweł's dirty work sweaters, his denim vest, which he used to iron meticulously, and his lucky Korona Kielce cap. Without a word Justyna lunges toward Elwira, pinning her with her body. She grabs a fistful of her sister's hair and yanks. Elwira screams and scrambles for a hammer.

'Oh, really? Is that your weapon of choice? What, don't have a knife on you?'

'What the fuck is wrong with you?!' Elwira screeches as Justyna slams her head against the floor. Finally, Elwira manages to wedge the handle of the hammer under Justyna's chin and presses with all her might against her throat, shoving Justyna off. Justyna lands on her ass, strands of Elwira's hair in her hands.

'What's wrong with *me*? Who gave you the right? Who gave you the right, you god-forsaken fuck?' Justyna's words slur, and she's gasping for air.

'Calm down!' Elwira stands up and rubs the sides of her head, feeling for the extent of the damage. 'You didn't even give me a chance to explain. God, how much have you had to drink?'

'Shut up, you *pizda*. You've got an hour to move all our stuff back, and if you don't, I'm gonna kill you. You're already dead to me as it is.' Justyna stumbles to her feet, starts tugging at the boards, but they don't budge.

'It's just a fucking bathroom. And it gives me the creeps every time I walk past it! I can't do it anymore, *rozumiesz*? Can you? Have you even taken a single fucking dump in there since it happened? Have you? You told Damian not to use the potty in there 'cause of the "spiders"! You and Damian can move down-stairs and I'll stay on the third floor with Cela. And this floor, we'll pretend this floor never happened.'

'And what, we'll sail through the house on a magic carpet? We'll *pretend* it all away?'

'You're such a hypocrite, Justyna. You haven't even told your son his father is dead. Who's the one pretending?'

Justyna walks over and grabs the Korona cap, twisting it in her hands.

'What scares me is that you've been planning this. Was this your idea of an early Christmas present? You didn't even ask me, didn't even broach the subject.'

'You don't let me broach the fucking *weather* with you. It's like I don't exist, Justyna. It's not my fault he did this!'

'You brought him into this house! He mooched off you and instead of kicking him to the curb, you let him beat you, you let him—You're not the landlord, Elwira. I don't turn to you for living arrangements and I never will. Go to *Babcia*'s. Go to fucking Timbuktu if you want, but you can't do this. I won't let you do this.'

Just then they hear *Babcia* Kazia's voice. 'Justyna! Justyna? You shouldn't leave the door open like this, *do jasnej cholery*!' They hear footsteps running up the stairs, and then Cela's there, buttoned up in her purple wool coat, a knit hat with a pom-pom bouncing on top of her head. Her cheeks are flushed from the cold. She's holding a small wire cage in her hands, with a rodent in it.

'Guess what? Guess what?' Justyna and Elwira stare at her and say nothing.

'*Babcia* bought us a hamster. A real live hamster! His name is Miki and he's so cute but he bit Damian's finger this morning.'

She laughs. 'And his *kupa* looks like watermelon seeds and I'm gonna have him for a week in my room and then Damian in his. *Babcia* said it's called "joint custody." '

Damian appears, gnawing on a *rogalik*.

'I was trying to see if he had teeth. They look like tiny knives. That little fucker.' He walks over to the pile of wood.

'Where'd you get these boards? Can I have some? I can totally build a skateboard. *Tato* can help me when he gets back.'

'You can have as many as you want.' Justyna looks at her son, at the poppy seeds stuck between his teeth, at Paweł's old *Knight Rider* sweatshirt he's wearing. He's swimming in it. She pushes past the kids but not before slapping Paweł's cap on Damian's head. It falls over his eyes. 'Help *Ciotka* clean up this mess, both of you.'

Downstairs *Babcia* Kazia is unloading food, slamming things left and right. The kitchen fills up with the aroma of fried *kotlety* and pickled beets. Justyna regards her grandmother with disdain. 'Nice one. You think a hamster's a proper replacement?'

'I stepped in egg,' *Babcia* Kazia replies as she bustles around. 'And I want you and Elwira to empty out this refrigerator. You've got crap in here that's expired, it's disgusting and I have no room to put all this.' She motions to the small pots on the counter, undoubtedly filled with tripe soup, dumplings, and all sorts of goodies. 'But first, sit down.' Kazia turns from the rancid fridge to face her granddaughter.

'We stopped at the *warzywniak,* and the checkout girl told me you were in there today, hammered. That you were knocking things off the shelves. *Wstyd!* A week in the ground and you're making a mockery of him, a mockery of this entire family. How dare you?' She walks over to Justyna and smacks her across the face. Justyna fights the urge to smack her grandmother back.

'Hit me, hit me!' Kazia shrieks. 'I'll have the police down here faster than you can say *mam cie*. I'm sure they remember the address. They'll take Damian from you.'

'Good.'

'If your mother were here, none of this would have happened. You're rotten through and through, Justyna, and you've been that way since you were little. I tried all my life, I tried to do right by Teresa. But she's no longer here and I'm tired, goddamnit. I didn't sign up for this!'

'And I was first in line?'

Justyna walks out to the front yard and sits on the steps. A light snow is falling. She is flooded with memories. Paweł proposed to her here. He was tipsy and she had laughed in his face until he fished out an actual ring from his pocket, a gold band with green stones placed like the petals of a flower. She once gave him a blow job in the bushes at the side of the house, which turned out to be rampant with *pokrzywa,* and they scratched their blistered feet and knees for days, giggling. Things rush at her, snippets from a previous life. Paweł rocking baby Damian to sleep for hours at a time, while Justyna naps on the couch. Paweł in the kitchen drinking black Nescafé, reading motorcycle magazines until she grabs him by the hand and leads him to bed. Paweł, on his knees, showing Damian how to tie his shoes. Paweł, bringing home a pack of smokes every day after work and tossing them into Justyna's open palms.

'You're so lucky, Justyna,' her friends would tell her. She had been lucky.

Thirty-six Witosa Road is now a Smithsonian of memories. The absence of her husband stuns her daily to the point of paralysis. There is no end in sight, no end to the sinking feeling she has every morning when she turns her head and sees no one there, and every morning the surprise of it is overwhelming. *Where are you?* she asks, when she opens her eyes.

Justyna hasn't cried once since it happened. She'd never been a crier, not even as a kid. Her mom used to joke that the last time her daughter wept was at her own birth. Now, when Elwira hears the wail, she comes running outside and stops in her tracks. She watches Justyna, head in her lap, shaking, rocking herself back and forth. She takes off her black sweater and drapes it on Justyna's quaking shoulders, and without a word, she goes back into the house.

CHAPTER SIX

1995

ANNA
WROCŁAW, POLAND

The morning of Anna and Kowalski's romantic getaway to Wrocław, Anna finds herself at it again, standing in the kitchen, spying on Lolek through the lace curtains.

Every morning, Lolek stands outside his *klatka,* staring straight ahead, in the same teal blue sweat suit he has worn for days in a row. Every morning since Anna arrived in Poland two weeks ago, she has peeked through the curtains and watched him. Sometimes he'd still be outside when she left *Babcia*'s apartment. She'd sail past him with her heart thumping, fearing that if she actually looked at him, she'd see the image of his naked torso and his sagging man tits, pressing onto her own breasts.

Three years have passed since that night in the tent with Lolek, and Anna hasn't been back to Poland in all that time. For three years she found excuses not to come back. She had to save money now that she was in college, and thanks to her father's depression, Anna's mother needed her more than ever. She didn't want to believe that the real reason she wasn't going back to Poland was fear.

When Lolek joked that night at the Sielpia campgrounds that he was finally going to have his way with her, Anna rolled her eyes and fended him off with playful swats. 'You're wasted, buddy,' she pronounced. 'Out of my tent!' When he started kissing her, she let him for a few seconds, because why not; he was her oafish best friend. But when she tried to stop him, he grabbed her face with so much force that he drew blood. She didn't even remember what he felt like inside her. She recalled only that the whole thing hurt and that it was over quickly.

Afterward, Lolek kept murmuring, 'My Ania,' until he finally passed out and Anna wanted so badly to escape but felt paralyzed. In the morning, just as Anna was about to sneak out of the tent, Lolek rolled over and said, 'Oh fuck, I feel like shit. Will you see if anyone's got some aspirin?' Anna had looked past him, past his stained sweatpants, and crawled out. She spent the day in a daze, wondering if she should press charges or if the whole thing had been a figment of her imagination. The rest of the summer, Lolek acted a bit sheepish but definitely not like he'd commited a crime. And so Anna never told anyone; truthfully, she didn't know what to say.

Anna started senior year of high school with a heavy heart. One night at a party a boy named Malachy Sullivan approached her. He was a senior too and they shared a few AP classes. They talked about Gabriel García Márquez, and then Malachy kissed her. It was a gentle kiss. They fell in love but broke up after graduation, and in the fall Anna went off to study theater in Pittsburgh.

A month before freshman year at Carnegie Mellon was over, Anna received a letter from Kamila. *Where have you gone, Aniusia? I miss you terribly. I'm still pining for Emil, and now, it seems, for you too. Please come back.* The letter made Anna cry and she did as told. She came back. Two weeks ago, her plane landed in Warsaw and Anna had taken the train to Kielce. She spent the three-hour ride sitting with her carry-on bag in her lap, staring out the window past the rolling fields and the sleepy *wioski,* past the birch forests and hay bales, and she couldn't stop smiling.

In the hotel room in Wrocław, Anna and Kowalski are lying around listening to the radio, and before signing off the announcer says *'and, finally, forty monkeys escaped the Vienna Zoo this morning. Authorities say they are headed west.'* Anna turns the volume down and looks toward Kowalski, who is sprawled on the pullout, buck-naked.

'Maybe they're running toward us.' Kowalski laughs and holds out his hand. Anna slinks toward him. He pulls her on top of him and wordlessly slides down her panties.

'Again?'

He nods his head; the condom is somehow already on. Yesterday, when she had interrupted their first frenzied go at it by asking him if he had protection, he was incredulous. 'Against what?' he'd panted, confused. Anna had quickly reached for her pack of Eros-O-Lex, praying they were as good as Trojans, and then demonstrated how to put one on.

'But it's like swimming with a cap. It doesn't feel natural,' he had whined.

'Does AIDS?' Anna snapped back and he shut his mouth. Anna didn't even want to think what his inexperience with the condom meant. He used to be the shy one, the hesitant one, always standing off to the side. Now there was no end to his sexual appetite, and, amazingly, no end to his ejaculations. It didn't turn her on as much as she thought it might.

Kowalski vigorously pumps for a few minutes and then she feels his body tense up and shudder. When it's over he falls asleep immediately and Anna gently removes herself from his arms. She throws on a T-shirt and goes out onto the narrow balcony. The hotel's neon sign, attached to a nearby railing, is already lit, even though it's barely dusk, and Anna goes back inside and grabs her camera. She snaps a photo of the blinking letters, spelling out H-O-T-E-L, with the steeples of Wrocław looming in the distance. The sunset has left the heavens smudged with red, purple, and cobalt, like the work of a finger painting. It's beautiful.

Maybe when Kowalski wakes up, they'll go to the Chinese restaurant near the hotel. Anna wants to take a picture of Kowalski holding a pair of chopsticks.

Back in the room, Anna goes to the phone. She crouches by the wall while Kowalski snores peacefully, his small, firm ass on display.

'Kamila? It's me.'

'Hi! How's your rendezvous?'

'Well, Wrocław is pretty, but the entire city is under renovation, so there are bulldozers and cranes everywhere. We went to the zoo this morning.'

'And?'

'The monkeys were cute.'

Kamila sighs on the other end. 'No, dummy. *And?* How's Kowalski? Are you in love?'

Anna mulls the question over silently. Somehow, after all these years, Mariusz Kowalski had grown some balls and a few days ago, he walked her back to her *klatka,* grabbed her shoulders, and started kissing her, just like that. 'I didn't think I'd miss you so much. Thank God you came back. I could eat you up, right here, right now.' Anna had been pleasantly surprised. She had always thought Kowalski was cute. Anna needed to get away from Kielce for a bit, and she invited Kowalski to take a trip with her.

'Where?'

'Anywhere,' she replied.

'Okay. How about Wrocław? I hear there's a great zoo there.'

Anna had smiled and nodded. 'Wrocław it is.'

Now, she glances at his rump, his *dupa,* on the couch. 'In love? With Kowalski? We're having fun, Kamila, but the man can't string together a sentence. And he only packed one shirt. For three days.'

'I told you!' Kamila laughs. 'Well, at least you're getting laid. Emil still doesn't wanna do it. I think I'm just gonna have to get him drunk and rape him and call it a day.'

'Desperate measures,' Anna says quietly.

'I'm serious, Ania. I just don't know anymore.' Kamila sighs into the phone. 'I love him, he says he loves me, but he hardly even slips me the tongue when we kiss. You'd tell me if my breath was the problem, right?'

'Your breath is fine, Kamila. That's not the problem.' Anna wants to tell Kamila that her problem is that she's probably in love with a homosexual, but you can't say *homosexual* in Kielce, not in the circles they run with.

'Well, have your fun and hurry back. Besides, I'm rotting here without you. And, we should go visit Justyna. You gotta get over it.'

Anna doesn't say anything. Justyna's baby made the differences between her American life and her Polish life so much more palpable. She didn't want to think about it. Just then Kowalski lets one rip. It's a long, laborious fart, like a foghorn.

'What the hell was that?' Kamila asks.

'A sign from God,' whispers Anna and blows a kiss through the receiver. When she hangs up Kowalski rolls over, and much to Anna's chagrin, he's ready for action, still cloaked in a used jimmie. Anna wants out. Out of the room, out of Wrocław, and out of his reach.

'No, thanks. I need a shower.'

'All right. But I gotta take a dump something awful,' Kowalski announces and gets up off the couch.

Anna stares at the wall. 'I was thinking, you know. Since we've gone to the zoo and all, maybe we should get back on a train tonight. Plus, I'm running out of cash. We can make the eight o'clock if we hurry.'

'No Chink food?' Kowalski calls out from the bathroom.

'I lost my appetite,' Anna says quietly and starts packing.

On the eight-o'clock express, Anna leans her forehead against the cool window, and closes her eyes. Kowalski burps and the air goes putrid with the waft of stale sausage.

'That *kiełbasa* from lunch.' He grins and waves a hand in the air, fanning toward her face. 'Want some?'

The train ride to Wrocław had been different. They had cuddled, exchanged brief kisses, and shared a glazed raspberry *pączek*. Now, she glances at him with obvious contempt.

'Jesus. What's the problem, Anka?'

'You're the problem here, Kowalski. This isn't working out. I need more than a willing lay. I need conversation.'

Kowalski looks at her like she's insane. His face flushes crimson.

'See, that's what I mean, you don't say anything. I mean, I don't need you to recite poetry but something other than a running commentary about the workings of your digestive system would be nice.'

Kowalski gets up and violently grabs his knapsack from the overhead bin.

'So you're just gonna leave? You have nothing to add? Nothing? What's wrong with you? It's unnerving. You're like an animal; you communicate through fucking, grunts, and farts. I need *words*.'

Before he slides open the compartment doors, Kowalski turns around. 'You want words? I've got two for you. *Odpierdól się.* How's that? You drag me on this trip, it's your idea, you fuck me, we stroll around the ape cages like fucking Romeo and Juliet, and then you switch on a dime, so what words do you want? I never said I was good enough for you, Anka, but you don't have to keep reminding me of it. Lolek was right.'

It is the most he has ever uttered in one breath. Then he is gone.

Anna gets home past midnight. *Babcia* is fast asleep on the *wersalka* in her little room. *Babcia* hadn't been too happy that Anna had run off with Kowalski like that. Maybe Anna should have listened to her and just stayed put.

The next morning, the ringing phone wakes her at seven. Anna shuffles to the foyer, wishing, again, that *Babcia* would finally let her buy a cordless phone for the apartment.

'*Halo?*'

'So *Babcia*'s in a huff because you ran off with some boy to Wrocław? Did you have fun, *córko?*'

'I did. How's *Tato?*'

'Don't change the subject. I wanna talk about the fun.' Anna can see the small smile on her mother's face, she can hear the wistfulness of her plea.

'He's the subject of our lives, *Mamo.*'

'Your father's a mess, but what else is new. He refuses to take his Prozac, he cut up all my credit cards.'

Over the years, Radosław has sunk into real depression. When Poland held its first democratic elections in 1991, he couldn't get over the fact that he wasn't there to celebrate with his old friends. His anger overwhelmed him, and in turn, overwhelmed his wife and daughter. One morning, they found him in the bathroom with a steak knife pressed against his wrists, and talked him back into bed, where he cried into his pillow and didn't speak for days.

'I'm sorry. The fun, huh? Well, Wrocław is gorgeous and the boy was too. Kind of.'

'Oh, Anna, I'm so jealous. . . .' Anna laughs but she knows Paulina isn't kidding. The depth of regret Paulina lives with is something Anna never wants to experience. Before her departure to Poland, she took her mother out for drinks, and when Paulina, sloshed on martinis, began detailing her awful sex life, Anna shouted 'No!' laughing. She didn't want to hear it.

'What did you want to be when you grew up?' she asked instead and Paulina had looked sadly into the bottom of her glass, dipped her finger in and swished it around absentmindedly.

'I wanted to own a *cukiernia*. I wanted to make candy.' It was that disclosure, more than anything, that broke Anna's heart.

After she hangs up with her mother, Anna walks into the kitchen, where *Babcia* is making pierogi. When the first batch is ready, boiled to perfection and drenched in onions and butter, Anna eats more than is good for her, stuffing them whole into her mouth. *Babcia* eats like she always does, over the kitchen sink, straight out of the pot.

When Anna walks downstairs at five forty-five, she notices someone has spray-painted the word *kurwa* next to *Babcia*'s mailbox. *Kurwa* like bitch, *kurwa* like cunt, like whore, *kurwa* like all of the above. She wonders if Kowalski did it.

Anna sits down on the curb in front of *Babcia*'s apartment building. She brings her knees to her chest, and suddenly, she's fourteen again. She remembers one summer when a neighborhood kid walked past her and muttered, 'Go back home,

Amerykanko.' Anna's face had flushed, but she caught up with the kid and swung him by the arm. 'I *am* home, you little fucker,' she'd hissed and the boy looked at her like she was crazy but he never bothered her again.

This place is her private corner of the world. No one can ruin this patch of sun-baked grass, these cobblestones, that *trzepak* in front of her, unfaltering as ever. No one can ruin Poland for her. Just then a flock of blackbirds flies overhead, in perfect formation. 'They're on their way to a wedding,' *Babcia* always said and that's how Anna had always pictured them: gathered round a white canopy, dancing till dawn. The birds disappear past the rooftops, flying quickly, as if they're late.

KAMILA
KIELCE, POLAND

Motivated by the account of Anna's lusty escapade in Wrocław, Kamila decided that she was finally, finally going to do something about Emil.

Her father was at some art historian seminar in Lublin for the weekend – and her mother was visiting Kamila's *Ciocia* Frania in Sandomierz. The stars were truly aligning. Yesterday *Ciocia* Frania had taken a turn for the worse, and Zofia had rushed off, hoping to positively affect the contents of her aunt's last will and testament.

Kamila told Emil that she was having a small party, since her folks were out of town. 'I only invited Lidka Frenczyk and Irek, bring some wine if you want. We can make pizza.'

When she opened the door, in her red bustier and high heels, Emil nearly passed out. He was cradling a bottle of white wine in his arms, with a green satin ribbon tied around its neck. The bottle fell from his hands and shattered, soaking the welcome mat and his shiny black loafers. 'Is this a costume party?' he stuttered.

'I'll get a towel. And get in here. I don't want the neighbors to see me like this. They'll tell my mother I'm running a brothel in her absence,' Kamila muttered. She scurried into the bathroom to regroup, trying to make herself believe that things could only go up from here. She sat on the toilet, which felt like an icicle against her bare ass, and whispered a small prayer. 'Please, God, let me have sex tonight and let it be everything I always dreamed of.'

Last month, she and Lidka had taken the train to Kraków, and found the Coco Erotik Butik. Kamila and Lidka giggled like schoolgirls at the dildos and vibrators, but Kamila felt excited surrounded by all those rubber cocks. 'Maybe you should just get one of these,' Lidka had suggested. But Kamila shook her head and headed toward the back of the store, where she found exactly what she wanted – a red lace body stocking with two silken tassels attached to the bustier. It was flamboyant, expensive, and most important, it was crotchless. For weeks, the outfit lay hidden underneath her bed.

Kamila got off the toilet and stood in front of the mirror. She had abused her newly dyed hair into an impressive bouffant and shellacked it into place with a can of Elnett. She'd lined her eyes with kohl, smeared glitter on her lids, and painted her lips blood red. She looked like a fucked-up version of Cleopatra. Glancing down at her auburn bush, she wondered if she should have listened to Justyna and shaved it off. 'Guys like it when you look like a little girl down there, Kamila, trust me.'

Kamila takes a deep breath and stares at her reflection. 'All right, Kamila Marchewska. Look at you. Look at you! Men are visual creatures and I bet you Emil's out there right now at full mast.' But when she comes out of the bathroom, Emil is sitting on the floor, Turkish style, his shoes off, one black sock in his hands.

'And don't stop there.' She motions to his bare feet, her arm outstretched, her pointer finger rising up, toe to head. She stands above him like a warrior, but she's a bit wobbly in her three-inch heels.

'Are Lidka and Irek here yet?'

'Look at me, Emil! This is for *you*. And I don't care if you don't make love to me tonight. I don't care if you don't have sex with me. But you are going to *fuck me,* Emil. Once and for all.'

Emil's voice actually cracks when he speaks. 'And if I can't?'

'Then you will never see me again.' With that Kamila struts into her bedroom, throws herself on the folded-out *wersalka,* and splays her legs open. When Emil finally toddles into the room, there is nothing left to his imagination.

Kamila worked all year for this moment. She dieted like mad, finally lost those last fifteen pounds thanks to the tiny heart-shaped appetite-suppressing pills. The results were impressive – she had a twenty-six-inch waist and even her toes had slimmed down. My God, she had actual ankles, for the first time in her life! Of course, the steady intake of Dexatrim had caused some of her hair to fall out, and she experienced odd palpitations every now and again, but it had all been worth it. She felt like a model.

Emil perches on the edge of the *wersalka* and doesn't say a word. She wants him to tell her that she looks beautiful, that he too has been waiting years for this moment, but he sits motion-less and silent, so Kamila reaches for his fingers and guides Emil's hand to her clitoris but it sits there, motionless. Kamila joins her fingers with his and shows him how.

'You should kiss me, Emil. Don't you want to kiss me?' He leans down obediently and kisses her lips with his closed mouth. Kamila has to blink back tears, but Emil hasn't run off scream-ing, and she takes that as some kind of victory. She gets down on her knees in front of him, arches her back, and unzips his trousers. His penis is soft in her palm, like a wounded animal. 'Hello, stranger,' she whispers. Emil's apprehension is natural, she tells herself; they are about to cross the boundary between friends and lovers. She works hard for a long time, flicking, sucking, tracing elaborate circles on his shaft with her tongue, just like the videos taught her, until finally, she gets on top of him and instructs him to close his eyes and picture anything he wants, anything at all.

Emil's eyes squeeze shut and his face contorts with concentration. He manages a few deep prods before slipping out of her. He sits up, hangs his head in embarrassment, and asks her if she is okay.

In the bathroom, Kamila peels the lace stocking off her body and stands there, naked and clammy from head to toe. She wipes away the bit of blood, sits on the toilet, and quickly masturbates. She feels accomplished; it isn't every day that one loses her virginity to her soul mate.

Now, Kamila figures she just has to wait for him to get on his knees and ask her what she has been dying to hear all these years. She tells herself that as awkward as the sex was, she and Emil will get better at it with time, and that eventually they will marry.

Kamila wakes up the next morning, fully sober. She doesn't have to roll over to know that Emil is not in bed with her. She is suddenly aware that the night before was a catastrophe. She all but forced Emil to have sex with her. She behaved like an animal, and treated Emil likewise. She doesn't even know when he left the apartment. In fact, the last thing she remembers is sitting on the shitter, playing with herself.

The phone rings and Kamila leaps toward it, praying it is Emil calling to forgive her, but it is Anna, asking if they are still going to Justyna's.

'I guess so. But I need a few hours here. Can we do it in the evening?'

'Yeah, sure. You sound tired.'

Kamila hangs up, and the phone immediately rings again. Kamila lets it ring.

'Kamila! Get out of bed. *Ciocia* Frania died. Pick up the goddamn phone! Hello?? They're gonna go over the testament in the afternoon and then I'm back on the bus. I want you to go to the *masarnia* and get a pound and a half of beef and some vegetables, but only if they're fresh. Don't let *Pan* Tadek talk you into yesterday's produce, I don't care about any discount. Kamila?!' Zofia lets out an aggravated sigh. 'She died screaming in pain. You should have been here with me.' Her mother breathes heavily for a few seconds. 'And, *cholera jasna,* wash the sheets!'

Kamila stuffs the remains of the bloodied bedsheet into a plastic garbage bag, but not before tearing off a pinkish swath, tucking it in the back of her underwear drawer.

When Kamila arrives at the bus stop, Anna is already there, looking effortlessly beautiful. Anna doesn't need diet pills and she doesn't need to bully boys into bed. Tonight, for the first time ever, Kamila feels acutely jealous of her.

Anna jumps to her feet. 'Kamila! God, you look so different.' For a minute Kamila panics, perhaps the old superstition is right, that you can tell a woman's had sex just by looking at her.

'It's such a drastic change every time I see you. I miss the carrot top.' Anna reaches out to touch Kamila's black frizz.

'I don't. Orange isn't pretty and you know it.'

'It was pretty on you.'

'No, it's pretty on a *cat,* Anna, but not on a person. Can't you be honest for a change?'

'At least your red hair was natural. This looks fake. It's so black it looks blue. And it just doesn't suit you.' Anna smiles. 'How's that for honest?'

When they board the bus, Anna takes two prepaid tickets and slides them in a slot, punching out the holes, in case *kontrola* comes. Anna smiles when she returns to the seat, waving the little tickets.

'Someone graffitied *kurwa* on my *babcia*'s mailbox,' Anna blurts out. 'I assume it was Kowalski, or one of his cronies. Maybe it was that fat fuck.'

Kamila doesn't say anything. Obviously something happened between Lolek and Anna, but Kamila doesn't know when it happened or what it was, and she'll never ask.

'When was the last time you saw her?' Anna changes the subject.

'Justyna? A month ago, I think. *Pani* Teresa was still in the hospital then.'

The topic of Justyna's mother's impending death is too much; they simply avoid the subject.

'The baby's cute. Small. But I'm not surprised. You couldn't even tell she was pregnant. It just looked like someone snuck a beach ball under her sweater.'

'Lucky bitch. I bet I'll blow up like a balloon.'

'Me too.'

'You'll look beautiful.'

Kamila sighs. 'Why do you always do that?'

'Do what?'

'Tell me how pretty I am, when we both know it's just not true. I'm ugly, I was always ugly, but I didn't care. I only started to care when you started telling me otherwise *all the time*.'

'Kamila—'

145

'I had sex with Emil last night.'

Anna's mouth falls open.

'I wanted to come here and tell you how magnificent it was. I wanted to lie, but I can't. Let's stop lying to each other, Anna. Last night was the worst thing that ever happened to me. I got so jealous of you, griping about Kowalski, I thought, *What a spoiled brat – someone eager to love her, and she's boohooing about the lack of conversation?* So I got drunk, dressed up like a whore, and basically forced him. I told him I would never see him again so he better fuck me. I *made* him do it. And do you know the worst part?'

Anna shakes her head.

'He could only get an erection – and it was just a partial one, just enough to make it work – when I told him to close his eyes and think of something else. *Just pretend it's not me.*'

'Kamila . . .'

Anna doesn't say anything more, and Kamila is grateful. They get off the bus and walk in silence up the street toward Justyna's. When they get to Witosa Road, Kamila stops in her tracks and grabs Anna's arms.

'I'm sorry. I shouldn't have told you I thought you were a spoiled brat. You're not; you're my best, closest friend.'

'Don't be sorry. Life's too short to always be sorry. The first time always sucks, Kamila. Trust me, mine was no picnic either. One day I'll tell you all about it.'

Kamila nods, relieved.

'You took the initiative. That's ballsy, Kamila. That's the goddamn stuff of life.'

Anna's right. Anna's always right. There had been one moment last night, when Kamila had stopped bucking under Emil's weight, clenched the length of her body against his, and kissed him on the cheek. 'I love you,' she had whispered. They lay like that for a brief minute, before Emil whispered back, 'Me too.' Emil will forgive her, because he's Emil. She'll just wait it out, and if there's one thing she's good at, it's waiting.

They walk up to Justyna's house at a quarter past seven. The lights are all on and the windows are open. They can hear clearly the cries of an inconsolable baby.

JUSTYNA
KIELCE, POLAND

When Anna and Kamila ring the doorbell that night, Damian is deep in the throes of his nightly tantrum. Justyna opens the door to the sight of her best friends, one of whom she hasn't seen in three years, standing side by side like frightened Girl Scouts.

'*Dziewczyny,* meet Damian Paweł Strawicz, jerk extraordinaire. He's just taken a steaming dump. Follow the smell of *sraczka,* and make yourselves at home.' Kamila and Anna clumsily take off their shoes and smile blankly. Justyna chuckles at their unease. She is a mother now, and Kamila and Anna, God bless them, had better get used it.

They follow her into the living room as Justyna plops down on the floor and places Damian in front of her, stretching his legs out and making them bend in circles, like he is a tiny bicyclist. 'Wipes!' she shouts and Paweł appears in the doorway with a tub of Bambino wet wipes. He is dressed in a black wife beater that shows off his muscular arms, and his long hair is tied back in a ponytail. He throws the baby wipes at Justyna, who sets to work, popping the snaps, scooping the shit, and fastening a fresh diaper onto the baby like she's been doing it her whole life. Kamila and Anna look on, stunned.

'It packs a wallop, right?' She tosses the dirty diaper to Paweł, who catches it with one hand, brings it to his nose, and inhales, an exaggerated, delighted *aaaah*. This is their routine and Justyna loves it. They perform best in front of an audience. Behind closed doors, when they realize Damian needs changing, they spend a few moments bickering about whose turn it is. In front of people, they work in mutual, tacit accord.

'We need some beer. Here' – Justyna thrusts Damian toward Paweł – 'make yourself useful.' He holds Damian in equal measure of watchfulness and adoration. Justyna notices the way her friends stare at Paweł, and she smiles to herself as she walks toward the kitchen. Let them see; let them see just how happy she is.

She opens the fridge. From the living room she hears Paweł's voice, an octave too high, aware that she'd be eavesdropping.

'You don't know love till you watch your wife shit herself and you think it's kinda cute. And then the head popped out and *I* nearly shit myself.'

Justyna walks back from the kitchen, four beer bottles expertly balanced in one hand, and she passes them out quickly.

She hands Paweł his Żywiec and he grabs her waist, kisses her on the mouth, and then takes a swig, with the baby between them.

'Maybe I should tell them how when you saw his little dick, you started bawling like a girl.' Paweł turns red and lovingly kisses the top of Damian's head.

'See this? My man's turned into a complete pussy,' Justyna proclaims, grinning from ear to ear.

'I can't get over how quickly you changed his diaper. Did your mom teach you?' Anna speaks up, in awe.

Justyna rubs her eyes and takes Damian into her arms. He has calmed down, and his eyelids hang heavy.

'*Dobranoc, kotku,*' she whispers and covers his face in dozens of small kisses. When she's finished she lets Paweł take him.

'Good night, girls. Don't let *Mamuśka* stay up too late. We've got a four A.M. dinner reservation.' As soon as Paweł is out of sight, Justyna flops back onto the floor, digs in her front pocket, and fishes out a flattened pack of cigarettes.

'My mother hasn't gotten out of bed in months, Anna,' she says after her first drawn-out drag. 'We have to change *her* diapers now.'

'I'm sorry,' Kamila murmurs as she holds the Żywiec between her bony thighs.

'I bring Damian upstairs every day and when I lay him down next to her she thinks he's Elwira.' Justyna frowns; she had forbidden herself to talk about her mother tonight. Who the fuck wants to go into the heinous specifics of cancer in its fourth stage? This is supposed to be a happy reunion.

They make small talk for a bit, and Justyna brings out the wedding album to show Anna.

'You looked like a princess or something,' Anna says, closing the album, smoothing her palms over its cover.

'I know. Some fairy tale, right? Baran, you look good. Your hair looks *ekstra* long. Every time I try to grow out mine, I end up cutting it,' Justyna says, touching her closely cropped hair, still worn in a pixie like Mia Farrow. 'But I'm not even gonna comment on yours, Kamila. What'd you dye it with, tar?'

Kamila pats her head self-consciously. 'It's so nice to see that motherhood's softened you.' The girls erupt into laughter.

'Let's get out of here.' Justyna stands up. Upstairs, she can hear Elwira, who is on Mom duty tonight. Neither sister takes particular pleasure in spoon-feeding their mother, changing her underwear, or injecting her with morphine, but they make do.

By the time the doctors had done all the ultrasounds and biopsies, the cancer, which had originated in her mother's left breast, had metastasized to Teresa's spine and lymph nodes. It was in her pelvic tissue and liver, and heading north to her lungs. Women didn't die from breast cancer like they used to, except the ones who ignored lumps and bumps and blisters. About a month ago, the hospital had discharged her because there was nothing they could do and there were other patients in line for her bed — other patients who were sick but whose recovery was still a possibility. They couldn't afford a hospice aide, so Teresa was sequestered to the guest room on the third floor, where she'd been about to take her last breath for weeks now.

Every time Justyna walked in to see Teresa, the smell made her gag. When people talked about death they talked about the sadness of it, the waste, but they never talked about the things that made you want to shut the door on the dying. Justyna would sit on the edge of the bed, talking nonsense while she clipped her mother's toenails. Teresa was unresponsive, teetering between sleep and God knows what.

'Should I see your mom before we go?' Anna sheepishly asks.

'She weighs forty-eight kilos, Anka. Have you ever seen bedsores?'

Anna shakes her head slowly.

'Well, if you're remotely curious, now's your chance. Otherwise . . .' Talking about a person's death was easy; coming face-to-face with it was a whole other gambit.

'Fine, let's just go,' Anna answers.

Ten minutes later, Justyna stands in front of Marex Bar and whistles three times. Moments after, Jacek Szuler comes downstairs. 'Fucking fifteen minutes and you're out. I gotta get up at five and go to the bazaar for my old man.'

'Sure, sure . . . and turn the music on.' Justyna smiles and waltzes past him, Kamila and Anna follow. On Sunday night most pubs in Kielce are closed. The people who want to get drunk on God's day of the week are the kind that brown-bag their liquor. But Justyna has connections.

Jacek rests his head on the bar; after a half hour of shuffling shots over to their table, he's given up. 'I used to date him.' Justyna leans in conspiratorially. 'Massive *siur,* I mean it fucking *hurt,* which further proved my theory that's he's half black.'

Kamila and Anna laugh in disbelief.

'I'm not kidding. Jacek used to do this clicking thing with his tongue, it was like Tourette's or something, but it might have been Swahili.'

'You're fucking crazy, Justyna,' Kamila shouts. 'Forever Young' starts playing and the girls all chime in. *'Let's dance in style, let's dance for a while, heaven can wait, we're only watching the skies . . .'*

'Remember how we used to force you to translate all those lyrics? You hated it!' Kamila recalls.

'She didn't hate it, she loved it. You loved it, right?'

Anna smiles and shrugs her shoulders.

'Hey! Do you remember when Lolek stole that Russian motorcycle? How old were we?'

'Fifteen,' Anna answers, looking into her empty glass.

'Fifteen. My God. He drove us all over town on that fucking thing. Remember, you burned your calf on the exhaust pipe, Kamila, and we put honey on it? And we sat on the bench in front of your *klatka* and all of a sudden these bees appeared and this one' – Justyna points to Anna – 'had like a full-blown panic attack. God, we were stupid.' Images fly at Justyna, swarming her head. She sees it all like it was yesterday, her whole wasted youth.

Jacek finally shuts off the stereo.

'You're a loser, Jacek!' Justyna shouts but gets up to leave. She watches Anna place a hundred-*złoty* bill on the table. When they step outside the night air engulfs them, the breeze balmy and summery, the sky lit up with stars. The aroma of freshly baked rye bread wafts from down the street where the *piekarnia* is preparing tomorrow morning's loaves.

'Let's go see if we can mooch a *bochenek*. A warm slice with gobs of butter melting on it! I bet you have some vodka at your house. We could have a picnic, under the moon.' Kamila giggles.

'Justyna has to get back to the baby,' Anna reminds them.

'No, she doesn't, Anna,' Justyna retorts hotly. 'The baby has a father and the father knows how to heat a bottle.'

'But it's already after ten and I just got back from Wrocław. I don't wanna piss my *babcia* off any more than she already is.'

'Then *you* go home. What were you doing in Wrocław, anyway?' Justyna asks.

'She was on a sexcapade with Mariusz Kowalski.' Kamila grins.

'Kowalski! Holy crap. You fucked Kowalski? He's like a fucking midget, but his . . .' Justyna glances at Anna. 'I heard his cock is colossal. His girlfriend used to brag about it all the time. She's married to a mafia guy now, from Czarnów.'

That summer was long ago but it's a thorn in Justyna's side. She's not afraid of looking like a chump, or even a backstabber, but she is afraid of looking like a coward. Because the only excuse she has for not intervening then was that she had always been inexplicably terrified of Lolek Siwa.

'I should go home, you guys. This doesn't feel right,' Anna says, kicking some pebbles out of the way.

'It doesn't feel right? What doesn't feel right?'

Anna squats down, hides her face in her hands.

'Your mother. Your mother is dying and you want to get wasted and talk about cocks? Don't you want to spend every last minute with her?'

'No! No, I don't! She's already gone! And I'll drink and cuss and discuss dicks if the opportunity arises because I'm nineteen fucking years old and sometimes I need a break. What do you need a break from, Anka? Homework?'

'You're in denial.'

Justyna paces around Anna and Kamila, arms swinging at her sides. 'You know what the most irritating thing about you always was, Anna?'

'Please, you guys—'

'You know what it was? The fact that you pitied us, but flaunted everything in our faces. The fact that deep in your little heart you thought we all wanted to trade lives with you.'

'That's not true. What did I ever flaunt?'

'Your clothes, your dollar bills, your fucking aspirations.'

'You raided my closet every summer, Justyna Strawicz!'

'Whatever. What gives you the right to get all weepy on my behalf? I haven't heard from you in years, Baran, and you show up on my doorstep with advice? Grow up! People are born, people get sick, and people *die*.'

For a moment, no one says a word.

'I fucked Emil last night.'

'I'm sorry, Justyna, I'm not perfect,' Anna whispers.

'That's the point, Anna. Whoever said you were? Marchewska – you what? You "fttt" what?'

'I *fucked* Emil. I FUCKED Emil!' Kamila holds out her hands toward Justyna and Anna. 'Now, come on, *pipki.*'

When Justyna sneaks back into the house to grab a liter of Siwusia, it's dark and quiet. She grabs the liquor and a blanket from the armchair.

They walk up toward the open field past Witosa Road, where they used to sit around bonfires, feasting on sizzling *kiełbasa.* The stars hang low, and the bottle of vodka gets passed around generously.

'My head is spinning. The stars look like disco balls, I swear to God,' Kamila murmurs, closing and opening her eyes. 'I wish we had Anna's old boom box. When's the last time you made a mix tape?'

'God, I still have all of them at home.'

'I wanna hear all the juicy morsels about last night, Marchewska. I can't believe it, you little slut. Does your *cipa* hurt? Did you shave like I told you to?' Justyna slurs.

'Yes, it hurts, but only from shock. He only managed a few, you know, thrusts. And no, I didn't shave. It was so bad.'

'You should have shaved! Did he cum?'

'No.'

'Great. At least you won't spend the next month panicking about your period.'

Kamila laughs. 'I guess there's a bright side to everything.'

'The first time always blows. I was thirteen, with my cousin Arek, in the bathroom at Relaks. I told you guys it happened when I was sixteen and I fucking lied.' Justyna laughs. 'It was so gross, ugh, I can still smell the wet toilet paper on the floor. We did it standing up and halfway, some old guy came in to take a piss. But then every time after, and with each new guy, it got better and better. You'll see.'

'Yeah, Anna said the same thing.'

'What, you fucked my cousin too?' Justyna laughs. She laughs because here's her chance, here's her chance to come clean, to say *I know, I know what happened.* But she just laughs and the sound of it echoes through the hills like bells.

'No! My first time was with this Spanish guy in high school. It didn't hurt that bad, but it didn't change my life, that's for sure. He had terrible acne.' Justyna stares at Anna, impressed by how smoothly the lie comes.

'I wish we could sleep out here. Hey, you guys' – Kamila raises her head and leans back on her elbows – 'we're like the three musketeers, together again.'

'Like the Summer Triangle,' Anna replies, pointing to the sky.

'The what?'

'It's a constellation made up of the brightest three stars in the universe, but it's only visible in July and August.'

'You're a fucking riot, Baran.' Justyna cackles. 'I bet you just made that shit up. *Marzycielka.*' Anna looks down, and for a second Justyna feels bad. She likes the fact that Anna has always been a dreamer, but being a dreamer was a luxury in life, and tonight the last thing Justyna wanted to do was discuss the fucking stars.

'All right, girls. One swig left. Let's make a toast. To the goddamn Summer Triangle, and to next summer.'

Justyna takes the vodka bottle last. Before she brings it to her mouth, she looks up for a moment, searching for something bright to call her own.

The girls make plans for lunch on Thursday in town. Justyna

watches her friends link arms and make their way toward the taxi stand farther down the road.

When she walks in the house, the kitchen light is on. Paweł and Elwira sit at the table, staring down into coffee cups. A bottle of formula stands on the counter. When they both look up at her, Justyna knows.

CHAPTER SEVEN

2002

ANNA
NEW YORK, NEW YORK

Anna blows on her frozen hands; it's cold and getting colder. Her fingers comb through the branches of the Christmas trees, feeling for the right one. And then she sees it. Taller than the rest, perfectly proportioned, deeply green, and regal. The bright yellow tape stuck to one of its impressive branches reads $140. She motions to the pot-bellied proprietor, and he ambles over.

'That's a beaut. I'll give it to you for $135.'

'$120?'

'No way. This is one of the best trees on the lot.'

'So why hasn't it sold? Tomorrow's Christmas, sir, and it's still standing here. . . .' Anna smiles coquettishly. Just then her father appears, dragging behind him a scrawny, sickly looking specimen. It's a Charlie Brown tree.

'Whatchu doin'? Let's go. I got it.'

'Dad, that's, like, a bush. I think we should get this one. It's beautiful. That one won't even hold half of Mom's ornaments.'

'A hundred forty dollar? Whatchu, crazy fucka? Ees the high robbery. I go to forest and get one the more beautiful for zero dollar.' The lumberjack shakes his head and walks off.

'You've been saying that every Christmas since I was eight. We're gonna drive upstate and chop down our own tree? Really? Just let me get this one! It's my money.'

'I your father and I say that's eet. *Nie pieprz głupot.*' Radosław hoists his tree onto one shoulder and starts walking. By the time she catches up to him on Columbus Avenue, he's close to the apartment building, smoking a More Red, and he looks pissed.

He speaks quickly and in Polish. 'Never embarrass me like that again. You moved back under my roof, and if you don't like my rules, get back on the fucking L train.' Anna wordlessly holds the lobby door open for him.

Two weeks ago, when she arrived at her parents' apartment in Manhattan with her duffel and announced that she and Ben were over, her mother raised her eyebrows but petted her shoulder reassuringly. 'He didn't have money anyway,' she said. Her father hadn't acted surprised, and had told her that living in sin had its consequences; a kick to the curb, he said, was what she deserved.

When they open the door, Paulina is on the living room floor, arranging delicate glass-blown ornaments, the Polish-made *bombki* she's collected over the years. She's amassed Santa Clauses from every continent, tiny glass mushrooms, glass birds with feathery plumes, wooden doves, and miniature cottages. Paulina takes pride in these baubles, and she gets excited when she can finally put them on display. Neighbors from the apartment building come by every year and proclaim that the Barans' tree is straight out of a *Gracious Home* catalogue, while Paulina, the super's wife, poses next to her creation and flushes with pride.

'I tried.' Anna unwraps her scarf and slowly takes off her coat.

'What do you mean?' Paulina asks, panic already rising in her voice.

Radosław heaves the tree into the living room and goes about securing it in the stand. When it is upright he rips the binding off with his bare hands and gives the trunk a good shake. Paulina and Anna assess its many shortcomings. The spruce is pallid green, it is short, ungainly, unruly, and altogether tragic.

'Is this a joke?' Paulina asks Anna. 'Did you leave the real one in the hallway?'

Radosław picks up a glittery glass bulb the size of a grapefruit, bright red and painted with pearly white doves, and he throws it to the floor. It instantly shatters into tiny pieces. Before Paulina has time to react he grabs another ornament, a Danish Santa Claus in a white robe.

'Should I keep going? Maybe if I keep going there'll be just enough left for the fucking tree. Pagans!'

Paulina starts crying and runs to get a broom.

'You're such a miser, Dad.'

Radosław shrugs and walks into the bedroom.

Later that afternoon, after the tree has been decorated to the best of their abilities, Anna and her mother sit on the couch, drinking tea and staring at the TV. The Polish satellite channel is playing an episode of Paulina's favorite soap, *Złotopolscy*. Anna couldn't care less about the dismally acted comings and goings of some fictional Polish upper-middle-class family, but her mother is enthralled, commenting on the action as it unfurls. Anna waits for a commercial to speak.

'*Mamusia,* what's going on?'

'Well, Katarzyna just found out she's pregnant but she's in love with Father Piotr, who's actually having an affair with *Pani* Hania from the bakery. I wonder if she's going to keep the ba—'

'With you, Mom. What's going on with you and Dad?' Living with them again, Anna has noticed the growing strain between them, evident in the fact that her father has taken over Anna's old bedroom, and is sleeping there nightly.

Paulina stares into her teacup for a moment before answering.

'Have you ever had your fortune read?'

Anna shakes her head.

'I did, when I was twenty, tea leaves in the bottom of the saucer. My *Ciocia* Alusia was the real deal. She warned us that my dad was going to die young, due to emphysema. Anyway, you know what it said? My fortune? "Things will break apart and it will always be your job to put them back together." '

Anna glances at her mother's hands. Paulina's fingers wrap around the porcelain Bayreuth cup. They are weathered beyond forty-eight.

'What if the broken thing is you, *Mamo*? Isn't it your job then, to put *yourself* back together? You need to divorce him.'

'He'd kill me.'

'And then he'd get over it.'

'No, *córko,* he'd hunt me down in the middle of the night and stick a knife in me. He's told me so.'

'He's full of shit. And you're afraid of dying? You're already dying!'

'Oh, cut it out, Anna! Life's not that simple.'

'It is! It is that simple. I packed a bag, I wrote a note, and I shut the door behind me. Stop being a *tchórz,* Mother – you are wasting your life.'

'A coward?' Paulina's face contorts and her eyes blink rapidly, fending off tears. 'What happened after you left that note for Ben? You ran here so you wouldn't have to look him in the face. You sneak off to get clothes when you know he's at work. So who's the coward?'

Anna doesn't answer because there is no answer. She *has* been evading Ben; it's been hard work to avoid phone calls, to hide out in her parents' living room. It's hard work but it comes naturally to Anna.

At six o'clock, Radosław emerges from his cave, wearing jeans and a wrinkled white shirt. The table is ready. An extra place is set for a wandering vagabond – it's a Polish tradition. If anyone knocked on the door tonight, they would be taken in, just like Joseph and Mary who begged for shelter on Christmas Eve and found it in a manger.

Before Anna and her parents eat, the *opłatek* is shared. Anna breaks off a piece of the square wafer, imprinted with a nativity scene, that she bought for two bucks at a Polish deli, and wishes her mother peace and money, as she's done for years now. Her father chews noisily, then engulfs Anna in a hug.

'I just want you to be happy, *Tato*.' Anna's voice quivers.

'Oh yeh, yeh, yeh,' he answers, goofy and glib, and shrugs his shoulders. 'Sorry for me. You should have the career and the guy who love you, eef you wanna, my dough-ter.' Her father was capable of poetry once. Anna has read the letters he wrote to Paulina from prison. *I dream of your naked body, of your hips, which slope shyly toward me, like two pearly seashells.* There must have been a love story, once.

Sharing the *opłatek* was always Anna's favorite part of Christmas Eve. The words and intentions were fleeting, but it didn't matter; Poles worldwide were soldiering on, and for five minutes the atmosphere was full of repentance and hope. Out of the corner of her eye, Anna watches her parents silently exchange a truce, her father's arm slung casually around Paulina's neck, her mouth pursed in a straight line. Then they eat, and after the dishes have been put away, they exchange gifts and small, gratified smiles. It's a nice hour and then it's over.

At around three A.M. there is a huge, shattering crash. Anna's eyes adjust to the dark and there it is, the cause of the ear-splitting ruckus. The tree has fallen, weighed down with too many ornaments. Her parents run in from their separate rooms and one of them flicks on the light. The tree lies across the coffee table inches from where Anna is sleeping on the sofa; glass debris is everywhere, like rainbow-colored shrapnel. Paulina starts sobbing and swatting at Radosław's face. He expertly grabs her wrists and shoves her away from him.

'That's what you get, *szmato.* Be glad God struck down the fucking tree and not you. But so help me, if you touch me again, I'll do it for him. Get a broom, Anka,' he orders, scratching his belly. Anna huddles on the couch, careful not to move, sure she is covered in tiny glass fragments invisible to the naked eye. She turns her face toward her father. '*You* get a broom. Or better yet, get back on your meds.'

'What meds?'

'Um, it's called Prozac and it's what makes you human.'

'Mind your business, and clean up this mess, *idiotko.*'

'You think I'm gonna run to my room and cry because you called me a name, Dad, like I did when I was twelve? I'm not scared of you anymore, *Tato.* In a few years, you'll have nothing left but visions of your bygone glory, dancing like sugarplums in your warped head. And you'll still be hosing down the sidewalk for the Americans.' Anna's voice cracks before she continues. 'You were my hero, my *bohater,* and I worshipped at your altar. I really fucking did.'

Her father's fists are clenched at his sides. His hands are purple. *Go ahead,* Anna begs silently, *give me something to cry about.* But he walks back into his room and slams the door behind him.

Moments later, it's as if nothing's happened at all. Paulina is quietly doing her best to sweep away the debris. The tree is already by the door and Anna can't recall how it got there. Anna grabs her coat and walks out of the back of the apartment, to the alley where her father sorts the recycling. After Anna graduated from college, her parents left Brooklyn and moved to the Upper West Side, when her dad lucked out and got a job as a superintendent in a fancy high-rise. 'We're like the Polish Jeffersons!' Anna had joked, but her parents didn't get it. She lights a cigarette now and as she smokes, she remembers the time Radosław told Paulina he was taking Anna to Costco, and instead they rented a car and drove to Atlantic City, where they played nickel slots. On the ride back home, her father shared stories about his wayward youth. They had been happy. She flicks the cigarette into the dark and walks back inside.

'There's glass in the cushions, but I can't vacuum now. Or should I?' Paulina is sitting on the couch, dustpan in her lap.

'You should go to sleep, *Mamo*. It will be okay.'

Anna sits down next to her mother and thinks about reaching for her hand.

'*Mamo*, I have a one-way ticket in my purse. I'm going to Polska today, booked business on the eleven P.M. flight. Come with me.' Paulina looks down.

'I can't, *córko*. I just can't.'

Anna nods her head. 'Tell me, then. Tell me what made you love him. Tell me something that will make me understand why you're still here.'

Paulina's eyes close. 'He used to mold me little figurines out of bread and water, when he was in jail. Little stars and a bear. I still have them. He was unbelievably handsome and everyone called him Ponderosa because he wanted to be a cowboy.' Her mother is crying softly and now Anna takes her hand and holds it.

When Anna wakes up, it is light outside and she is parched. She walks to the kitchen and is startled to find her father sitting at the table, playing with a match. He lets the flame burn down to his fingertips, till there is only a hiss, a small puff of white smoke. When Anna was little, her father brought *kasztany* back from his trips to Europe – shiny, smooth chestnuts, oversized and beautiful – and he'd make little animals from them, using matches for legs, horns, and hooves. Anna lined them up on her windowsill, and stared at them in the mornings, imagining their lives, till they began to rot and her mother threw them out.

Radosław takes another match and lights a cigarette. He tilts his head back and exhales a plume of blue smoke toward the ceiling. 'I never wanted this.'

'Yeah,' Anna replies, not wanting to cry.

Suddenly, Anna remembers taking Radosław to see *Braveheart* the year it came out. Her father was riveted, laughing happily when the barnyard Scots mooned the ruthless Brits, and wept like a child when Mel Gibson died in the end, and then every day afterward Radosław walked through the house bellowing out, 'Freeeeeeedom!' It was in his blood, and yet now, he sits hunched over like a child.

Her father looks down at his knuckles. 'I never wanted your mother, or marriage, or you. I wanted to be a fighter, like my father, like his father before him. I *was* a fighter. But she made me stop. I called the wedding off three times. But she wouldn't let me go.'

'I don't believe that. You're either lying or you don't remember. No one can "make you" when it comes to that.'

Her father slams the tabletop. 'Goddamnit, I'm telling you – *she made me.*' His eyes brim with redness, and he squeezes them shut.

'Just leave me alone. *Zostaw mnie.*' His voice is shockingly pleading and so Anna complies.

★

168

At eight o'clock, Anna finishes packing, puts on her coat, and sets her duffel bag by the door. Paulina watches her every move.

'Tell *Babcia* I miss her. Tell her I'm going to come visit this summer, this time for real. And give her some money, Anna, please.'

'I don't get how you've never been back to Poland, in all these years, *Mamo*. Money's not an issue. Just come with me,' Anna pleads one last time. But her mother shakes her head.

'I'm afraid if I go back, Ania, that I'll never want to leave.'

Anna smiles. This, she understands. She walks over and hands her mother a wad of cash. 'This is for you, Mommy. Get a nice haircut. Not at Supercuts, okay?' Paulina takes the money and stares at it.

Before leaving, Anna cracks open the door to her father's room. Radosław lies on the bed, propped up on his elbows, tapping ashes into a saucer which rests next to his Polish newspaper, its inky pages spread like a blanket before him.

'I'm going, Ponderosa.'

Her father's face registers surprise at his old nickname and he raises his eyebrows. 'Where you going?'

'Home.'

Outside, it's dark and quiet. Anna hails a cab and quickly gets in.

'JFK, please.'

There is barely any traffic as they head east toward the Queensboro Bridge. In her pocket, her cell phone vibrates. In a few hours, she will be unreachable and she can't wait. But she hasn't spoken to Ben since running off, and she figures that everybody deserves a goodbye.

'Anna?' Ben's voice is familiar and foreign at once. She remembers the first time they made love and how hungry she was for it, and how, when he passed out exhausted next to her afterward, Anna stared up at the ceiling, somehow still wanting more.

'Merry Christmas, Ben. *Wesoych Świąt*.'

'Anna. Oh, fucking Christ. You picked up! You finally picked up, and I'm leaving. I'm in a cab and I'm flying to Omaha. Oh, Anna.'

'I'm leaving too. On my way to JFK. You?'

'LaGuardia.'

Under the bridge, the East River shines black, tiny frozen lakes shimmering on its glossy surface. Ben is silent and for a minute Anna thinks that the call was dropped.

'Anna.' Ben sighs. He's groping for an answer, or holding on for dear life, but isn't that the same thing, really? 'Are you going to Poland?'

'Yes.'

'Anna. Why? We have to deal with this, with us. You wrote a fucking note. After years with me, you left a note. I'm surprised you didn't leave a twenty by the bedside while you were at it.'

'I have to go home.'

'It's not your home, Anna. Your home is right here.'

'Well, what if I told you I'm going to see a boy? Would that make you feel better?'

Ben doesn't answer; he just hangs up.

Anna closes her eyes and presses her fingertips over her eyelids. When she was a little girl, back in Poland, she would shut her eyes at nap time, and do the same thing, till the blinding billows of white she'd see would turn to colors, like a kaleidoscope. 'You'll damage your corneas,' *Babcia* used to say.

The inside of JFK is quiet. Footsteps echo, shadows fall; it's like a movie set. Anna walks up to the business-class counter at

LOT, and the Polish airline attendant hands Anna her ticket and doesn't say anything.

An hour later, sweating and ready to drop, she boards a plane that is already occupied with passengers traveling from Chicago. The cabin interior smells Polish, like *krakowska* ham, cheap floral eau de toilette, and sweat. She finds her place in the third row, and plonks into it gratefully. It's at times like these she thanks God that the world all but overlooks the existence of her country. You mention Poland to an American and they think three things: *kiełbasa,* the Pope, and Auschwitz, probably in that order. No one really gives a shit about her homeland. So why would anyone bother messing with a planeload of Polacks? Anna convinces herself that no Al Qaeda crazy would give a fuck about hijacking LOT Flight 76, direct to Warsaw, and she takes a deep breath, clutching her father's medallion around her neck.

When the captain announces that they are ready for takeoff, and the engines rumble toward their full throttle, Anna grips her hands together. Her thighs jiggle. Her neck goes rigid. The man sitting next to her cracks a wide smile.

'Scared?' he asks in Polish.

Anna nods her head.

'Don't be, *laleczko.* If it happens, you won't even know.' The man is smug, openly judging her head to toe.

'Thanks,' she replies in English. *Thanks,* in a perfect American accent, because sometimes that puts these types of assholes in their place.

Miraculously, Anna falls asleep. She dreams in fits and starts, dreams of the roily *zalew* waters. When the plane touches the ground Anna's eyes fly open, and she lifts the window shade and is greeted by the blinding white glare of snow.

'Where are we?' she asks, bewildered.

'Tahiti,' the man next to her answers. 'Where do you think we are, lady? Polska.'

Anna turns back to the window. The sky is white and gray, just like the ground. Where is the sun, the green fields in the distance? Anna is confused and then she realizes that this is Poland in winter, something she hasn't seen in eighteen years, something she has no recollection of at all. Around her, passengers start to stir and gather their things. And yet, she is aware of only one thing: that old feeling, that old rapture, bursting in her heart.

'Polska,' she repeats to herself. 'Polska.'

'Really, Natalia, my eyes. I can't take it . . .' Kamila tries to wave away the cigarette smoke that is visibly settling in gray layers in the stinky green Peugeot.

'What? The fucking window's open!' Natalia laughs and takes another puff, turning her mouth to exhale the smoke toward the tiny crack in the driver's side window.

'I'm trying to quit, but gimme a break. Besides, beggars can't be choosers, Kamila. It's either this or the 10:25 *osobowy* from Warszawa to Kielce.' Kamila rolls her eyes and then closes them. She wasn't able to sleep on the plane, terrified not of the turbulence, but at the thought of landing in one piece and having to face Emil. She was actually doing this.

Her parents had begged her to give them Christmas, their first one together in almost six years, and Kamila agreed. Two days ago, she accompanied her father to midnight mass. They walked silently in the snow and as they got closer to the Polish church, more and more people fell into step with them. The mass was long and solemn, but the carols were as beautiful as Kamila recalled them from her childhood. Her father stood beside her, mouthing all the prayers, shaking hands with acquaintances, kissing their cheeks. On their way back, Kamila glanced at Włodek, who seemed more alive and content than she had seen him her entire visit.

'You miss it, don't you? You miss home.'

But her father just patted his heart and smiled. 'I don't miss home, Kamila. Because it's always right here.'

Kamila didn't know if she bought that, but she linked her arm through his and put her head on his shoulder.

'What I miss is *you, córciu*. But I'm glad you're going back. It takes courage to go back to anything.'

Natalia flicks her cigarette out the window and rolls it up. 'I think you should get a dog.'

Kamila opens her eyes and squints at Natalia through the smoky haze.

'You know, when the smoke clears. Hahaha.'

'A dog?'

'A puppy. A little yellow puppy.'

'A puppy?'

'Yeah. A fucking puppy. When my dad died last year my mother was this close to slitting her wrists. So Stas and I got her this little dog, a *miniaturka* poodle, you know, the ones that don't grow? I swear to God, that thing saved her life.'

'My husband didn't die, so I'm sorry to say I won't be replacing him with a dog.'

'*Dziewczyno!* It's called *dogoterapia* and it works in fending off major bouts of depression. Like the ones that might follow the breakup of someone's marriage due to her husband's closeted homosexuality.'

'I'm fine.'

'You're a skeleton. I thought America fattened people up. All right, forget the puppy for now. What's your plan of attack?'

'I thought I would stay with you and your mom for a few nights, to get my bearings.'

'Wrong. I'm dropping you off at the doorstep of your fucking apartment and you are gonna walk in and order that *głupek* to pack up and hit the road.'

Kamila sighs. How can she explain that it's not Emil's sexual preference that has destroyed her, but the years of shrouding, when really, he could have just told her a long time ago.

'Natalka, you're a dear friend for chauffeuring me today but I can't deal with it now, I just can't. And if you won't let me stay with you I'll check into a hotel.'

Natalia suddenly swerves toward the roadside and pulls over. She turns to Kamila. 'Marchewska, you did not fly across half the world to go cower in a hotel room. You'll just lose momentum. And I'm sure you have dozens of speeches prepared, so when you see him just pick one and let him have it.'

'I don't have any speeches prepared.' But Natalia is right. She does have speeches prepared, diatribes and monologues that have been brewing for months. There's a speechless option too, the one where she walks into the house unannounced, doesn't even look at Emil, but just matter-of-factly starts chucking all his belongings off the balcony.

'Your life is passing you by, minute by minute. I wouldn't be a friend if I let you hide,' Natalia insists. 'And I'm not driving until you agree.'

'Then I'll walk to Kielce. I'm tired and jet-lagged and I don't want to see him now. I need to sleep some of this shit off.'

'You're going to confront him today. End of story.'

'The story ended months ago, Natalia. There's no story left.'

This time Natalia doesn't say anything. She steers back toward Route 7. Kamila stares out the window, past the snow-capped roofs of the huts that line the roadway, each one stooped under the weight of snow. The homes break her heart and she realizes how much she's missed Poland.

★

When Kamila opens her eyes, the car is parked and Natalia is gone. She glances at her wristwatch, set to Polish time because she never bothered to change it. It feels later than half past one. Natalia appears, juggling two coffees and a paper bag. She mimes for Kamila to lean over and open the door for her.

'We're just forty kilometers out but I needed a jolt. Doesn't help having Sleeping Beauty in the passenger seat. Here.' Natalia divvies up the goodies, a scorching coffee, fries, and a box of chicken nuggets.

'I fucking love McDonald's,' Natalia says, stuffing a handful of *frytki* into her mouth as she turns the engine on again. 'Homo, here we come!' she bellows.

'Stop it,' Kamila admonishes and turns up the radio, in time to hear the familiar strains of 'Jolka Jolka.' Immediately Natalia starts singing along.

'*Z autobusem Arabów zdradziła go, nigdy nie był już sobą o nieeee!* Can you believe it, cheated on the poor bastard with a busload of Arabs? They don't write songs like this anymore, eh, Kamila. . . .'

The song gets to Kamila, haunts her, and she doesn't care if Natalia catches her out of the corner of her eye, crying.

It's good that Kamila's having this moment now, instead of an hour from now, when she will be standing face-to-face with Emil. She can't help wondering what Anna Baran would say. She'd hug Kamila and tell her it was all going to be okay, that Kamila was strong and deserved better, the very things she told Kamila time and time again, every summer since they were fourteen. Did Anna remember the anguish and the elation of those summers, the way they held hands on their way down Toporowskiego to meet Justyna by St. Józef's Church? Did she remember the hours they spent on the steps, ogling boys, cracking up over nothing and everything?

'Good, have your cry now, Kamila,' Natalia says softly, eyes on the road.

When they drive up to her apartment building, Kamila can feel her heart thumping throughout her whole body. Even her toes are pulsating. Suddenly Kamila knows that Natalia's right; it's now or never.

'Take my credit card and book me a room at the Hotel Pod Róża. A suite, with a balcony, if they have it.'

'For him?' Natalia's eyes grow incredulous.

'No, Natalka, for me. I'm going to have my say, and then I'm checking into the hotel. I can't stay here, and I don't want to. I'll sell this apartment and in the meantime you and Stasiu can move in. Give your mom and that dog a break.' Kamila smiles.

'*Na serio?*'

'It's the most lucid thought I've had in days. Take it or leave it.'

'I take it! I take it!' Natalia throws her arms around Kamila's neck.

'I'll be back for you in an hour?'

'Half hour.'

'And if he's not there?'

'He's there. Look.' And she points with her chin toward her apartment, where the kitchen light is on.

'Kamila. *Trzymaj się.* You'll feel so much better afterward.'

'Well, I can't feel any fucking worse, right?' Kamila gets out of the car and watches Natalia drive off, waving at her as she heads up Wiejska Boulevard. Kamila feels her coat pocket for her keys. They jangle reassuringly. The stairwell is dim and alive with *obiad* aromas.

She slowly turns the key in the lock to her apartment and the door clicks open. She pushes it with her foot and steps into the *przedpokój,* and just like that she sees Emil, his broad back, at the kitchen sink, scrubbing dishes. Wojtek's head pops in from the bedroom. When he sees Kamila, he yells in surprise.

Emil drops a dish at the sound. He turns his head and sees Kamila, who glances away quickly. The apartment is spotless and warm.

'Honey, I'm home.' Kamila doesn't plan on saying it, and certainly doesn't plan on saying it in English, but there it is. Right away, Wojtek is scrambling to find his shoes, retrieving his coat from the rack next to Kamila. She grabs his shoulder. 'You're not staying? By all means, stay. I won't be long.' There are tears in his eyes, and Kamila feels a pang of pity and regret.

'Kamila. Please.' It's all he says and then he's out the door. Kamila shuts it behind him.

'Take off your coat.' Emil's first words to her are spoken quietly but firmly. Kamila obliges, allowing her Calvin Klein wool coat to drop to the floor.

'Tea? I've got a fresh pot ready. As soon as I sweep this.' He points to the shattered plate at his feet.

'Sure.'

Kamila sits down. There's a small plastic Christmas tree replica on the table with tiny plastic ornaments dangling off its skinny little branches. She feels the fight in her die. Emil brings over a cup and saucer and sits down across from her. He's grown a beard and put on a few pounds. Love allows for a lapse in personal maintenance.

'I know. I got fat.' Emil smiles sadly and starts to cry.

'Why didn't you tell me before?'

'That I gained weight?' His laugh comes out like a hiccup.

'You should have just told me, Emil. When we were twelve, or when we were sixteen and I tried to dry hump you at every sleepover we had.'

Emil wipes his eyes. 'I thought you'd figure it out and leave me on your own. But I prayed you wouldn't.'

'*Dlaczego?*'

'Because I didn't want to be alone. Because I couldn't name it, Kamila. I didn't even know what it was, not till a few years ago, I swear to you. I thought it was a phase. Like pimples, and that in time it would clear up on its own. Please don't hate me.'

Kamila sips her tea. She doesn't hate him. She wants to believe him. She also wants to chew him out, rail against the injustice of being spurned all those years. But they are somehow having an adult conversation, meaningful and quiet. It isn't any of the ways that she imagined this moment, but perhaps this is better.

'I can't even go into what I'm feeling, Emil. I could have spent my teenage years running around town with some deserving guy, who would have *wanted me*. Who would have used me, or pined for me, or just . . . fucked me at the very least. You led me on.'

'You let me,' Emil says, quietly. For a moment, Kamila wants to slap his face, but instead she gulps down the rest of her *herbata*.

'You were everything to me, Kamila. You still are.'

'No, I wasn't. I'm not. Isn't that clear? There wasn't anything real about it, and a lot of that was my fault, I suppose.' Kamila pauses. She reaches for his hand and holds it briefly.

'It's going to be hard for you here, now that . . .'

'I know. It's already hard. Maybe Wojtek and I will pack our bags and go somewhere else. Warsaw, or London.'

'Well, wherever you go, just don't go "back in the closet,"' Kamila says in English.

'*Bek een da clazet?*' Emil smiles, confused.

'It's an expression I picked up in America. It just means, don't hide anymore.' Emil nods, grateful. Kamila smiles and finishes her tea.

'Here's the deal. I can't stay here, Emil. But neither can you. You have a week to find someplace. I won't throw you onto the street, but please, a week is not a long time, so you better get cracking. I don't want to see you for a long time. I wish you well and I'll call you soon so we can talk about the divorce.'

'Divorce?'

'Absolutely. What else can there be? Live your life, Emil. Obviously, you don't need me anymore to do that.' Kamila picks up her fancy coat, dusts it once, and drapes it over her shoulders. She walks out the door but turns around, one last time. Emil stands up.

'You look beautiful, Kamila,' he says, and she believes him.

JUSTYNA
KIELCE, POLAND

They say you fall in love with your child instantly. They say it's a sudden-impact situation and that it happens moments after birth, right when they place the baby on your chest for the first time. They say that love bears down on you like a stone, till you can't breathe. And it does.

But Justyna doesn't talk about this love. She tucks it away, beneath her bravado and fear. She talks about her son as if Damian was a stray she took in years ago. In public she yells at him, to shut up, to scram, go away and find something else to do. She smacks his rear in grocery stores, pulls on his earlobe to hurry him along, while older women purse their lips and scowl in her direction, as if they had never felt the same impatience. Other mothers, Justyna has found out, are the most judgmental of them all.

Justyna didn't fall in love with Damian moments after birth. Moments after birth she was dying for a cigarette, and left him simpering in his bassinet to sneak down to the lobby for a smoke. When Justyna returned, the nurse on duty was cradling her son and feeding him a two-ounce bottle of formula. 'Smoking inhibits your milk flow,' the nurse warned. Justyna shrugged her shoulders, got back into bed. 'Well, then, turns out it's good for something. I'm a mother, *proszę pani,* not a cow.'

She didn't fall in love with him when they got home either. He was colicky and fussy and the last thing Justyna wanted to deal with, as her own mother lay sick and dying. The moment it happened, the moment she finally felt her heart surge, was when Damian was two and a half and landed in the hospital with a bad case of pneumonia. Justyna watched him as he struggled for breath, hooked up to IVs and heart monitors, all but lifeless for a day. Justyna felt like she too was fighting for her life. When his eyelids fluttered open, and his hand reached out as if searching for hers, she ran to his side, crushed Damian in a hug, and placed her ear against his rattling chest. That's when it happened. That's when she finally felt it.

It took a brush with death for Justyna to realize her love for her son, and it took death itself to realize something else; life was fleeting and meaningless. Weeks after Paweł's murder, Justyna yearned to take Damian aside and clue him in so that when he headed out into life's open jaws, he would be equipped with a steely heart and a clear head. 'Your father died because nothing matters,' she wanted to tell him. But even though Justyna was sure that in the long run her son would thank her for the heads-up, she had a niggling suspicion that she'd be robbing him of something. So she let him believe that life was fair and perhaps Daddy was coming back.

On Christmas Eve morning Justyna and her sister wake up groggy but determined to rise to the occasion.

Babcia Kazia brings a small tree with her that afternoon, and when she walks through the door, dragging the *choinka* by a rope, the kids cling to her stockinged calves, yipping their *dziękuje,* and covering her knees in sloppy kisses, like their grandmother is *Święty Mikołaj* himself. Justyna goes up to the attic, finds the small cardboard box labeled *Bąbki,* and brings it downstairs.

Celina and Damian hang ornaments as Justyna and Elwira sit on the couch, watching them and smoking. *Babcia* Kazia keeps busy in the kitchen defrosting pierogi, red *barszcz,* and cabbage *bigos* and setting the table for Christmas Eve dinner. At three o'clock, Justyna comes to the table still dressed in her pink sweat pants and T-shirt. *Babcia* shares the *opłatek* she brought with the kids and Elwira, but Justyna refuses to take part, and for once *Babcia* doesn't argue. Justyna eats a little of everything but doesn't comment on the food. When *Babcia* Kazia starts clearing the table Justyna tells her, 'Leave it. Just let them open their gifts.'

Celina receives two Barbies – a stewardess and a pet shop owner – and a pink tutu that is too expensive but worth the look of jaw-dropping happiness on Cela's face when she tears off the gift wrap. Damian gets a couple of Hot Wheels cars and a yellow digger. Elwira hands Justyna a Spice Girls CD and a bottle of cheap perfume. 'Sorry,' Justyna mouths to her sister, because she has nothing to give her.

When Justyna tucks Damian in later that night, he asks her if 'Święty Mikołaj didn't bring *Ciocia* Elwira anything because her boyfriend did something bad?' Justyna is blindsided by the question and scrambles for a diversion.

'You know what? Tomorrow we can go to Puchatek and you can pick something else out for yourself. I like what Mikołaj brought you, but honestly I think you're way too old now for that plastic digger. What the heck was he thinking, right?'

Damian frowns. 'Is it because he did something bad to *Tata*?' he asks again.

Justyna answers quickly, confidently. 'Listen, *synu*. Mikołaj didn't bring *Ciocia* anything because silly *Ciocia* forgot to write him a letter. He can't read minds, you know? Kinda shitty, right?' Justyna chuckles.

Damian stares at his mother, his big blue eyes fixated on her, and when he finally speaks it is one word, exhaled like a sigh. 'Oh.'

The next morning, Justyna waits in the kitchen for Elwira to come downstairs. Her sister is prone to six A.M. cravings for ham and butter sandwiches, and, like clockwork, Elwira shuffles into the kitchen, in a dirty bathrobe. When she sees Justyna, she gasps, clutching her chest. 'Fuck me! Jesus, are you trying to give me a heart attack?' She walks over to the counter and grabs the rye bread.

'Did you tell Celina what Filip did?' Justyna speaks, quickly and to the point.

'No. Of course I didn't! What do you think, I'm crazy?'

'So how come my son knows something is up? How come my son thinks that asswipe did "something bad" to his father?'

'I have no fucking idea! What are you talking about?'

Justyna walks over to Elwira, snatches the bread from her and throws it on the floor. 'Did you tell her?' Justyna's hands grab Elwira's chin and squeeze until Elwira starts to cry.

'I swear, Justyna, I would never tell any kid that, let alone my own. But Celina is sleeping in my room now, and I call friends at night when I can't sleep. I mean I'm quiet, and I make sure she's out, but who knows? Oh fuck, maybe she overheard something, maybe . . .' Elwira's voice collapses into a whisper. 'Listen, Justyna, I can't do it like you. I have to talk, you know, it helps me process.'

'Process? What's there to process? Filip killed my husband. What can't you process? And he's still out there. It's been twenty-nine fucking days and—' Justyna stops talking, barrels over to the phone, and quickly dials a number.

'*Tak, halo,* may I please speak with Officer Kurka? You can tell him the widow Strawicz is calling. Yes, I'll hold, I'll hold, goddamnit.' She stares at Elwira, who is cowering by the fridge.

'Yes? I understand it's *Boże Narodzenie* today, I got it. How's your Christmas been, *proszę pani*? You wanna know how mine is? Pretty fucking dismal, what with my husband dead. No one over there gives a fine crap about—Yes, I'll hold, but I know he's there and I have his mobile number so maybe I should just fucki—' And that's when Justyna notices a large plastic bag on the floor, peeking out from the corner of the living room doorway. She drops the receiver to the table. Echoes of *Halo? Halo?* fade into the background as she makes her way toward the bag.

'What? What is it?' Elwira's voice whispers.

Justyna stops at the foot of the plastic bag and wills herself to peek around the bend. The door leads straight into the kitchen. Why hadn't she noticed it sooner? Her dog, Rambo, is lying motionless, a bloody shoelace round his neck, securing the plastic bag over his head. She stoops down, shaking. She wants to untie the bag but can't bring herself to do it.

'What the fuck is that?' Elwira starts creeping toward Justyna, who holds out her hand.

'*Don't!*' Justyna blurts out, and Elwira immediately shrinks back.

There are no locks on the windows in the house. The balcony doors on the second floor don't close all the way, and no one's bothered to repair them.

'Run upstairs and check on the kids. Right now.'

Elwira scrambles upstairs, crying. Silently, Justyna strokes Rambo's torso, her hands hold his paws. She knows she shouldn't touch the victim, shouldn't fuck with the fingerprints, but she can't help it because Rambo was her mother's dog and now he's gone, just like Teresa's gone, just like Paweł is. One by one, everyone is dropping like flies.

In a daze, she walks back to the kitchen, and she picks up the telephone. The line is dead so she redials the police station. 'Yes, *halo*. Tell Officer Kurka that the person who murdered my husband came back last night, while we were all sleeping – and that includes two kids, miss. Our dog has been butchered and left with a plastic bag tied around his neck. Tell Kurka that I will personally drive myself and my family to his house tonight, right now, and we will stay there, camped out on his fucking *wersalka,* until the police stop jacking off and start doing their job. Do you understand what I am saying? Have you been writing this down? I fucking hope so.'

Elwira comes running into the kitchen as soon as Justyna hangs up.

'They're fine. *O Boże,* Justyna. What is it?'

Elwira is sobbing, the fear in her eyes is astounding. Justyna lights a cigarette and points toward the dog.

'He was here. And he left us a gift.'

Elwira shuts her eyes and shakes her head. 'Let's call *Tata*. Please. We'll tell him he has to come back. I can't be here alone anymore. I'm scared.'

'Don't be pathetic, Elwira. It's embarrassing.' Justyna stares at the remains of the dog. Someone will have to move him, bury him. It would be a job for Paweł, just the kind of thing he was good at, taking care of stuff that no one else wanted to do, like changing lightbulbs or cleaning up the trash bins.

'I want you to go upstairs and pack bags for Cela and Damian. I'm calling a cab, and you are taking them to *Babcia*'s and you are not to leave there till I tell you to. Don't tell *Babcia* what happened, tell her we had a fight.'

'What about you?' Elwira asks.

'I'm staying.'

'No! Justyna, please, *proszę cię*! Oh my God, why would he come back? Do you think he knows I talked to the police?'

'He's fucking crazy. That's all.'

'But you don't come back to the scene of the crime unless you wanna get caught, right?'

'I don't fucking know, Elwira! Maybe he's trapped, or it's cold as fuck out there, or he just couldn't help himself, so he came back. I'm not a fucking criminal psychologist! Point is, he was here.'

'So, does that mean he'll come back again?'

'I don't know. But next time, I'll be ready for him.'

'Stop it! Who do you think you are, for fuck's sake, Kojak? He snuck in here during the night and *killed our fucking dog*. You're coming with us. We'll call the police and they can stake out this house and wait for him.'

'And what? They'll cuff him and haul him off in a van and we'll live happily ever after? The police give fuck all about what happened to Paweł, and what happened to our dog, and what is going to happen to you and me. You're scared and I don't blame you. I swear I don't blame you but I'm not scared.'

'Yes, you are. Don't fucking lie to me.'

'*I'm not*. I'm not scared. I'm not *anything*. There is nothing left in me, nothing left to even properly take care of my son.

Do you understand that?' Justyna sits at the table and reaches for her pack of cigarettes. She offers Elwira one.

'So, what? You're gonna stay here and wait for him and have it out?' Elwira smokes the L&M, taking quick puffs one right after another.

'If I'm next, so be it. I don't care. But I want to look that psycho in the face, I want to—'

'You're sick. You're in denial. You just went insane at the thought of Damian knowing what happened to his father so don't tell me you don't care. Please, Justyna, fucking on my knees, I beg you, just come with us!'

Justyna looks down at the kitchen table. Every morning before school she'd come down and her mother would be sitting at the head of this table, filing her nails and smoking a Marlboro. *Eggs or eggs, ptaszyno?* Every morning, the same, calling Justyna her birdie, scrambling half a dozen *jajka* in gobs of butter, serving it up on rye bread. Every fucking morning. *Eggs or eggs?*

'Remember the summer we all went to the Croatian sea, *na wczasy*? The first day we went to the beach, the waves were so high. Mama dared us to jump in the water. And you stood by the shore, crying. You wanted to jump, but you just couldn't do it.'

Elwira speaks softly. 'I remember how you dove in and went under. You swallowed a ton of water, and we thought you had died, and then Mama told you you were stupid for actually jumping in, that she'd just been kidding.'

'The thing is, I don't think she was kidding. I still believe that she wanted me to jump in. And I'm jumping in now, Elwira. And I don't expect you to join me. I don't want you to. But I have to do it.'

Elwira walks up the stairs. In a few minutes, Justyna hears the kids waking, hears Elwira gathering their things. *They'll be fine,* thinks Justyna, and she dials the number for a taxi.

CHAPTER EIGHT

1998

ANNA
KIELCE, POLAND

After another three-year absence, Anna arrived in Poland that August with zero fanfare. Her cousins Hubert and Renata had made lives for themselves in Dublin and Naples, respectively, and her aunts only came by once in a while. *Babcia* had been happy to see her again. 'You look like a woman now, Anna,' she said, wiping away tears. *Babcia,* on the other hand, looked old. She'd apparently given up on her dentures, and the sight of her toothless mouth threw Anna. 'Why, *Babciu*?' Anna asked, and *Babcia* just grinned wider. 'Oh, *córciu*! They click and clack and it doesn't feel natural. Besides, I'm not afraid of growing old.' For the first time ever, *Babcia* Helenka's apartment seemed huge and empty.

Besides *Babcia,* nobody seems to care that Anna is here. Nobody has called since her return a week ago. Kamila is in Warsaw with Emil, spending the summer at some seventeenth-century villa. 'We'll try to come back before you leave, Aniusia. It's been ages, hasn't it, darling?' Kamila had sounded so cosmopolitan and grown up on the phone. When Anna called Justyna, she said she was busy with kid stuff. 'He'll shit anywhere in the house: the carpet, on the balcony, in our fucking cactus planter, but not in the goddamn toilet!' But she promised to see Anna before the summer was over.

'I'm only here for two weeks this time, Justynka.' The whole conversation made Anna's heart sink.

Szydłówek is a ghost town. In the mornings, Anna gets up late, eats a *parówka* dipped in mustard for breakfast, and goes jogging around the *zalew*. In the afternoons, she sits on the curb by the church, watching traffic. She saw Kowalski once, from a few blocks away, recognized him by the silk shirt he had on, the one he used to wear in 1995. Anna had to stop herself from calling out his name. She'd wanted to apologize for their last exchange, for the way she had spoken to him on the train. But instead she looked away and prayed he wouldn't notice her.

When it rains – and it's been raining the whole week – Anna spends her days on her grandmother's balcony, staring past St Józef's steeple, hoping someone will see her sitting there and spread the news that she is back, but no one does. When the rain lets up, Anna goes on walks, mining information from the neighbors. When she ran into *Pani* Nowacka by the *trzepak* a few days ago Anna called out to her.

'*Pani* Nowacka! Where is everyone?'

'Oh, you know, probably in the *skwerek,* getting drunk. All your old pals, they're criminals now, stealing in broad daylight. You had better tell your *babcia* to hide your dollars, that's all I'm saying.' But *Pani* Nowacka had continued, gleefully informing her that Lolek had just been released from prison, after serving time for aggravated assault. 'That's what his father says anyway, but there's another rumor floating around. . . .' Anna had given *Pani* Nowacka a hasty wave goodbye and hopped onto the rug beater. She didn't want to hear any more.

Anna's seen Lolek a few times. Standing around the neighborhood, smoking and swigging malted beer with the same group of local guys she recognizes from her youth. They've grown up to be the kind of guys that she'd never associate with in the States – guys who don't read books, or discuss current events, guys with corroded teeth and black fingernails. The very same guys she'd been buddies with for all those years now made her cringe when she waved hello but hurried past them, feeling all kinds of sadness. When she was fourteen and handed out clothes and candy to the beholden post-Communist children, there was magic and power in it. When she was sixteen and rallied her girlfriends to follow their dreams, she was their ally and, more importantly, one of their own. '*My Polaki,*' she'd say. She *was* one of them. But she was better, and until this summer, she never felt there was anything wrong with that.

Anna began to notice things this year that threatened to collapse her idea of Polska. The neighborhood bums – who huddled around lampposts at all hours of the day, passing bottles of home brew around – bugged her. The desperate wives and mothers, who had to search behind bushes for their wasted sons, bugged her. People who cut the line at the local *warzywniak* bugged her. Everyone seemed dismal, hurried, and hungover. Had Anna always been this blind? She felt utterly alien, as if Kielce was a place she no longer understood.

Today, the most exciting thing Anna did was help *Babcia* move the credenza. At four o'clock the phone buzzes and Anna leaps up from her dog-eared copy of T. C. Boyle's *Water Music*.

'*Dzieńdobry.* Is Anna there?' a deep baritone voice inquires and Anna's curiosity is instantly piqued.

'This is Anna. Who's this?'

'Guess.'

'I have no idea.' Anna laughs, scrambling to figure out who the voice belongs to.

'That's a shame. But I'll give you a break. *Będziesz moją dziewczyna.*'

Anna's mouth falls open. 'Sebastian?'

'*Ja, das ist Sebastian.*'

'I, I thought you lived in Germany,' Anna stutters.

'Moved back two years ago.'

Anna is silent for a beat, surprised and thrilled.

'Can I take you out for a drink?' he asks.

'*Tak.*'

Sebastian tells her he'll pick her up in an hour and Anna hangs up grinning like a fool.

Two hours later, Anna hears a car honk and peeks through the kitchen window. There's a beat-up old truck — one of those Star 200s from the eighties — parked in front of her grandmother's building. When she walks out of the stairwell, Sebastian Tefilski is leaning against the driver's side door, smoking a cigarette.

'Did someone call for a limo?' Sebastian jokes.

'You look like some kind of Adidas ad,' Anna tells him. He's tall and sporting an Adidas baseball cap, Adidas polo shirt, and black Adidas sneakers. He's also more handsome than Anna had imagined. Sebastian laughs, showing his white teeth, which throw her, because white teeth like that are definitely not a Polish thing. He eyes her up and down.

'My, my. The *Amerykanka*'s all grown up.' He flicks his cigarette and smiles. 'Get in.'

They drive past Staszica Park, on their way downtown, past the lake that's teeming with ducks and swans. At a red light, Sebastian turns to her. 'Did you know that swans mate for life?'

Yes, she says, of course she knows.

'But did you also know a male swan — a cob — is the only bird that has a penis?'

Anna laughs. The words *for life* echo in her head, and she feels dumb for reading into things already.

At an outdoor pub on Sienkiewicza Street, they are making small talk over some beers when Sebastian says, 'And then you had to go ahead and ruin it with that fucked-up letter. Man, Baran, you could have been my wife by now, instead you drove me out to Berlin, where I filled up on spaetzle, trying to forget you.'

She laughs wildly. 'What "fucked-up letter"?'

Sebastian winks at her and stands up to get some more Zywiec. Anna has no recollection of a letter. When she left in 1989, she remembers handing Sebastian a note with her address, and he promised to write to her but he never did, and that was that. Maybe he has her mixed up with some other girl. When he gets back with two *kufly* of beer, Anna takes a sip, wipes the foam from her mouth.

'I wrote you a lot of letters, Sebastian. Just never mailed them. I don't know what you're talking about.'

'All right, Anna.' Sebastian winks at her again and grins.

Emboldened by the alcohol, Anna kisses him lightly on the mouth when he drops her off at Szydłówek. He doesn't kiss her back, but he doesn't duck either. 'I'll call you in the morning. Maybe we can drive to Kraków for the day or something.'

The next day, Anna wakes up with a sore throat and butterflies in her stomach. By eleven A.M., she's on the balcony, looking for his truck. At five o'clock, she is ready to give up, but when *Babcia* draws the curtains for the night, Anna refuses to change into her pajamas. At ten P.M. Anna hears it: a single honk. Suddenly, she's scrambling down the stairwell like a madwoman, calling back to *Babcia,* 'I won't be late but don't wait up.'

On the hilltop, where Sebastian parked the truck, he refills Anna's glass. The wine is sweet and cheap. 'Just like the company,'

Anna joked when she took her first sip. They are fifteen kilometers outside of Kielce, past the little village of Masłów nestled in the Swietokrzyskie Mountains. The night air feels damp and chilly. The tickle in Anna's throat has been bothering her all day, and it's an effort to swallow every sip of wine.

Sebastian and Anna don't say much, just clink glasses and stare up at the sky. You can see it all up here, every possible configuration, from the Big Dipper to Orion's Belt. When she got in his truck, he promised her the best view of the city, and he wasn't kidding. In the distance, Kielce glimmers, aglow with what look like dozens of tiny flashlights.

'It's a pretty sight, isn't it?'

Sebastian smiles and nods his head. 'Sure is.' Anna still can't believe she's here with him, on a date that's been ten years in the making.

'I had a dream about you last night,' Anna tells him as they lounge in the back of his pickup truck.

'Oh, yeah?' Sebastian is noncommittal, breezy.

'Yeah. You picked me up in the truck at *Babcia*'s and told me you were gonna drive me to America. You were wearing a white hat. And when we got in the car I was like, "Wait, you know there's an ocean after Paris. How are we gonna drive across the ocean?" And you said, "Don't worry about it, we'll make it."' Anna immediately regrets telling him.

Sebastian takes a swig from the bottle and closes his eyes. 'That's it?'

'No, hotshot, and then I told you I loved you and we made out all the way to France.'

He laughs out loud. 'That's better.'

Anna flushes pink because that *was* the dream, goddamnit. *Kocham cię*, she had whispered three times in a row, as they sped down Toporowskiego and he had turned to her and started weeping.

'So what are you doing tomorrow, Baran?'

'You tell me. Maybe we'll go to Kraków again.' Anna rolls her eyes at him.

'Ha ha.' He opens one eye and takes a final gulp of wine, chucking the empty bottle over the side of the truck. 'So, let's get to the crux of the matter here, Baran. You have a fella back home?'

Anna shakes her head. She's pretty sure he's not asking because he's dying to know the answer.

'I want a career, and then I'll worry about "a fella."'

'You Americans do it all backward, huh? Look at your best buddies. They're way ahead of you in the game.'

'What game? And what best buddies?'

'Marchewska, Strawicz. Kamila's as good as married, Strawicz already has a kid.'

'You don't think I know that?'

'I don't know what you know. You might be too busy with Hollywood to keep up with the local newsreel.'

'I still don't know what your point is.' Anna sits up, irritated now. This was not how she had imagined the night unfolding.

'Point is, love is in the air, Baran, up for grabs. But you have loftier goals, I guess.'

'Loftier goals? I don't want a husband or a child right now, what's so lofty about that? There's an expression in America, "whatever floats your boat." So it's my boat and I don't need anyone telling me how to float it.'

'Till it sinks, right?' Sebastian laughs.

Anna fusses with her jean cuffs. 'And wouldn't that be great? Wouldn't it teach me a lesson, huh? That I should have settled for mediocrity? "Lofty ambitions." You say that as if it were a bad thing. Why is that? The minute you try to rise above the fray, what are you? Cocky, stupid, lucky? But it's never admirable, so explain that to me. Maybe that's why this country's so fucked. 'Cause you'd rather sit on your asses, judging others and griping about life, than work to change your circumstances.'

Sebastian stares at her, eyebrows raised. 'Wow, if your acting thing doesn't work out, you could always run for mayor, Anna.'

'You're happy? You're happy being a truck driver at twenty-one? Why don't you just knock up one of the wide-eyed fawns that are probably lined up around the block for you, and call it a day?'

'It's easy to visit, Anna. Try living here and then talk to me.'

Sebastian leans toward her and and touches the small medallion dangling from the chain around her neck. *'Patriotka,'* he murmurs, and suddenly they're kissing. It's not how she envisioned it, but the moment grabs hold of her and doesn't let go for a long while. Anna parts his lips with her tongue. They kiss hungrily, their mouths still tasting like cabernet.

And then, just as suddenly, Sebastian stops, stands up, and jumps off the side of the truck, dusting his hands off on his jeans.

'There's a woman,' Sebastian offers quietly. And Anna knows that it's over. All of it.

They drive back in silence, the rickety truck speeds down the hill, and in eleven minutes they are pulling up to Toporow-skiego, where Anna jumps out before Sebastian can make a full stop.

'We really should drive up to Kraków,' he calls out after her and she turns around and stares at him, memorizing his face, his hangdog expression and churlish little smile, his black curls that are matted to his forehead. She knows this is the last time that he'll be this close.

'You carried my bag,' she whispers. 'You were thirteen years old and you hoisted that duffel over your shoulder in front of everyone.'

Sebastian leans his head out the window. 'What? I can't hear you, Anna. Just come here for a second.' But Anna turns and runs into the building, runs up the three flights of stairs, almost knocking down *Pani* Nowacka, who's heading to work.

That afternoon Anna wakes up on the couch with *Babcia* sitting beside her. *Babcia* has a wet washcloth folded in her hands, which she gently places on Anna's forehead. The handkerchief sends icy hot shivers down Anna's neck, and she weakly moves her head from side to side, trying to slide it off.

'You have a fever, *córeczko,* and a bad one at that,' *Babcia* informs her. Anna opens her mouth and winces in pain; the skin on her lips is cracked and brittle. 'My throat,' she croaks in English, hoping *Babcia* will guess, because if she tries to stretch the open vowels for the Polish words *moje gardło,* she might draw blood. Her grandmother shakes her head and places her hand on Anna's chest. 'Your heart.'

Anna stares into her grandmother's loving face, into her gray eyes that shine like titanium. 'Cut it out, *Babcia,*' she manages.

'I saw the way you ran down those stairs last night. Tell me, *córeczko,* did you sleep with him?'

Anna shakes her head, surprised at the question. If Anna could talk, and if she could talk of such things with *Babcia,* Anna would confess that she was the one who wanted to make love with Sebastian last night, she was the one that didn't want to stop kissing him.

'Were you able to say everything you wanted to tell him?' Anna shakes her head again. Tears are gathering in her eyes and she feels stupid and confused. She wishes Sebastian had never called her.

'No wonder your throat is sore.'

'I caught a cold, that's it, *Babciu*. It was freezing last night.' Anna tries to sit up.

Anna just wants to sleep everything off, but *Babcia* continues. 'Did I ever tell you what happened to me after I met your grandfather for the first time?' *Babcia* wipes her hands on her apron and folds them on her lap. 'I was seventeen. It was summer and I was on my way back from town. My hands were full of shopping bags, and I was tired and hot and not paying too much attention to where I was headed. As I crossed the street I tripped on the curb and skinned my knee. I should have been wearing stockings but it was too darn hot that day. My mother had admonished me, but what did I care?' *Babcia* smiles at the memory.

'Anyway, my bags spilled every which way and suddenly there was a shadow over me. I looked up and there he was, your grandfather. Oh, Aniusia, he was so dapper then. He knelt down and, without a word, licked his finger and blotted the blood from my knee. He stood right back up, tipped his hat, and said, "Stefan Chmielinski, at your service," and then sauntered off, leaving me on the pavement to clean up the rest of the mess. That would turn out to be his modus operandi when we were married, but back then, what did I know.' *Babcia* divorced *Dziadek* Stefan years and years ago, long before Anna had been born.

'Well, the next day I woke up covered head to toe in a terrible rash, itchy red hives everywhere. Doctors came and examined me and not one of them could explain what was the matter. But my grandmother, your *pra-pra-babcia* Walentyna did. "This Stefan, he got under your skin, Helenka, and until you see him again, the rash won't heal." And she was right.'

To Anna, the story is a good one, but that's all it is. Anna is not lovesick, she has a throat infection that's been brewing for days now, that's all it is. But she can't argue with *Babcia*. This is the same woman who swears up and down that cancer is an actual crab that hibernates in the body, and if it 'wakes up' it preys on its host. Anna wants to laugh at the story but she's too tired for an argument, so she closes her eyes.

When Anna boards the plane back to JFK five days later, her throat is still throbbing. As the wheels lift off, she wipes away tears; saying goodbye to Poland would never be easy. But Anna spends the next nine hours replaying the trip in her head, wondering if summers in Kielce are worth the hassle anymore. Somehow, her hometown has lost its luster. This time, when the customs officer hands Anna back her United States passport and says, 'Welcome home,' she doesn't roll her eyes.

'And so, after what felt like a lifetime of skirting the issue, I finally got down on one knee, right in the middle of Zamkowy Square, and asked Kamila if she would allow me the honor of being her husband. And thank God, she said yes. I hadn't really planned on it, even though I'd been thinking about it for years.'

'*Years,*' Kamila chimes in, because she just can't help it.

'Okay, okay, *koteczku*' – Emil turns red, but plows on – 'but I didn't think it would happen yesterday! When we were packing, I thought, lemme bring the ring, just in case the mood strikes me. And boy, it struck me. It sure did. Tourists were taking pictures of us and everything.' Emil ceremoniously throws his arm around Kamila's shoulder and brings her in for a rough squeeze as if she were a goal-scoring player on his soccer team. 'We have to refit the ring, that's why she's not wearing it right now – it was my great-grandmother's and she had tiny fingers. Kamila's got paws, right, *kochanie*?'

'Well, that's the most romantic thing I have ever heard,' squeals Jola, and elbows Norbert's side.

Kamila takes a sip of her daiquiri and sloshes the drink around in her mouth before rolling her eyes. '"Kamila's got paws"? *That's* the most romantic thing you've ever heard?' Everyone laughs.

Norbert lights his girlfriend's third consecutive Vogue

cigarette. All night long, Kamila's made it a point not to stare at his hair plugs, but she's failing miserably. They look fresh, like little black turnips sprouting in rows on his scalp.

'Let's have a party at the country house before you guys leave on Monday. An engagement party. It's been too long since we partied up at the *chatka,* don't you think, Jolusia?' Norbert winks.

Jola twirls the skinny cigarette between her fingers, her French manicure gleaming, and nods vehemently in agreement. '*Za długo!*' she thunders. Kamila is fascinated by her cousin Jola, by her two-inch-long nails ('Acrylic tips! Asian-owned salon. Kamila, I'll tell you what, those Orientals know what they're doing'), by the way she flounces into a room in three-inch high heels, and by the fact that Jola is schtupping her forty-two-year-old boss, a bona fide Polish millionaire, who has his own plastic surgery practice, as well as his own wife and two kids.

'But my procedure is scheduled for tomorrow,' Kamila reminds them.

'Then we'll reschedule it for Monday. Jola, you can set it up, can't you, *kotku*?' He laughs loudly because of course Jola can. If she could, Jola would pull up the office calendar now. She'd do anything to keep her job with all its perks, including weekend getaways at the '*chatka*' Norbert has in Suruck, on the outskirts of the city. Chatka, *my ass,* Kamila thinks. It's not a hut, not even close. The vacation home where she and Emil have been staying for the past two weeks is more like a castle, with turrets and balconies and a stable in the fields surrounding the grounds.

Norbert motions for the waitress, and Kamila excuses herself. Jola hops up and follows her. 'It's like they need help with wiping or something,' Kamila hears Norbert say to Emil. Kamila cringes as Emil erupts in a fit of giggles.

The bathroom is all polished porcelain with perfectly folded hand towels. White cans of Rexona deodorant perfume and Elnett hairspray sit in neat rows next to the sinks. It's like a five-star spa, not a bathroom; even when it comes to its shitters, the Warsaw area is shiny, effusive, and impossibly chic compared to Kielce. Kamila is suddenly overwhelmed. She stands in front of the enormous mirrors and examines, among other things, her painfully short bangs and big paws.

'I can't believe you're getting married, Marchewska. I didn't wanna say it back there, but it's about fucking time.' Jola snickers, reapplying her bright pink lipstick.

'Joluś, please don't call me by my last name. "Marchewska" wears a kerchief and brings jars of cabbage to the bazaar every Sunday, okay?'

'You're so fucking funny, Marchewska – I mean, Mrs. Ludek!' Jola laughs.

'No. I'm so fucking nervous,' Kamila whispers, as the bathroom attendant does her best to appear occupied.

'It'll be *superosko, kochanie.* You have to come back here to buy your dress, obviously. You won't find anything couture in Kielce. Who's gonna be your maid of honor, huh?' Jola widens her eyes theatrically. 'Okay, don't answer that now, but keep in mind, *kuzynko,* that I'd throw a fucking dynamite bachelorette party. There's this place that opened last year called Fantom. It's like a gay nightclub where you can watch guys go down on each other! There's no sign or anything, you just ring a little bell. And some of the guys paint their balls with glitter!' Jola scoops and rearranges her breasts. For a moment, Kamila doesn't know what to say, about any of it.

'I'm nervous about *tomorrow,*' Kamila corrects her cousin.

'Oh my God, Kamila, Norbert's the best there is. You're

gonna love your new nose! Let's face it' – Jola titters – 'the *nochal* you've got doesn't do you any justice. Out with the old, honey, and in with the new. You're in Warsaw now.'

'My *nochal*. Right.' She wonders what her father will think next time he sees her. She is getting rid of *his* nose, his genetic stamp. All her life Kamila has dreamed of transformation, of physical metamorphosis, because beauty was not just skin deep; it burrowed underneath tissue and muscle. Kamila liked her personality just fine, thought of herself as insightful and enterprising; but ever since Maciek Toboszycki told her she was ugly, calling her *brzydula* in front of the whole fourth grade, Kamila has wanted to erase her face and start over. And now, she is going to do just that. She thinks about the picture she has had tucked in her wallet for weeks now – a close-up of Michelle Pfeiffer's tiny, button-sized nose. When she nervously showed it to Norbert last week, he smiled. 'Well, I'm not a miracle worker, Kamila, but I'll try.'

Jola straightens up and looks at herself one last time in the bathroom mirror. 'We better get back, Kamila, they'll think we drowned.'

'Would you marry Norbert, if you could?' Kamila asks. Jola stares at her for a minute, before bursting out in a peal of laughter.

'Are you kidding, *dziewczyno*? He's like a hundred years old.' In that moment, Kamila realizes that she's underestimated her cousin. Jola's dalliance with Norbert is dirty and wrong, and it will all probably end quite soon, but that's why it is so good. Kamila briefly tries to imagine a life where nothing else matters but the thrill of living.

★

By the time Norbert and Jola drop them off at the villa, Emil is sloppy drunk, falling into Kamila's lap in the car and groping her. It's all for show, and it's what Emil does best. Whenever they get behind closed doors, Emil curls up on the couch and complains about headaches or bellyaches. Kamila is used to it, and yet she is still constantly disappointed.

'We'll stay at a hotel tonight, *kochanie*. You two can have the house to yourselves.' Jola winks at Kamila.

'Let's not reschedule tomorrow, Norbert. The idea of a party is tempting, and we appreciate it, but I just want to get this over with, okay?' Kamila asks, lightly tapping the tip of her nose before getting out of the car. Norbert concedes quickly, his hand already somewhere under Jola's dress, and then speeds off into the night.

The villa is dark but Kamila refrains from flicking on any lights. She's suddenly feeling lost and worried, wishing that she could just flop into her bed back home.

'I should shower. I can still smell those cigarettes,' Emil says and makes his way toward their bathroom.

Kamila helps herself to some whiskey from the bar and goes out onto the terrace. The night sky is speckled with stars. She listens to the sound of the cicadas chirping and the running water upstairs, and somewhere underneath all that noise, she can hear the sound of her own pounding heart. On the eve of what she has dreamed of for years – a marriage proposal today and a new face tomorrow – she feels uncertain.

In the hushed night, she can hear Anna's and Justyna's voices, she can see their sixteen-year-old faces, on the cusp of real life but not quite there yet. The last time she saw Justyna was months ago, randomly ran into her on Sienkiewicza Street. She had Damian in tow, but she had stopped and grabbed a beer with

Kamila. *Pamiętasz, pamiętasz?*, they laughed and sipped their *piwo*. They didn't talk about Justyna's mother or Kamila's problems with Emil. They talked about the only thing that they had in common now: the past. The conversation was nice but in the end neither of them mentioned meeting up again.

Kamila pours the rest of her whiskey over the balcony and walks back inside. She finds Emil in their bedroom, reading a book. Kamila undresses quietly and slips under the covers, naked, shivering. She can't even remember the last time they made love. It was months ago, maybe years.

She finds Emil's penis with her left hand and with her right she begins to fondle herself. Emil turns a page of his book.

'You *have* to. *We* have to. What will we tell our children about the night we got engaged?' Kamila pleads.

'Children? We won't be telling our children anything about this sort of thing,' Emil answers.

'Well, then, it would be a personal travesty, my husband-to-be, if you left me yearning on the night of our betrothal. Don't make me go hunting through this castle for a banana.' Kamila laughs, hoping to lighten the mood.

'*Fe*, Kamila.'

'You know, they say sex goes out the window once you're married. So I guess we're ahead of the game,' and then she dissolves into a fit of laughter. Emil sighs and puts his book down on the nightstand.

'Kamila, Kamila,' Emil whispers, and his fingertips trace the contours of her nose with its dips and valleys. When he parts her lips and leaves his finger in her mouth, she stops laughing.

'Kamila, you are my soulmate. Let's not debase that. In the second grade you stood up for me and I knew then that we were destined to be together. I didn't need a blow job as proof of that then, and I don't need one now. Animals fuck for the sake of their existence. But we are more than animals. We are beyond skin, beyond flesh. And if that isn't enough for you, then I don't know what to tell you.'

Kamila feels her heart hammer in her chest. She thinks back to the spectacle in the square earlier that day. Emil was grinning like a fool, flailing as he spoke, the sweat flowing down his face in torrents, as he clownishly exclaimed, 'Marry me!' Kamila had always imagined him proposing during a private moment, because Emil was most truthful and most himself when they were alone. She had imagined him quiet and focused, vulnerable in his desire to make her his wife. She imagined happy tears, and a kiss. She never imagined a gaggle of Saudi tourists snapping their picture as he got down on one knee.

She wants to flat out ask him if she is signing her life away to celibacy. Is that what he means? That they will never have sex again? But Kamila is afraid to ask, afraid to know more. Emil strokes her forehead.

'I'm nothing without you, I want you beside me forever, and I can't imagine not having you as my wife. And I'm sorry I called your hands paws tonight. That sounded callous because it *was* callous. But your hands, Kamila . . .' He reaches under the covers and retrieves both of them and places them on his face, till she is cradling his head. 'Your hands are my armor, my comfort, my everything. And they are meant for better things than that,' and he smiles.

'Okay, *kochanie*. Another night.' She sighs and closes her eyes.

In the morning, Kamila wakes up to the smell of coffee and sausage. Emil is in the kitchen, already dressed.

'Sweetheart, I can't eat or drink before the surgery, remember? But thank you.' Emil serves himself a big helping and chews his food in silence. She can tell he's jittery too.

'Turns out I can't eat before the surgery either. But I sure could use a drink.' He laughs his giggly, high-pitched laugh.

'Kamila, I'll say this once and I'll say it here because I'll be too anxious at the clinic, but listen, I love you the way you are. I love your face. And I know you aren't doing this for me, that this is something you want for yourself, but I want to reiterate that I will not be more attracted to you afterward and therefore . . .' And he lingers, leaving things unspoken, but she hears him, loud and clear. A better nose will not guarantee better sex. And for a minute, Kamila just wants to go home.

On the cab ride over to the clinic, Emil calls their friend Wojtek, who is staying at Kamila's while they are away, watering plants and such. Emil gushes to him about the coolness of the capital, the racy nightclubs and the swanky restaurants, already planning a mini vacation for the three of them, perhaps in October.

'*Mówię ci, superosko!* And maybe Norbi will let us stay in the villa again. *Brachol,* and when I say *villa,* I mean castle . . . *tak!* A freaking turret and everything . . . Now? Now, we are off to see about a new nose for my gal here.' Emil turns to Kamila and winks exaggeratedly.

'For my fiancée, you mean.' Kamila corrects him and Emil's hand flies to cover the speaker as he shakes his head vehemently and mouths, *Not now.* 'Wojtuś, I gotta go, we're almost there. I'll call you after . . . I'll tell her. *Buziaki.*' He hangs up and sits back. Kamila stares at him.

'It's strange that you say *buziaki* like that. *Buziaki* for him from who? From me? Kisses from us? I don't get it. It sounds — *weird.*'

Emil glances at Kamila from the corners of his eyes.

'I want Wojtek to be my best man. So I didn't tell him because

I want to tell him in person. Because I know that's what you're getting at.'

'Nothing gets past you.'

Immediately, she feels remorse.

'I'm sorry. It's my nerves. I'm all twisted with them, *kochanie*. I won't say another word.' And she doesn't, until they get to reception, where Jola greets them with a giant grin.

'Norbert is taking me to Ibiza!' she whispers giddily to Kamila and then continues full voice. 'Now get started on this paperwork, it's a fucking bitch, but we gotta do it. After that Kinga will take you in the back and prep you. You didn't eat or drink anything, right?'

Kamila nods as Emil drums his knuckles on the front desk. She wishes he could be stalwart, but he's even more nervous than she is. She places her hand on his to calm him but he flinches.

'*Chłopie,* you're not the one going under the knife. Settle down,' Jola orders and directs her next question back to Kamila. 'So nothing, right? Not even a little liquid protein.' Jola winks at Kamila, who turns red.

'Nothing.'

Jola laughs and hands Kamila a clipboard and pen. She sits down in the empty waiting room and Emil plops down beside her, peering over her shoulder. After a few minutes of trying to concentrate, Kamila feels like swatting him away like a fly who is buzzing in her face, and suddenly Emil jumps to his feet, as if she had.

'Hey! I'm gonna go grab a *herbatka* from next door. You want one?'

Kamila glances up from the papers, incredulous. *'I can't eat or drink—'*

'Right. Sorry. Right.' And with that, he pecks her cheek and sprints off, giving her a preposterous thumbs-up before he disappears through the front doors.

'Ibiza, Kamila! We're staying at a nude beach resort!' Kamila smiles as she continues filling in the blanks: name, age, date of birth, allergies, sign here, sign there, sign away your life on the dotted line, please print. Her head spins.

Jola smiles and presses the intercom. 'Kinga, *Pani* Marchewska is ready.'

Fifteen minutes later, lying on a metal slab, dressed in a paper gown with a hairnet on her head, Kamila waits. She wants the drugs already. She wants to close her eyes and be done with it.

Norbert walks into the room, in his scrubs, fussing with a pair of beige latex gloves.

'Kamila! On your back and ready for action! Just like your cousin!' Norbert laughs uproariously. *'Gotowa?'*

Kamila nods her head weakly. 'I'm ready.'

'Okay, Doctor Gniazdo will be here soon to pump the juice. Once you're out, the whole thing should take about forty-five minutes, depending on how compliant your cartilage is.' Norbert smiles.

'Here's the spiel, and I gotta give it to you now, because afterward you'll be too drugged up to comprehend any of it. Jola will give you an after-care packet. You're gonna clean your nose with Q-tips soaked in hydrogen peroxide about three times a day. Apply Vaseline because everything will be dry and sore. I'll give you saline spray; use it with abandon. Sleep elevated, on your back, for about a month. And for the first few weeks – and you can give my apologies to Emil in advance – you should sleep alone, in case he elbows you or something.' Norbert futzes with his gloves. 'And no sex. No sex of any kind. Once again,

213

apologies to the mister. No bending over, no lifting. No tweez-ing eyebrows, no lipstick. No excessive grinning.' Norbert grins and plows on. 'No sneezing. No alcohol, no caffeine, no nico-tine. There will be bruising and swelling and some bloody nasal drip. If there's a lot of blood, call me. A week from now, I want you to get that splint off, but you can do that in Kielce. Typically you'll see results in about two weeks, but it takes up to a year to see the full effect. Oh, and you might experience some depres-sion, but God knows why because you'll look a whole lot better than you do now.' Norbert flashes Kamila another fulsome grin. 'You got all that, *Pfeiffer*?'

'No sneezing?' Kamila feels stunned. She's waited for this her whole life and now, it's happening too fast.

'No sneezing!? No *sex*, Kamila! That should be your concern. Four weeks is a long time to go without.' Kamila cracks a smile. Four weeks is a drop in the bucket for her. The anesthesiologist walks in, nods politely, and starts turning dials. He injects Kamila, and instantly her eyes roll back. She's aware of her breathing slowing down, and it feels so nice, this momentary awareness of one's own spiral into complete and total darkness.

JUSTYNA
KIELCE, POLAND

'It's your turn,' Justyna grumbles.

'But I did it yesterday,' Paweł groans back.

'Yeah, but I got up twice during the night.'

'Whattya mean?'

'What do I mean? I mean, twice, last night.'

'Twice when?'

'At one-thirty and again at four. He wanted water. So, it's your fucking turn.'

Paweł mutters, '*Kurwa mać*,' as he heaves his body upright, and sits on the edge of their bed for a moment, postponing the inevitable. He rolls his neck, cracks his back, and shakes his head as if he's got water in his ears.

'Paweł!' Justyna growls and tries to kick him in the behind. He pulls his sweatpants on and grabs his crying son from the middle of the bed.

'Ah, goddamnit, he peed through the diaper again.'

Justyna silently points toward the door and rolls over. She hears Paweł ripping off the wet diaper while Damian squirms.

'You gotta hold your pee till the morning, *synku*! You're a big boy now, okay?' His voice turns stern and he prods Justyna with his foot. 'No more Pampers at night, Justyna! We're sending mixed messages.'

'Mama! Maaamaaa! *Wstawaj!*' Damian screeches, trying to wriggle free from Paweł's arms.

'He wants you.'

'And I want a Lamborghini and a deep-tissue massage. But that doesn't mean I'm gonna fucking get it.'

'Next time he crawls in here in the middle of the night, we take him back to his room. He's three, for fuck's sake. He needs to be sleeping in his own bed. 'Cause I can't take this. I have work in an hour, *kurwa mać*.'

'I have work in an hour too. It's called motherhood, *cwaniaku*, and it doesn't pay shit.'

Shaking his head, Paweł grabs a change of clothes for Damian, and walks out of the bedroom, closing the door behind him quietly. Justyna gets why he's angry with her. She shouldn't let Damian get in their bed like she does; but at three A.M., it's easier than listening to him throw a tantrum.

Justyna makes sure that Paweł and Damian are out of the room before she opens her eyes. There is no way she'll fall back asleep now, but she'll sure as hell lay here till 6:55 – five minutes before Paweł has to leave. Sometimes, on days when Justyna feels close to strangling Damian, she will deposit him in his room, toss him a sippy cup and a *smoczek* to suck on, and lock the door behind her. Her son will wail for an hour, but if Justyna is downstairs and turns the TV up high, she can just about drown out his misery, and she does.

Before Damian, Justyna would sleep till noon if she felt like it. Now, Justyna lives for every Friday, when she throws some shit into a backpack and they take the bus to *Babcia* Kazia's apartment in Szydłówek, where Damian spends the weekend. She milks her freedom for every fucking last drop, till Sunday at three P.M., when she has to get back on the bus and retrieve the snot-nosed, overeager toddler who throws his fat little arms around her neck as if she's been away for weeks and months instead of seventy-one-and-a-half sublime hours. Thank God today is Friday.

Last weekend, she and Paweł loaded up in a van with some friends and drove to Kraków where they partied their asses off till Sunday morning. Justyna and Paweł couldn't keep their hands off each other on the ride back, and as they drove into Kielce, Justyna whispered into Paweł's ear, 'Don't you wish we could go back?'

'We'll go back next weekend, *myszko*.'

Justyna shook her head. *No, no,* she wanted to say. *Not back to Kraków, but back in time, all the way to sixteen.*

It's not that she regrets having Damian. Damian happened when he was supposed to happen, he happened out of love. She felt no regret, but she harbored plenty of resentment. The difference between the two is small, but Justyna understands it the way only a mother can.

The truth is, Damian keeps getting in the way. Like last week, she had to drag him to the pediatrician's because he had a cough. Ever since that incident with the goddamn pneumonia six months ago, Justyna starts to panic at any sign of a cold. The death of Justyna's mother had stunned her but she was able to sort out her grief and move on. The mere thought of her son dying, however, almost annihilates her, so she schleps her kid to the doctor's anytime he has a sniffle.

The *poczekalnia* at the clinic had been packed and Damian ran wild, crying, laughing, spilling water, and throwing his shoes around. At first, Justyna tried yelling, and then she tried pinching his arm and holding him down, but she resorted to the tactic she relied on most days: she gave up and reached for a magazine. One of the mothers, whose daughter sat by her feet in silence, turned to Justyna and cleared her throat. 'If you can't rein him in, perhaps you shouldn't have had him,' she said.

Justyna blinked her eyes. 'Excuse me?'

The woman leaned in conspiratorially.

'I'm sorry, I just see that you're struggling.'

'You see that I'm struggling,' Justyna repeated slowly. The other women in the waiting room averted their eyes.

'Yes, I do. Look at him. Look at *you*. I see this all the time, you know. And it gets worse. Soon he'll be a boy and then a teenager and then a man, and you'll *still* be in over your head. My heart just breaks for him.'

Justyna stood up and clenched her fist. She hadn't punched someone in a long time.

'You see me struggling, *kurwo*? You don't see me, period. You see a statistic. If my son weren't here, you'd be laying on the floor in a manicured, pedi-fucking-cured heap. Damian, *idziemy*!' As soon as Damian heard the words *we're leaving,* he scrambled out from his hiding place, shouting *Hura! Hura!* Justyna grabbed his sandals and his hand.

'And one more thing, *pizdo*. You know who else had a kid when she was a teenager? Holy fucking Mary, Mother of God! And that shit turned out fine, that shit saved the world, didn't it now?'

But the woman's words had haunted Justyna. She never felt in over her head before, but that bitch was right.

At ten to seven, Justyna rolls out of bed and glances at herself in front of the full-length mirror that hangs on the door. Her breasts bounce perkily midair. At least by forgoing breastfeeding, she's saved them from doom.

She lives for these Fridays. She lives for going out. Downtown Kielce, while no downtown Warszawa or Gdansk, is nonetheless *her* downtown. The orange-domed bus depot, the wild parks and dark alleys, the homegrown boys; Justyna loves it all. But she lives for the nightclubs. Pod Krechą, Vspak, and Disco Park, these are her sanctums. There was sorcery in the opening of drawers to search for the right *stringi* underwear, in selecting a tight white outfit because white turned fluorescent under the club lights; it was in the way she sashayed down the porch steps, legs gleaming with baby oil, the smell of summer mixing with the scent of her Giorgio Beverly Hills perfume. Suddenly Justyna *was* sixteen again. Sixteen, and howling 'Wannabe' into the heavens, holding her heels in her hand, back when she *was* a Spice Girl, when she was free and tipsy and nothing could stop her.

People fawned over toddlers, but the truth was that they were primordial beasts, living exclusively according to their needs and desires, and sometimes, nothing but a smack to their heads got through to them. Yes, Damian gave her satisfaction in small ways that she knew she'd miss one day, like his slobbery kisses and his dimpled smile. But Damian also deprived her, and his new, boorish disposition was too much to handle. Prior to the pneumonia, Justyna coasted by, biding her time till he was old enough to fix his own lunch and wipe his own ass. But after his illness, she finally understood the depth of her wretched love for him. More and more often she'd pinch his arm a little too hard, smack him on the head, or shove him off her with a little too much force. Those impulses scared her but she couldn't stop them.

'Justynaaaa!' She hears Paweł summon her from the kitchen. Once again, she won't have time to shower before Paweł takes off. She throws on a Reebok tank and her black denim shorts – the same thing she wore yesterday – and thunders downstairs.

The kitchen is a mess, a cataclysmic mess. Damian is squatting in the middle of the floor, attempting architectural genius with a pile of pots and pans.

'I'm late. I'm fucking late.'

Justyna blows Paweł a desultory kiss and he rushes out the door. Justyna stands there, wishing she was going with him.

'Damian, wanna watch a show?'

But Damian is too busy stacking the unstackable, biting his lip in solemn concentration, because everything is a matter of life and death to him, including getting the frying pan to balance on top of the eggbeater.

So Justyna leaves him to his work, pours herself a cup of Jacobs instant, and lights her first cigarette of the day. Its effect is instant and she feels herself relax. They'll make it through until three o'clock somehow.

As she puffs contentedly, glancing at Damian from the corner of her eye, Filip walks into the kitchen, wearing underwear and nothing else. The old tighty whities are no longer white and are hanging loosely at his crotch. He sits down across from her and helps himself to one of her smokes.

Filip Bednarczyk is Elwira's latest find, and where she found him God only knows; he's in his late twenties, with no ties to anyone or anything. The sisters' taste in men has always differed, and this guy was worse than all the rest.

'Jesus. Put some pants on, will you?'

Filip laughs and taps his ashes into the ashtray.

'You don't like what you see? Then look away, Strawicz.'

'*Kochanie,* if you handed me a telescope right now, I still wouldn't see much.'

Filip lets loose a jarring laugh.

'*Oj, dziecko,* where's my breakfast?'

'Probably getting cold over at your *mamuśka*'s. Why don't you go back there.' Justyna stands up and motions to Damian. '*Chodz synu,* let's go outside, okay?'

Damian doesn't even look her way but he scrambles to his feet, and runs to the hallway.

'By the way, do us all a favor, and kick my sister to the curb before you get her pregnant, all right? If my father were here, you'd be gone yesterday.'

Six months after their mother's death, their father had packed up a suitcase and hightailed it to Naples, where he said work was rampant for the Poles. Justyna knew it wasn't money he was after, but escape. He could no longer function after Teresa died. At first he called them regularly, then just mailed some lira every few months, and in the end even that stopped. Justyna had no idea if he was alive or had drunk himself to death. In her mind, he was dead anyway.

Filip takes a long drag of his cigarette.

'She loves me. She's like him.' Filip points to the foyer, toward Rambo, her mother's dog. 'You kick 'em and they still come back for more.'

Justyna wishes she could walk over to his self-satisfied mug and whack him across it. But she doesn't, because this guy would whack her right back. You can tell just by looking at Filip that he would have no qualms about hitting women. Justyna is sure of it.

'Don't you have to go stand on some fucking unemployment line, *kretynie*? Get the hell out of my house.' She hears his rasping laughter behind her as she walks out and sits down on the porch steps, where Damian is already building pyramids out of pebbles and rocks, and apparently chewing on one.

'Damian, take that crap out of your mouth, right now, *jasna cholera*! It's probably covered in Rambo's piss! You wanna eat doggie's pee pee?!'

Damian spits out the stone and laughs. 'Doggie's pee pee!' And then in an instant, he gets to his feet and commands belligerently, *'Do parku!'* He runs to their picket fence, rattling the slats with impressive force, like a monkey in a cage.

Justyna sighs. *Do parku* again. Sitting in a park watching him slide down the rusty slide eight hundred times in a row does not sound appealing. 'No, thanks,' Justyna murmurs. She closes her eyes and enjoys the sun against her skin, warming her face. 'Let's just bake in the sun, till we're two brown loaves, how about that? 'Cause *mamuśka* just doesn't feel like doing fucking anything.'

Damian smiles at the sound of a cuss word. 'I'm the bread. You eat me!'

'Sure, I'll slice ya, and butter ya, and eat ya up, all right? Good idea, because I've got nothing but a tomato for lunch. So, Damian and *pomidory* sandwiches it is.' Damian laughs, raking his small fingers through the lawn, ripping up fistfuls of grass and hurling them into the air, where they fall on his face like raindrops.

'Mama jest smieszna.' Mama is funny. There's still plenty of time on earth, she reminds herself, and one day Damian will be fifteen and she'll get her life back.

After she drops Damian off with *Babcia* Kazia, Justyna returns home to find Paweł there. 'I decided to play hooky.' Justyna claps her hands in delight and pounces on him. Their love-making is invigorating and quick, like getting doused with cold water. That night they take a cab to Desperados. Paweł sits behind a banquette, sipping on a beer, ogling his wife with fire in his eyes. Justyna twirls, undulating to the music. When the song is over, she points toward the bathrooms and motions at him with her index finger. They used to fuck in bathroom stalls all the time. Paweł raises his eyebrows and nods, and Justyna knows that he'll follow a few minutes behind her.

In the bathroom, Justyna glances at herself in the mirror. Her eyeliner is smudged, her hair is sopping wet, and her tank top clings to her braless chest like a Band-Aid. And just then a face appears next to hers. Black bob, jutting collarbones, and small gray eyes made up with frosted white shadow.

'Holy fuck! *Marchewska?*'

It's Kamila. Or is it? Something is different about her – but when was the last time they saw each other? Has it been months or years? Justyna can't recall. She turns from the mirror and then it hits her.

'You got a fucking nose job!'

'I did. I did get a fucking nose job,' Kamila says, eyes scanning the floor. 'Hi. How are you?'

'I'm fucking awesome. My kid's away for the weekend, I get to sleep in tomorrow. And right now, Paweł and I are gonna screw in the stall right there. But afterward, come to our table. Let's catch up. You look so good! You here with Emil?' Justyna doesn't mean half of what she says. The sight of her old friend undoes her momentarily, brings with it a thousand memories that for some reason she wants no part of. When Justyna had Damian and when her mother died, Kamila dropped her, as if birth and death had so altered Justyna that she was no longer the same person. Justyna never quite forgave Kamila. Not so much for the distance, but for the assumption that Justyna had become a sad and broken thing.

'No. I came with some girlfriends. Emil asked me to marry him,' Kamila blurts out.

'Fucking finally!' Justyna laughs. 'Congrats.'

'Thanks. My nose, it's just a subtle change, right? It's still swollen and stuff. I, like, just had it done. The doctor says it won't take on its true shape for another year or so.' Kamila is wearing expensive clothes, not anything she could have bought in one of Kielce's boutiques.

'Subtle? Are you on drugs? I mean good for you, *dziewczyno*, but you're, like, unrecognizable.' Justyna says it like it's not a compliment and that's how she means it. Kamila flushes bright pink.

'Did you see Anna Baran when she was in Kielce?'

'Nah. We were supposed to get together but I was busy. You know how it is. We moan about those fucking summers, we plan on getting together, and it's all kind of bullshit isn't it?'

'No, it's not,' Kamila counters halfheartedly.

'Really, Kamila . . . ?' Justyna is no longer smiling. Kamila retreats without another word.

A minute later, Paweł joins Justyna in the last stall, where they go at it against the wall, but somehow Justyna's heart is no longer in it. When she and Paweł leave the club later, Justyna doesn't bother looking for Kamila. A few days after their awkward run-in, Justyna gets out her address book, and thumbs through it until she spies the old entry. *Kamila Marchewska 33-97-18.* She stares at the page before tearing it out and crumpling it.

CHAPTER NINE

2002

ANNA
KIELCE, POLAND

Anna can't get used to it. Can't get used to the sun that sets at four P.M., the snowy sidewalks, and the goddamn cold.

She arrived in Kielce two days ago on a train from Warsaw that stopped and stalled at every village they passed. She dozed, and when she woke, she spent her time staring out the window. The green fields she used to pass on her way to Kielce were now covered in white and it unsettled her.

When her cab turned down Jesionowa Street, the old neighborhood came into view and Anna's heart sank. Szydłówek was empty and covered in snow, and the thought of *Babcia* in her dark apartment was too much. If her mother had told *Babcia* that Anna was flying to Poland, *Babcia* would have to wait.

'Actually, I changed my mind,' she informed the cabbie as he made a right onto Toporowskiego Street.

'About what?' The cab driver exhaled loudly.

'I want to go to a hotel.'

'Which one, lady?'

'I don't know, *proszę pana.*' She smiled meekly. 'The nicest one.'

He made an abrupt U-turn, wheels skidding in the slush. Ten minutes later the cab was parked at Moniuszki 7, under the black copper awning of the Hotel Pod Różą. Two decorated Christmas trees flanked the entrance. A few steps away, Anna could make out the steeples of the *katedra* and a little farther down, the beginning of Sienkiewicza Street.

'This is perfect, thanks,' she said and handed him a generous tip. He sped off without a thank-you, and Anna smiled, finally finding something familiar about Poland.

From the main entrance, she walked up one small flight of stairs, following the signs to *Recepcja,* and at the small front desk Anna rang the chrome bell. A minute later a young Polish girl appeared. Her nameplate read Wiola.

'*Słucham Panią?*'

'Yes, hello, Why-ola. I was wondering if you had a room available?' Anna surprised herself by speaking in English, not knowing why she did it, but knowing it felt right. The girl at reception stared at her in surprise.

'You have the reserve?' Her phrasing was awkward and she had a slight British accent.

'No, I'm sorry, I don't have a reservation. I'll need a room for a few nights, any room you have will do.'

'Yes, we have the rooms. Smoke?'

'Yes, please, with pleasure, smoke.'

'I please just need the identification from you.'

Anna pulled out her American passport and slid it across the marble slab.

'Is this you first time in Kielce, miss?' Wiola asked, as she tapped a keyboard and printed out a sheet of paper for Anna to sign.

'It is.' Anna smiled.

The key to room 217 was copper and dangled from a wooden handle, like a key from a children's book. She got in the small elevator where there were only three buttons to choose from. Her room was narrow and neat, although it smelled a little musty from cigarette smoke that had embedded itself in the velvet curtains. It smelled like her aunt Ula's house, like her father's room back in New York, and like her own apartment on Lorimer Street. The walls were painted a burnt orange and there was a small television, which sat precariously on the windowsill. The bathroom was tiny but immaculate and there were ashtrays set out everywhere, even one on the back of the toilet. Anna plopped down on the twin bed, held her face in her hands, and felt a profound relief wash over her.

That night more snow fell. She watched it settle on the bare tree branches outside the hotel room while she called her mother to let her know she had arrived safe, if not entirely sound.

'I can't even believe you're at a hotel. When *Babcia* finds out she'll be devastated! Anna, you have to at least call her and tell her you're in Kielce,' her mother reprimanded. Anna promised that she would call, and that the hotel was just for a few nights, until she slept off her jet lag.

'What's Poland like in the winter, Anna? Is it the same like when we left? Is it snowing? God, I remember how beautiful everything was in *zima*.'

'It still is, *Mamo*.'

That night Anna tossed and turned, falling victim to jet lag. She finally gave up and showered at four A.M. She was out the door by six.

Anna walked up and down Sienkiewicza Street all day. It was still so strange to see people in hats and furs. She popped into pubs for fries and warm spiced beer. She bought books at the *ksiegarnia* and looked at pricey furs in fancy new boutiques. And for a long time, she stood in front of the Teatr Żeromskiego. Like every summer, the theater was on hiatus for the holiday. She had always dreamed of one day standing on its stage, in the footsteps of the great Kielczan actress Violetta Arlak. But that seemed silly now. Later, she sat on a bench across from the Puchatek mall and stared at the bustling crowd, full of faces that were so Polish – set in frowns, wrinkled, and moon-shaped. She felt separate from them, but her heart swelled with something akin to pride; these were *her* people. Back at the *hotelik,* she hung the Do Not Disturb sign on her doorknob, and went to bed early.

Anna wakes up when it's still dark outside. Today she plans to simply show up and knock on Justyna's door. 'I just flew here, and, boy, are my arms tired.' It would be good to start with a joke, because Justyna was always laughing at the unlaughable. Besides, things tended to happen when one just showed up, and she desperately wanted things to happen.

When the sun comes up, Anna orders a cup of coffee from room service and finally calls her grandmother.

'*Babciu? To ja,* Ania.'

'*Słońce, moje!* How are you, *córeczko?*'

'I'm good, *Babciu.* I'm in Poland.'

'*O, Jezus Maria!* Ania! *Naprawdę?*'

'Yes, *Babciu,* really. I'm in Warsaw for a few days and then I'm coming to Kielce.'

'A few days? That's not enough time! *O, mój Boże,* I have to cook and clean. I have to call Ula so she can—'

'*Babcia,* calm down, *Babcia.*' Anna smiles, feeling a slight pang of guilt for lying.

'How can I calm down, *córeczko?* You've just given me a heart attack.'

Anna hangs up and showers. The water is cold and smells like sulfur. An hour later, she turns the key and locks her hotel room behind her.

'Your taxi is here, miss,' another hotel clerk informs Anna on her way downstairs. 'You need the directions for anywhere?'

'No, thank you, I know where I'm going.' Anna smiles.

Will Justyna slam the door in her face? Will she still even be in that house? *'Lulajże Jezuniu'* is playing on the radio now and Anna hums along. It's a lullaby, sung to baby Jesus, and it's one of Anna's favorites. Growing up, Paulina would play the carol all day on Christmas and it always soothed Anna, reminding her that Mary had been just a mother once, trying to lull her restless child to sleep. Anna knows there will be babies, beautiful, healthy babies in her future, who will speak Polish, who will know where part of them came from. One day, she'll forget the abortion. She'll forget Ben. *Lulajże, lulajże.* Even God started out wide-eyed and afraid. It's a comforting thought.

As the cab makes its way up toward the neighborhood of Sieje, Anna's heart starts racing in anticipation. The last time she saw Justyna was the night Teresa died, when Kamila, Justyna, and Anna sat in the middle of a field, drunk on vodka, and happy. Anna remembers the bright sky, how romantic it seemed. She remembers the stars, and how the Summer Triangle was out that night, visible only to her. It feels like eons have passed since then, and yet it feels like yesterday.

KAMILA
KIELCE, POLAND

'Good morning. This is your wake-up call.'

'*Tak, dziękuje,*' Kamila answers briskly. She lies back down onto the sofa bed, and closes her eyes. She can tell that it has snowed without even looking. The sun is high outside, its rays, reflected off the snow, are blinding.

Yesterday, after her confrontation with Emil, Kamila felt oddly triumphant. Downstairs, Natalia high-fived her, but had refrained from asking Kamila about the details. 'Your face says it all. Now down a stiff one, and get thee to sleep.' And Kamila had done just that. At the Hotel Pod Różą, where Natalia had booked her a room, she asked for her key and promptly ordered a martini, on the rocks, one olive. Kamila fell asleep in her clothes, using her coat as a comforter. She woke up once during the night. She had been crying in her sleep, her cheeks were wet and puffy, but she had no recollection of any dreams.

The alarm clock on the dresser reads 13:01. To Kamila the hour is irrelevant. It could be three in the morning, and it kind of feels like it. Kamila fumbles for her mobile phone. She finds it lodged under her back. The battery is dying but her charger is in her suitcase and Kamila doesn't feel like looking for it. The thought of unpacking her lingerie into the hotel dresser drawers fills her with melancholy. Instead, she reaches for the hotel phone and orders room service: scrambled eggs and blood sausage, with breakfast rolls and a side of Nutella. Kamila is ravenous and when the meal arrives at her door twenty minutes later, her mouth waters. She eats slowly, but she finishes everything. *I don't care anymore,* Kamila thinks. She chews the doughy *bułeczka* and imagines herself years from now, soft and pliant, with a belly that sways as she walks, and somewhere there is a man who loves every last curve on her body. Once she's done eating, Kamila licks her fingers.

She cracks the window open and breathes in the crisp air. She uses the hotel phone to call Justyna, who picks up on the third ring.

'*Halo? Kto tam?*' She greets Kamila with a strangled *Who's there.*

'It's Kamila Ludek. Marchewska . . .'

'What's going on?' Justyna says lightly, as if they had just talked the day before, as if it was no big deal to hear her old friend's voice after so many years.

'Nothing much. I was in the States, visiting my parents.'

'Really? I heard you ran away from your husband 'cause he cheated on you or something.' Kamila cringes. Justyna's not going to make this easy. She hadn't made it easy the last time they saw each other in the bathroom at Desperados, when she had openly mocked Kamila's new nose and insulted her.

'Right. Well, yes. He did cheat on me. With his best friend, a man named Wojtek Marszałek. They've been together for the last three years. I found out in October, and then I fled to America. But I'm back now, and I'd really love to see you.'

There is a silence on the other side of the line. She can hear Justyna breathing. Her friend is stunned and Kamila doesn't give a shit. It's out in the open now, and she liked the way it sounded coming out, like a confession, and not an apology.

'Holy fuck,' Justyna finally allows and starts laughing. 'Holy fuck!' she repeats loudly.

'So can I come over today? I heard what happened to you, and I want to tell you how sorry I am in person.'

'Nothing happened to *me*. And why are you sorry? Were you an accomplice?' Justyna's laughter settles, and she continues, not giving Kamila any time to interject. 'Yes, Marchewska, come over. I'm sitting home alone. Bring some *winko*.'

Kamila hangs up, somehow both satisfied and confused. She's used to hemming and hawing. How strange, then, to just open your mouth and say what you mean. That is the biggest thing that Kamila always envied in Justyna – more than her perfect body and her cute little nose – Justyna never spared anyone, including herself.

In the shower, Kamila works lather all over her body, and for the first time she winces at how sharp she feels, at how her bones stick out after years of deprivation. Kamila can still somehow smell the American on her. She'll tell Justyna everything about him, about his fat stomach and his strange hands, about how beautiful he made Kamila feel. She's going to tell everyone everything from now on. Because today Kamila feels like a new woman. This Kamila will eat when she wants, will ask men to take her home on the first night, and will rid herself of her old, squandered life. After she dresses in a purple Anne Klein sweater and her favorite pair of jeans, pulled from her luggage, Kamila calls Natalia, to tell her she survived the night, and to tell her that she feels better than she has in a long time.

'Give me a few days to get most of my stuff out of the apartment. I'll leave all the furniture for you and Stasiu. Even the TV.'

'But it's forty inches! Are you sure?'

'I'm sure.'

'*Dzięki,* Kamila. I guess I can tell you now that you're a god-
send, Kamila Marchewska, because I'm fucking pregnant. Four
months.' Kamila erupts in congratulations. When she hangs up
she sits by the window, remembering the time, two and a half
years ago, when her period had been very late. When she was
waiting for it to start, Kamila felt her heart ignite, said her
prayers, and knew, knew deeply that a baby would be the thing
that would save her and Emil. A week later, she peed on a stick,
and she and Emil waited. When the two minutes were up, he
grabbed the pregnancy test from the sink and hid it behind
his back.

'Kamila! Kamila!' he cried desperately. 'We're not ready! You
can't be pregnant anyway; you're too skinny, *kotku.* That's why
your period's late. Okay? Okay, Kamila?' Kamila laughed and
tried to grab the stick back. Emil squirmed until it wasn't funny
anymore. Finally, he opened his palm and when they looked
down and saw the results, Emil laughed and hugged Kamila.

'See? We're not ready yet.' Kamila walked past him, curled
up on her bed, and cried herself to sleep. Looking back, Kamila
calculates that it was around this time that Emil started his affair
with Wojtek. She wonders if the thought of having a child with
her frightened Emil so much that it had driven him right into
Wojtek's arms.

In the lobby Kamila asks the girls at the concierge desk to call
her a taxi.

'Oh, a cab just left, *proszę pani.* Our *Pani Amerykanka* took off
in it.'

'No matter, I'll wait for the next one.' Kamila says it blasé,
but her insides spark like someone set a match to them.
Amerykanka. That word brings to mind only one person, but

surely the Rose's *Amerykanka* is not the same as Kamila's. She sits on one of the two chairs next to the concierge desk, and idly tears at her cuticles.

'*Amerykanka?* In Kielce? Where's she from, do you know? I have family in the States.'

'New York. She says it's her first time in Kielce but I didn't ask why on earth she's here and not in Warsaw or Kraków. My English is totally remedial, but it's fun to practice. She seems nice enough.'

'If you ask me,' pipes up the blond girl with impressive cleavage and a pouty mouth, 'I bet she's having an affair with a Polish man. She's got that look about her, you know? That *pining* look.'

'Well, no one asked you, Wiola,' Danuta answers with a professional smile.

Kamila makes a show of yawning. Her leg jerks up and down and she doesn't quite know how to stop it.

'Jet lag,' Kamila announces, now checking her leather boots for smudges. 'You called the cab, correct?'

'Yes, yes,' promises Wiola, and then she leans in across the desk. 'It's gotta be a man. If she were here on business it would be in Warsaw, like it is for every other American.'

'That's enough, Wiola!' Danuta hisses. 'Mrs. Ludek, will you be needing anything else before you go?'

'Do you have some water?' Kamila asks quietly. 'I don't feel very well,' she says to herself, as Wiola rushes over a bottle of mineral water, Nałęczowianka.

'Thanks. It must be the jet lag. I just got back from America myself.'

'Oh, how exciting!' Wiola exclaims.

'That's funny, isn't it? Two guests arriving from the States, at the same hotel . . . Tell me, are you sure she's American?' Kamila asks and takes a long swig of water.

'Yes, of course. I saw her passport. She doesn't speak Polish. And anyway, she *looks* American, you know?' Wiola answers. 'And when I told her that her last name meant *ram* in Polish she thought that was so funny. Oh! Your cab's here, miss.'

'*Baran?*' Kamila whispers the word, and it cracks in half.

'*Baran!* Except in English it sounds like Berrin or something. Like I said, my accent is horrible.' Wiola laughs.

The sound of a horn blares. Kamila stands up and walks toward the door. Her steps are deliberately, painstakingly slow. 'Thirty-six Witosa Road, over at Sieje.' The driver nods and revs the engine. Kamila rolls down the window and breathes in the frosty air, but it does little to calm her.

When the knock comes, Justyna can't quite hear it. She is upstairs, lying on her bed, staring at that one spot on the ceiling,
by the pipe, the one that's swollen with moisture. The pipe
Paweł was supposed to fix as soon as the snow let up, because
there were black patches of mold forming. The lights are off.
The electric bill is coming soon and Justyna's account is empty.
There's just an old pillowcase now, filled with some loose bills.
There's Damian's *skarbonka* clanging with *złotówki* that she'll
have to break open if things don't get better quickly. She's
already decided that when Kamila gets here she'll ask her for a
loan. She figures Kamila must be doing all right if she can afford
plane tickets to America. Besides, Kamila owes her, and she
knows it.

For two days now Justyna has held the fort down. Elwira and
the kids have been at *Babcia* Kazia's, and there are patrol cars
parked in front of both Kazia's building and Justyna's house,
from sunset to sunrise. It was the most that Officer Kurka said
he could do. 'Holidays, Mrs. Strawicz.' Kurka had explained
why she couldn't have twenty-four-hour surveillance. 'Besides,
in my opinion the dog was his last hurrah.'

Justyna wondered if she would ever be able to stop waiting.
Not just waiting for Filip to show up, but for Paweł to return.

When the knocking at the door turns to full-on pounding,

Justyna bolts up in bed. She runs down the stairs and when she reaches the foyer she exclaims, 'Christ, didja fly here? That was' — she opens the door — 'fast.'

'I did fly here. But that was three days ago.'

The woman standing before Justyna looks like her old friend Anna, only better.

'I was about to leave.'

'Hi. I was upstairs, napping. . . . Hi.'

And then Justyna pulls Anna in for a hug, a messy, jubilant hug.

With her arms still wrapped around Anna's neck, Justyna laughs. 'What the fuck is that perfume? You smell like a grandma, Baran.'

'Patchouli,' Anna says, twisting herself free. 'Let me look at you, Strawicz. But let me in first, it's cold as hell out here.' Justyna leads Anna into the house, and locks the front door. She quickly ushers Anna into the kitchen, runs to the kettle. 'Tea? Holy hell, I wasn't expecting a movie star to visit me tonight. I would have cleaned up a bit,' she says, referring to the kitchen and to herself.

'*Dobra, dobra.* Movie stars don't weigh 140 pounds.'

'It suits you. Bitch.' Justyna laughs again and Anna smiles. 'Anyway, you can lose the weight. But you can't lose the face.'

'Is that a good thing?'

'Baran, you're *śliczna* and you know it. Fuck the tea, right? You want a shot?'

'Yes, please.'

Justyna watches Anna take off her leather jacket, watches as she unwraps the silky blue scarf from around her neck, until it hangs from her hand in cascading sheaves, like a waterfall.

'That's some scarf.'

'Ralph Lauren.'

'*Rafloren?* What's that?'

Anna doesn't answer. She looks at Justyna, looks her up and down. There's not much to look at, but Anna takes her time and Justyna stands her ground in her rumpled Nike tracksuit, her dirty crew socks, her unwashed hair sticking up in short tufts around her face. She knows she looks like shit, but there's good reason for that.

'Did you sew those shoulder pads into your shirt?'

'I did.'

'Still? Still with the shoulder pads?' Anna smiles sadly.

'Always.' Justyna takes a cigarette from her pack on the kitchen table. 'All right, enough. You might be used to people ogling you, but I'm not.' Because Justyna knows it's not just her outer layer that Anna's taking in – she's trying to get at something deeper.

'Are you kidding? Who used to lay out on the Tęcza benches, one hand in the air, *begging* for someone to walk by and whistle?'

'I didn't have to beg.' Justyna grins. And then the grin fades, but just a little. 'Anyway, *dziewczyno,* that was a long ass time ago. I look like shit now.'

'Well, who can blame you . . .' Anna's voice trails off and she looks around the kitchen, avoiding eye contact. 'Where's that shot?'

'We're still waiting for one more guest.' Justyna winks.

'Who?' Anna asks guardedly.

'Who else?'

Anna's mouth drops open. Justyna sits at the table and lights a second cigarette off the dying embers of her first one. 'Weird, right? When was the last time all three of us were together?'

'Seven years ago,' Anna answers quietly.

'Right. I remember a bottle of *wódka*. And that's about all I remember.' Justyna grins.

'And your mom. Your mom died that night.'

'Oh, yeah. Riiiiight.' Justyna smiles and stands up. She never heard a word from Anna regarding her mother's death back then and she sure as hell doesn't want to hear one now. She starts walking into the living room.

'Bring some shot glasses, okay? And I think there's some Pepsi-Cola on the counter. And ice!'

They say every seven years the tide turns, the world shifts. Seven years of fucking crap. Tonight Justyna will drink to the next seven.

When Anna comes in, balancing everything in her hands, Justyna is on the *wersalka*, smoking a cigarette.

'What are those?'

'*Papierosy*,' Justyna drawls. 'I believe your term for them was always cancer sticks.'

'A girl can have a change of heart. Can I bum one?'

'*Ja pierdole!* Or as *you* say, "Fak meee!" Anna Baran smokes . . .'

'Anna Baran does a lot of things she shouldn't do.'

'Take a pack, I have a whole carton in the *barek*.' Anna sets down the glasses onto the coffee table. 'And get a bottle of *bimber*, and that bottle of Luksusowa vodka. The *bimber*, my uncle brewed in his bathtub. It'll destroy you.'

The knock on the door startles them both. Justyna looks at Anna.

'You wanna get it?'

'And give her a heart attack?'

'Why not?'

Anna laughs quietly, smooths the front of her jeans, and heads to the door. Justyna cocks her head and smiles to herself. It's so easy to pretend, it's so easy sometimes.

A moment later there's a squeal, and Anna walks in with a hyperventilating Kamila. She's skinny – painfully so – skinnier than she was in the bathroom at Desperados four years ago. Fucking Kamila, just beside herself.

'I stopped at the gas station on the way! Wine and stuff.' She takes a gulp of air, and then, 'I knew it! I fucking knew it! Those dumb girls at the hotel were talking about some *Amerykanka*! Fucking knew it! God! *Mój Boże! Dziewczyny!* This is incredible! Like, *kurwa mać*!' And then Kamila rushes over to Justyna, who is still sitting on the couch grinning from ear to ear, and Kamila kneels on the floor in front of her and clasps Justyna's hands.

'*Jezus Maria,* Justyna. I don't know what to do. Wait! I can't even get over Ania Baran over there, looking gorgeous as ever. *Jezus!*' And then Kamila's smile dissolves. 'Justyna. I'm sorry. I'm so sorry.' Kamila starts crying, fingers flying to her face, to wipe away the tears, but she can't quite keep up. For a while, no one says anything. Anna leans in the doorway and Justyna looks at her.

'Fucking Kamila. We were doing fine till you got here,' Justyna says. And when Kamila raises her head from her lap, Justyna Strawicz is crying. No one has ever seen her come undone, or apologize, or crumple, or beg for mercy. Even when Teresa died, she saved the waterworks for late at night, when she knew everyone was sleeping. Now, Justyna quickly covers her face. She takes a deep breath.

'Okay. So we started the evening like pussies. But we're not gonna end it that way. *Zgoda?*' She holds out her pinky.

And they answer in unison, loudly and clearly.

'*Zgoda.*'

Justyna pours the first round of shots. They sit on the floor and catch up on everything they want to talk about, and forget everything else.

When the bimber is gone they start on the wine Kamila brought. They go around in a circle, one-upping each other, their words breezy, bright, honest.

'My husband's a homo!'

'My husband's dead!'

'I never had a fucking husband to begin with!'

They don't let up, and they don't want to. It's too soon, and not soon enough to joke about it, but that's what Justyna needs because saying it like that, like it was a big fat joke, made everything surreal, and yet more real than ever. They are hardcore, breathless, and wasted on Uncle Marek's moonshine.

'Wanna know why I'm here alone?' Justyna asks when the clock strikes midnight.

'Yeah, where's Damian? Poor Damian, I wanna see him,' Anna drawls.

'He's at *Babcia*'s. With Elwira and her kid. 'Cause that fucker snuck in the house the other day. Strangled my dog and left him gift wrapped,' Justyna says quietly and her friends fall silent.

'Rambo?'

'Wait,' Kamila exclaims, 'you're not serious?'

'Oh, yes, I am. I'm so serious. Look how serious I am!' Justyna widens her eyes in exaggerated fear, brings her hands under her chin in fright, teeth chattering. And then she grows still.

'Rambo was your mother's dog,' Anna says quietly.

'Yes, he was. The last bit of Teresa I had.' Justyna says this like she says everything else, matter-of-factly.

'Is that why there's a police car outside your house?' Kamila asks, and Justyna can tell she's spooked.

'Yes! I'm not the only one with a bodyguard now, how about that? Huh, *gwiazdo*?' Justyna turns to Anna and winks.

'Wait a second.' Kamila's not smiling. 'So he's not in jail?'

'Nope.' Justyna gets quiet, wishing she had never brought up the fucking dog.

'Do you miss Paweł?' Anna asks. Of course it would be Anna to ask that. The question lingers in the air.

'I *will*. Once I stop believing he's coming back.' And with that, Justyna downs the last bit of the Luksusowa and stares into her glass. 'Kamilka, go upstairs and go into my room. Remember which one it was? Second floor. There's another bottle of *bimber* under my *wersalka*.' Kamila gets up with effort. She looks scared.

'Are the lights on?'

'Kamila!' Justyna barks and Kamila scuttles out of the room. Justyna sidles closer to Anna and leans her head back against the couch. She can feel Anna's eyes on her.

'I'm okay, Anna. I'm okay.' Anna nods and closes her eyes, tucks her head in the crook of Justyna's shoulder. Justyna smiles. This is the kind of night she had hoped for. And maybe the light of day would bring a bit of regret with it, regret at how wasted they got, and how disrespectful they had been, to both the living and the dead. Or maybe they'd continue in the only way they knew how; at once shielding their pain and sharing it, brutally, in revelatory spasms, but always with a wan smile and a wink.

Tomorrow, they'll make plans for *Sylwestra,* because undoubtedly they'll be spending New Year's Eve together. It's already been decided that they won't leave Justyna's side, and for that Justyna is grateful. They'll help clean the house, they'll babysit Damian while she goes out and tries to find a job, and they'll lend her a little money until she does. They'll make Anna pick up the phone and fucking call Tefilski. They'll help Kamila go through her belongings at her old apartment. It's already been decided.

When she hears the footsteps in the foyer, Justyna opens one eye. Anna has fallen asleep and Justyna has no idea how much time has passed and why it's taking Kamila so long to find that fucking bottle.

Justyna hears him before she sees him.

'Shhhh. Don't wake her. She looks so sweet.'

He's standing in the doorway. Shaved head, thick beard, dirty jeans, and dirty hands, no coat. She sees all these things in a flash and for a moment Justyna thinks he's an apparition, except apparitions don't talk. They don't have fresh snow on their boots.

'You having a party? Tsk tsk tsk. Is that how a widow is supposed to act?' Justyna is frozen, except for her hands, which start to shake.

'I guess your pretty little friend forgot to lock the door behind her. Didn't you tell her? About the bogeyman?' Anna stirs beside her, and Justyna shudders. She knows the minute Anna pops open her eyes, she will let go of a scream that might move Filip to action.

'The police are right outside,' Justyna says quietly.

'I know they are. I would have said hello but I didn't wanna wake them.' Filip smiles and looks around the room, looks up toward the ceiling. 'Where's Elwira?'

Justyna has spent her whole life talking her way out of shit. She knows people; she understands how they operate. She has rarely been afraid of confrontation or of dying. But now, face-to-face with a life-or-death situation, the only thing she wants to say is a pleading *jeszcze nie jeszcze nie*. *Not yet*. But she can't open her fucking mouth.

It happens in the blink of an eye. Kamila slams the bottle down on top of Filip's skull. The bottle doesn't break, but it's enough to send him to the floor. That's when Justyna scrambles to her feet, and takes over; five more blows, one right after the other, as Anna screams her fucking head off. Thank God for Anna's vocal cords, for their decibel-shattering powers, because she is loud enough to wake up Officer Leon, who runs in, pistol cocked.

An hour later, Justyna sits on her front steps, smoking a cigarette. It's cold, but she can't really feel anything. She watches Kamila and Anna drive down Witosa in a cab, on their way to Szydłówek. They begged and begged for her to hop in the backseat with them, to leave that fucking house.

'I'll be there later, I promise,' she told them. 'I have to go get Damian anyway.'

'You sure?' Anna asked as the three of them stood on the porch and watched the cop car drive off with Filip in the backseat, soaked in bimber from the sixth and final blow that finally shattered the bottle, just as Officer Leon tried to grab it from Justyna's hands.

'I'm sure.'

Justyna stares at her cigarette. Did she ever really believe that Filip would come back again? Justyna speaks softly, imagining Paweł sitting on the steps right next to her.

'I think I'm gonna sell the house, Paweł. It wasn't ours to begin with. And there's nothing to keep me here anymore. Who's gonna fix the fucking ceiling, anyway?' She exhales again, feeling like a fool, but she continues.

'I guess it's over. I mean, there'll be a trial, but I think it's done, *misiaku*. And I hope he gets it up the ass on a daily basis in there. And I hope they never let him out. There. That's it. I just wanted to say that, just put it out there in case someone else is listening.' Justyna closes her eyes. Everything is incredibly still, and quiet, the kind of winter stillness that promised snow.

'I miss you. Every day. I miss you not because you're not here. I miss you because I'm still waiting for you to come back. How fucked up is that?' Justyna stops talking for a moment, just to catch her breath, because she knows she could go on forever. But that's the idea, she supposes, that's what he wants her to do. To go on, forever.

EPILOGUE

'That's the last of it,' Kamila says. Satisfied, she sits down on top of the cardboard box that's now taped up like the others. Anna and Justyna sit at the kitchen table and survey the handiwork. It took them three hours to pack up Kamila's life into six boxes and two suitcases. Now, the clock hanging above the table reads 23:37.

'Are we seriously going to ring in midnight here?' Anna asks, finishing her cigarette. She stubs it out into a teacup saucer; Kamila doesn't own ashtrays.

'I'm sorry, you guys. I'm beat. I just wanna lay down and wake up next year,' Kamila says.

'Me too,' Justyna says, yawning.

Last night, when the three of them got to Kamila's apartment, they boiled *parowki* and made scrambled eggs, and decided they'd wake up early the next day, start packing up the place, and then spend New Year's Eve at a nightclub. Maybe Desperados. Anywhere with music and people, anywhere they could dance and let loose, just like in the good old days.

At first, Justyna wasn't interested in going out. The last two days had worn her out. The night the cops took Filip away, she stayed out on the front steps for a while. She didn't go to Szydłówek to get Damian, and she didn't call or talk to anyone. Justyna needed one night alone in her house, one last night. She went upstairs to the bathroom, sat on the floor, and cried for a long time.

In the morning, she finally called *Babcia* Kazia and told her what happened; that the police had informed Justyna they'd apprehended Filip thirty kilometers outside of Kielce, standing at a bus stop. Justyna heard Elwira crying in the background as *Babcia* relayed the news.

'I'll clean this shit hole up a bit,' Justyna said, 'and come get Damian tomorrow. All right, *Babciu*? I just need one more day.' *Babcia* Kazia didn't protest, didn't ask, admonish, or pry. 'Whatever you want, Justynka,' she said.

Later, when enough time had passed, Justyna would tell her sister and grandmother the truth. She'd tell everyone; how Filip had returned to the house. For now, it was nobody's business and she preferred it that way.

Anna stands up and walks to the fridge. She opens it and takes out the bottle of Afrodite sparkling wine, the closest thing to champagne Kamila had in the apartment.

'Well, someone needs to make a toast before we pass out.'

When Anna and Kamila had left Justyna on her porch two nights ago, they were both reeling. The prevailing emotion was relief, but Anna also felt giddy. Something momentous had happened. It wasn't just the fact that the three of them had braved a fucking psycho. It wasn't just that Filip would finally be imprisoned for his heinous crime. It was more than that. It felt like a final farewell to the past.

Anna's instinct was to go to *Babcia*'s apartment. She didn't want to spend the night in some hotel room and neither did Kamila. *Babcia* Helenka had almost fainted when she opened the door and saw Anna and Kamila there.

'*Jezus kochany!* What's happening? Anna! Who is that?' she asked, not recognizing Kamila.

Anna stepped into the apartment, pulling Kamila along by the hand.

'*Babciu,* this is Kamila Marchewska. Remember her? My old friend?'

'Kamilka!' *Babcia* had exclaimed. 'I wouldn't have recognized you in a million years.'

It was easy to lie to *Babcia* about why Anna had showed up now, without luggage, at two in the morning, and why she had brought a friend. *Babcia* didn't seem to care. She was just happy to have her granddaughter back. Anna slept on the floor in the living room next to the *wersalka* she'd offered Kamila. They didn't say a word to each other, but it took a long time for either one of them to fall asleep.

Anna didn't know how long she'd be staying in Poland. She didn't know much of anything, except for one thing, which she had decided as the sun was coming up. Before she left, she'd go down to the travel agency on Sienkiewicza and buy her parents two round-trip tickets to Poland, whether they liked it or not. Anna wanted to see what this place would bring out in them, whether or not it would save them, revive them. Sometimes, going back to the beginning was the only answer.

'All right,' Justyna says back in Kamila's kitchen, 'we'll make a damn toast.' She smiles. 'But first let me go check on Damian.'

Babcia Kazia had dropped Damian off at Kamila's that evening. Suddenly, Justyna hadn't been able to bear being away from him for another night. When he walked into the apartment, dragging his backpack on the floor, Justyna knelt down and hugged him for a long time, breathing in the scent of his hair.

'I don't wanna sleep at *Babcia*'s again,' he said gruffly, and she told him not to worry.

'And I don't want Miki anymore. I gave him to Celina.'

'Who's Miki?' Justyna asked, feeling a wave of remorse for everything.

'The goddamn hamster. I want a turtle now, but only if I can walk him on a leash.'

'Jesus, demanding, aren't you?' Justyna swatted his cheek, blinking back tears, and led him to the bedroom. She offered to help him get in his pajamas, but he held out his hand.

'I can do it on my own.'

Now, she cracks the bedroom door open. She sees his face in the moonlight coming in through the window. For the first time ever, she's glad that Damian, with his pale blue eyes and fair hair, looks nothing like Paweł. It would make things easier.

Kamila stares at Justyna standing by the door.

'She's a good mom, right, Anna?' Anna nods her head, as she uncorks the wine.

One day, Kamila would be a good mom too; she was sure of it. She would fall in love again. She would gain weight and find a new job. That morning her boss at the pharmacy left her a message: 'Your vacation was over weeks ago, Mrs. Ludek. We regret to inform you that your position has been filled.' It didn't matter. Somehow, life would go on. She wasn't looking forward to finding a new place to live, or sitting down with Emil at some lawyer's office. She wasn't looking forward to many things. But there was nothing easier in the world than getting knocked up, and for the first time in her life, she'd have fun trying. When Justyna joins them at the table, Anna has already poured three glasses. They each pick up one and take a pause.

'All right, *dziewczyny*. It's 23:51. Someone better fucking say something profound real fast.' Justyna smiles. It won't be her. Kamila and Anna stare at each other before Kamila sighs. 'Anna. You have to do it. You're the resident speechmaker here.'

'No,' Anna demurs. 'I'm good when someone hands me the lines, not when I have to come up with them on my own.'

'For fuck's sake, Anna!' Justyna points to the clock.

'Fine, fine. *Dobra.*' Anna takes a breath and raises her glass.

'I want to make a toast not to what's happened, but to what will. To our future. May it be bright and happy. May we never have to smash a bottle over anyone's head again.' Kamila and Justyna smile and wait for Anna to continue. 'I want us to find the place where we belong . . . One day, I want the three of us to stand off to the side, and watch our kids do *fikołki* on the *trzepak* in front of my *babcia*'s house.' Anna stops abruptly, looks away.

'*Na zdrowie!*' Justyna finishes for her. 'That wasn't bad, Baran. A little on the sappy side, but not bad.'

'You got something better?' Anna smiles.

For a moment Justyna considers the question. Tomorrow she will wake up and it will be a new year and Paweł will still be gone. And that's the only thing she can count on, so she shakes her head and brings the glass to her lips.

'Not yet,' Kamila says, pointing to the clock, and the three of them turn their heads. '*Jeszcze nie.* We've still got a little time.'

ACKNOWLEDGMENTS

Huge thanks to everyone at Quercus and to all my UK ladies, including Kathryn Taussig, Lucy Ramsey, Jenny Richards and Mary Pachnos. Thank you also to my entire team at Spiegel & Grau and everyone at Random House, including the meticulous Loren Noveck, who caught some big ones, and Greg Mollica, who gave me my pretty Polish girl on the cover.

To my editors, Julie Grau, Hana Landes, and Laura Van der Veer, the ultimate smart-girl trifecta – you helped me sculpt and whittle down and refine without compromising my vision, and I will be forever grateful.

Thank you to Laura Nolan, my amazing literary agent, who got it right away, and who took me to lunch where we feasted on *kiełbasa* and fell in love.

Huge, unending thanks to the awesome Adriana Trigiani, who read an unfinished draft, told me *you are a writer,* and gave me a deadline. Your encouragement and insight were crucial to my hunkering down, finishing this thing, and sending it out into the world.

Thank you to Mary K and John Wilson, who introduced me to Adriana and who have always loved and believed in me, even though I suck at returning phone calls.

To the fabulous Bill Butler and Chris Highland, who let me go off and be a mom and then go off and be a novelist . . .

To Kasia, who helped watch over the boys so I could write.

To Christine Onorati, my staunch supporter, for her words and her WORD – books brought us together, and so much else keeps us that way. . . .

To Adrian Karatnycky, who led my family to America.

Thank you to my countless teachers, who saw something in that immigrant girl and who told her to keep writing – especially Mrs. Conti, Ms. Carroll, Mr. Feigelson, and Mr. Levitsky.

To Judy Blume, Ann M. Martin, Lois Lowry, and V. C. Andrews; to Eva Hoffman and Lorrie Moore; to Barbara Trapido, Toni Morrison, and Dostoevsky; to TC Boyle, and Miłosz and Szymborska; to Frank McCourt and Francine Prose; to Márquez and Bukowski – my first loves, my mad loves, my many loves, too many to name.

Thank you to everyone who read the revised-one-last-time-delete-all-previous-attachments-this-is-IT-I-swear drafts – including Maggie, Krista, Anya, TJ, Vinnie, Scott, and Crispin Borfle.

To all the Polish boys who broke my heart, and vice versa.

To all the Polish girls I know, with their own dreams and their own stories, which have inspired mine, especially Karina, Iga, Aneta, and Augustyna – life goes on but we'll always have those *wakacje*. . . .

To my California Foleys, Malina and Keller – *ciocia* loves you.

To my family in Poland: *zobaczymy się za rok . . . zawsze tak bylo i zawsze tak będzie*. . . .

To *Babcia* Krysia, who took care of me every summer – may you read this book over and over again as well. . . .

Thank you to my mother, Aleksandra, who bravely left home to go start a new life, and to my father, Mirek, who keeps longing for his old one – you taught me sacrifice, you scrimped and saved to give me Polska every summer, and without that, there would be nothing. . . .

To my sister Marika, who read some of these pages a decade ago and told me I was sitting on gold – I'll never stop dreaming about us-down-the-block . . . and to my sister Veronika, who came home in a fruit basket when I was ten and changed my life . . . No one will ever understand like we do, and the three of us will always be walking down Toporowskiego, forever young . . .

To my sweet, beautiful sons, Kalin and Kassian – Mama's finally finished writing 'that book.'

And finally, thank you to my husband, Patrick, who said his vows in Polish, who never tells me no, even when he should, who always listens, who loves me beyond and despite, who lets me sneak off to the porch to scribble just a little while longer . . . *you saved me* and there are no words to show my love & gratitude, but here's a few thousand anyway.